AGELESS EROTICA

EDITED BY JOAN PRICE

Ageless Erotica
Copyright © 2013 Joan Price

Seal Press
A Member of the Perseus Books Group
1700 Fourth Street
Berkeley, California 94710

Library of Congress Cataloging-in-Publication Data

Ageless Erotica / [edited] by Joan Price.
     pages cm
  ISBN 978-1-58005-441-6
 1. Older people--Sexual behavior--Fiction. 2. Erotic stories, American.
I. Price, Joan, 1943- editor of compilation.
  PS648.E7A37 2013
  813'.01083538--dc23
                              2012041938

Cover design by Elke Barter
Interior design by Tabitha Lahr

Distributed by Publishers Group West

CONTENTS

INTRODUCTION

Joan Price

Older folks still enjoy sex—boy, do they!—and you might be startled by the diversity of plot, characters, theme, and imaginative sex acts in this anthology of erotica by, for, and about women and men ages fifty to eighty-plus.

How did this collection of senior erotica come about?

Since 2005, I have been on a mission to talk out loud about senior sex, and I've become known as a spokesperson and activist for older-age sexuality. I've written award-winning books and a popular blog about sex and aging, I give talks and workshops, and I'm pulling senior sex out from under the covers and showing people of my age, as well as those older and younger, that we don't need to give up our sexuality just because our bodies are older. Yes, there are age- and health-related challenges that we need to face, but with knowledge and creativity (a sense of humor helps, too), we can dance to our sensual music and leap over every barrier—even with arthritic knees.

But where is the erotica for and about our age group? Personally, I don't respond to erotica that's all about sopping-wet panties, rock-hard erections, and instant orgasms. I know the brain is our primary sex organ, but my aging brain wants to be stimulated by sexy stories that reflect *my* experience and the realities of *my* age group in a way that's both truthful and racy. I neither wish nor need to go back in time to spark my fire, even in my fantasies.

With much encouragement whenever I shared this idea with readers and audiences, I began envisioning an erotica anthology by senior writers featuring sexy senior characters. The stories could be fiction or memoir, but they had to reflect the sexual experience of our age group with some accuracy—not just slapping wrinkles and an arbitrary age on the same old, youth-oriented erotica.

I put out the call for submissions on my blog, on Facebook, and on sites that attracted writers of erotica, and I encouraged others to pass it along. I knew that erotica writers over fifty, sixty, seventy were out there, but would they be willing to write for our older audience specifically?

They were not only willing—they were enthusiastic. I received 106 completed submissions by the deadline, and close to a hundred additional inquiries. The variety of characters, sexual events, interactions, and attitudes thrilled me. Skilled writers—many widely published, some new to this genre—sent me erotica about sizzling sex in long-term relationships, new encounters, and solo pleasure. Some were tender, some were rough, some were lyrical, some were raunchy. They wrote about women with men, women with women, men with men, and women pleasuring themselves. You'll even meet a woman with a jaguar. The writers in this anthology bare the challenges of sex, relationships, love, and living in an aging body with accuracy and compassion, and sometimes with humor. Many of these stories are based on true experiences; others are fiction; many are a combination. All are sexy and proud.

I know my vision of senior erotica will be challenged. You may not want to know the realistic details of sex at our age—that we may need pillows under our creaky knees, that we're sometimes embarrassed about how our aging bodies look, that our medications may affect our libido, that sometimes we can't reach orgasm without a vibrator or have erections without a pill. You may question the eroticism of comparing HIV medications or enjoying a sexual encounter that does not end in orgasm.

You may, in fact, question the whole premise of this anthology, that "senior erotica" needs to be different than the traditional genre, as erotica writer Tsaurah Litzky did in an open letter to me:

> I am a senior, a proud sixty-eight-year-old senior who still responds to and is excited by rock hard erections, be they real, virtual, or imagined. I don't consider my golden years a time to abandon faithful and fulfilling fantasies but rather a time to cherish them and acquire new ones. As for the "sopping wet panties," while it is true that my panties now rarely get wet enough to be

considered "sopping" or even damp, my mind is as wet
and wild as ever, maybe even more so.

I don't challenge anyone else's view of erotica—I applaud every way that your imagination stimulates you. I do think it's time to embrace a new notion of erotica or to expand the old one, so that we includes details of what actual sex is like at our age, and how we don't just accept it—we celebrate and eroticize it. That's what our *Ageless Erotica* writers did here.

I hope you enjoy these stories as much as I do. Please email me at joan@joanprice.com and let me know.

TO BED

Erobintica

We undress. You stand, unbuttoning your heavy flannel shirt while I sit on the edge of the bed, unzipping my black suede boots. We talk about the movie we just watched, sitting together on the sofa, sharing a lap blanket to ward off the January chill. Every now and then I reach over and take your hand, wishing our sofa were more snuggle-worthy. Mission-style furniture, for all its aesthetic appeal, is not at all encouraging of eroticism. Straight, hard lines don't allow for loose wrapping of limbs.

I watch from the corner of my eye as you undo your belt and slide your jeans down to reveal oh-so-sexy army surplus long underwear. Swedish blue, and seen better days. You've never been a snappy dresser. Clothes are just practical coverings that have to somewhat match the activity. You unbutton your shirt, remove it, then slip your T-shirt over a mostly gray beard and receding hairline. Still so handsome to me. I watch you slip your wool socks off. We both know we're going to have sex. It's been almost a week, and there is a subtle charge to the air.

But there is no overt suggestiveness. Often I want that, longing for the enticement of candlelight and the slow progression from small touches to all-out ecstasy. But not tonight. Never good at seductive disrobing, I slip out of my jeans and pull my sweater over my head. As I undress, thoughts of unattractiveness creep in. My body has seen births and weight fluctuations. It is not the body of the young woman you married. My large breasts hang close to my rippled belly, which is streaked with stretch marks. But your familiarity with the skin I'm in helps me overcome my self-consciousness.

The bare wood floor is cold, and by the time we both climb under the covers of our waterbed, my feet are cold, my toes icy. Yours are too, but not like mine. We laugh about our "popsicle toes" and tuck them all together, seeking warmth. We spoon, my back to your belly, and you wrap an arm around me and gently knead the softness of my stomach. I recognize the affection of this little gesture. In the past, I might have taken it as critical, me never having a flat stomach, even before children, and always wishing for one. But you have loved me in my body through thick and never-ever-thin, and I'm finally able to appreciate that. I snuggle closer as we talk a bit more.

It is dark, only hours from a new moon. Often I like some light. The gentle flicker of candles or the bluish glow of moonlight, especially reflected from snow, something we've had little of this winter. Despite the stereotypes, I am the more visual of the two of us. We've talked about this. Especially as I explored my sexuality, unbridling myself from residual shame as I've aged. For years I took your preference for dark as your preference for not seeing. But you said you most enjoy focusing on touch, and sound, the changes in breath. They are your turn-ons. I like the dark as much as the light now, and tonight I don't even think of setting match to flame.

As we talk, we both comment on how quiet the house seems. I even wonder if the power has gone out, it's that quiet. Tonight is the first time we've had the house to ourselves in over a month. Though our two oldest moved out years ago, our youngest, still in college, was home for winter break. There is a subtle inhibition I feel when others are in the house. Even though we made love often through all the years our kids were growing, I hadn't realized until now how much I like having our privacy back.

Our conversation slowly drops off, and I feel your fingers on my belly, more deliberate as they make small stroking movements, then brush against the curls of my pubic hair. I smile in the dark. This small gesture lets me know that you, too, want sex. Since we sleep in the nude and are cuddly and affectionate most of the time, we have subtle signals to communicate desire.

There was a time when just the slightest touch from you— on my lower abdomen, the side of my breast, or along the line from the nape of my neck to my lower back—would turn me on instantly. And sometimes, if I've been reading or writing erotica, priming the pump, so to speak, it still does.

But we're both at that age: We're slowing down, and our reactions are slowing down. Our desires are no longer hair-trigger, and I'm thankful we've learned to give ourselves time to warm up, to let our bodies catch up. When I went through menopause and arousal began to take longer, I often would get discouraged and give up. I think of this as your fingers find a nipple and give it a slight pinch and I can feel my response, not quite as electric as before. But I love sex and could not imagine living without it. Neither can you. With time, we found that if we just kept going, eventually our bodies would get the hint, and the end result would be worth the effort.

You play with my breasts, and I can feel your cock begin to stir against me. I reach a hand back, stroke the outside of your hip and down your thigh to let you know I know. By this time we've stopped talking. I often wonder what is going through your head, and I have asked you, wanting to hear your fantasies, but you tell me you're just concentrating on what you feel—my nipple hardening under your fingers—and what you hear—the small catch in my breath as you touch me somewhere unexpected.

These days my mind is often a jumble as we begin our lovemaking. I remember the load of laundry I forgot to move from the washer to the dryer, or I think about the erotica story that I've been working on. I've found that, just like my physical erotic response, my creative erotic mind has slowed down too, and the erotica does not flow so easily from my imagination to my keyboard. My hope is that, just like with our perseverance between the covers, if I work past the it's-not-happening stage, the sex will also happen on the page as it does in our bed.

It helps that you support and enjoy my erotic writings. I remember when we sat in bed, you snuggled against me, and I read to you the first erotic piece of mine to appear in print. I was nervous, worried you wouldn't like it, even though you'd read it several times. But you liked listening, and it turned you on. I smile and roll over, turning towards you.

With my head resting on the pillow next to yours, I stroke your chest and brush against one of your nipples as I press my crotch against your upper thigh. We often take turns, you doing to me, me doing to you, though I realize that as of late, I've not been as bold as I've been in the past. While part of my brain wants to examine that more closely, your hand tracing my curves draws my attention back to the here and now. It is time to concentrate.

Your cock is still not fully hard, so I play my fingers around it, through the curls around it, along the crease of thigh, over your hip, and around to the small of your back. As I hear your breathing quicken, I feel my arousal. I press against you, move my hips, and then take you in my hand and stroke the underside of your now rapidly hardening penis. I cup your balls and press several fingers against your perineum, rubbing and listening to your breath get raspy. This turns me on even more, and I grind against you, find myself aching for you to be inside me.

Sometimes I roll onto my back and you reach down between my legs. There is a sound you make when you first feel my wetness that sends me to a joyous place. It does not seem to matter to you if it is my own natural lube or if it's from a bottle. You slip a finger inside, two, even three, and you stroke and press and I begin to lose the thoughts and just experience. Sometimes we play with our arousal, bringing each other close and then backing off, a zigzag path up the mountain that can seem to go on for hours since we know each other's bodies so well.

But tonight is different. You have yet to place your hand between my legs. Have yet to finger my soft folds, tickle my clit. And while I love all that, tonight I want the immediate sensation of your cock in my cunt. I raise myself and straddle you, not an easy move anymore on our waterbed. With my hand, I guide you to the entrance and slowly sink onto you. You make that sound, the one you make when you find me wet, but it's more intensified, and I sense that if I wanted to, I could just come right then and there, just from hearing that. But I love the feel of you inside me, so I refocus and start moving my body with yours.

As I ride you, moving up and down, sliding back and forth, or the stirring motion I like so well, you grip my ass, my hips. You reach up and take hold of each nipple, and I lean back and reach behind me and caress your balls. We both sense that orgasm won't take long, and we give in to the animal in us, and just fuck. I can feel my peak approaching. I do this thing with my hips, a press into you that makes my clit and g-spot happy at the same time. I feel a little surge of fluid escape me as we press and press into each other. It's almost as if we're trying to fuse with each other, and then, I'm there.

I try to hold still, just feel the rush, but you are bucking and soon you grab my hips and hold me to you as you orgasm, too. Suddenly I am aware of the noise we've been making, the moans and cries and gasps that haven't been stifled, because suddenly they cease and we're both just panting. I feel the pulsations of you inside me, and I twitch a few times, the aftershocks of my orgasm. Then I climb off you and drop onto my back as we both catch our breath.

I have a fleeting regret that it's over so soon. I've grown to love the long, drawn-out lovemaking that we do. But these "quickies" are a rare treat and remind me that we are not machines with an obsolescence date. It is in these moments after we've done the work to arouse each other and ourselves, after we've copulated like the best of animals, after that moment of "little death," that I feel most thankful.

SOMETHING BORROWED, SOMETHING BLUE

Nancy Weber

If the name Victoria Delvaux rings a bell, you probably read about me in *Avid and Ribald Pensioners Monthly*: "Oldest Living Tantric Goddess Says, 'Skip the Gym if You Must, but Wiggle Your Kegels Every Day.'" The story—which was published on my seventieth birthday—drew twice as many emails as the Jane Fonda cover. The server crashed for two hours! How's that for celebrating with a bang? An ob-gyn said I should get a Nobel Prize in Medicine.

Instead I got a summons to divorce court. My lawfully bedded Lewis, "the luckiest man in America," had found another woman. No matter that seventy suited me fine. I was triumphantly lithe and lubricious; let the numbers fall where they might. But Lewis, on the verge of seventy-five, couldn't deal with having an "old" wife. My big round number shrunk his psyche. And his penis wasn't far behind.

For whom, you ask, does a bald, white, commodity trader leave a Tantric goddess, albeit one with some mileage? A teen with tip-tilted tits and smart-phone savvy? Hold onto your hats, my darlings; it was worse. He ditched me for a fiftyish frump who didn't know kundalini from Kandinsky. Here's what she had: season tickets to the New York Giants. Her uber-connected husband had died and gone to the Skybox, bequeathing her a pair of premium seats on the fifty-yard line. Plus parking in the players' lot.

I was mad and sad and a little sorry for Lewis. But mostly I missed his parking in *my* lot. Putting his hot dog in *my* roll. (Hold the mustard.) My guilty ex had left my bank account stuffed, but my yoni was a ravenous hollow.

I needed a man. Not buzzing plastic nor organic cuke would do it; nor my fingers, such use of which makes me feel like a twelve-year-old. Anyway, we tantrikas tend not to be clitocentric, which also pretty much leaves out the L thing, although some of my best friends are women.

Call me old-fashioned, but I'm mad for the male body, every un-pretty inch of it. I like putting my hands and lips all over a man, from the top of his head (especially if it's bald) to his ugly but suckable big toes (well scrubbed, if you please). Oh God, it makes guys wild when I wrap my tongue around those mock cocks, especially if I reach up my hand and pump the real thing while my mouth is doing the toe. And I like making them wild, because then they give me what I crave.

Where to find one of the darlings? Online trolling and the bar scene weren't for me. Then a batch of snail mail brought inspiration via a glossy catalogue from a grand old midtown menswear shop where I'd picked out countless presents for Lewis. I flipped the pages and ogled the models, delicious silver-haired specimens with alluring lines around their eyes. They looked like the CEOs and senators I'd seen buying tennis sweaters in the store. One of those masters of the universe was just what I needed as a present for me.

I was on fire as I conjured images of starched, striped shirts crumpled on the floor and power ties leading a double life as cool, silky restraints. But I couldn't just dash up to the venerable shop and stand there exuding pheromones. I had to have a cover.

The next day I dolled up in layers of cashmere and pearls and stormed their employment office. More accurately, I proved myself as a saleswoman by selling them on me, never mind that I had no retail experience and clearly didn't need a paycheck. Charm and passion for their brand covered the holes in my resume.

Of course I wanted to be on the second floor, where suits and slacks are sold and titans of industry submit to having their inseams measured. (Oh, God. The measuring tape.) But I had to play it cool and be gracious when management posted me near the famous bronze front door at the ground floor hosiery counter. I quickly saw why they wanted me there. If I quirked a smile at someone walking by toward the elevator, he suddenly needed to buy argyle socks for a country weekend or black silk hose for a night at the opera. And if I threw back my shoulders and jostled my breasts under my gray cashmere sweater, he had to have tennis socks, dozens of tennis socks—anything to delay his departure from my turf. *Cha-ching!*

The accessories manager, a great-looking jerk, loved how I made his numbers rocket. By the end of the second week, I despaired of getting off the ground floor and close to the dressing rooms. The *un*-dressing rooms. I dropped hints, to no avail.

But Monday brought a beautiful surprise. Almost.

"Well, Victoria, you're getting your wish," my manager greeted me. "Three people called in with the flu, and I've been ordered to send you upstairs."

"Upstairs? That's fantastic! Of course I'm sorry about people being sick—"

"Of course," he agreed solemnly.

"But I'm on my way to the second floor!"

"And then right on up to three," he sang, with what I can only describe as vicious merriment. "Women's." he added, as if I didn't know.

"Mr. B, you're kidding, right?"

The women's department is the reincarnation of Peck & Peck. I don't think they've changed a thing since 1959. It would have been closed long ago, except that the owner's beloved Aunt Mabel buys her chocolate brown tweed suits there.

He wasn't kidding. Up I went. Past heaven to inferno.

The morning was so slow among the dust motes on three, I considered not coming back after lunch. Would anyone even notice? My sole colleague, who'd had the foresight to bring a crossword puzzle book, could handle any traffic that strayed our way.

But a deal is a deal, and so at two o'clock I assumed the position behind the sweater counter. The colors ranged from soy latte to cocoa bean. And then my life changed forever.

She walked in.

As I've made clear, I don't look at other females as objects of desire. There was something about her, though. Her boldly silver-streaked hair. The confident set of her shoulders. I felt alert in a way I don't usually feel unless there's a man present.

"Good afternoon, madam," I said politely. "May I assist you in any way?"

"Oh, thank you, no, I'm just looking," she said. But as I busied myself refolding a pile of cardigans that didn't need refolding, I realized she was mostly looking at me.

And smiling. And saying, "I can't help noticing that you and I have the same coloring. What do you think about this sweater on *us*?" She unbuttoned the trench coat she was wearing. She picked up a mud-color turtleneck, held it under her chin, and stepped back so I could get a good look.

I saw three things.

One: Not only was she just my coloring, she was just my build. The reason her looks had struck me was that she was a mirror reflecting my past: She was me at fifty-four or fifty-five, aglow—as I had been—in the menopausal meteor shower of hormones. Wow! I wondered if I struck her as a mirror of her future. I hoped she was happy with what she glimpsed.

Two: The mud-color turtleneck looked terrible on us—not that I could imagine it flattering any skin tone.

Three: Her stunning straight black skirt was bulging.

Bulging.

As in *C-O-C-K.*

Yes, gentle reader, beneath her skirt, where her long legs joined, what could only be an erect male member was saluting me.

My knees turned to jelly. I grabbed the counter.

"So what do you think?" She winked. "About the sweater?"

"I think . . . I have to say honestly . . . I'm not sure . . . the color . . . um . . . "

She cut me off with a little wave. "I know what you mean, but it may look better on. You know, you can't always separate the color from the fit. Which way are the dressing rooms?"

Wordless, I pointed, finger trembling.

She nodded thanks, started away, and then looked over her shoulder. "Would you mind coming to give an assist?" Brilliantly matter-of-fact. "The sweater I'm wearing has one of those diabolical back zippers that you can't quite reach yourself. My husband gave it to me with a card that said, 'So you'll never run away from home.' Isn't that charming?"

"Charming," I muttered deliriously. I tried to keep my eyes above her waist, but it was no use. She had a cock, and I was under its spell.

I signaled the other clerk to mind my half of the department. I led my customer and her *thing* past the flannel nightgown display into what must be New York City's least frequented suite of dressing rooms.

My mind was racing and empty at the same time. Nothing in my life had prepared me for this deep mystery. If you're thinking the lady was the beneficiary of gender reassignment, fuggadeaboutit. Some of my best friends had done the deed or were in process. *She* was something else. I would have bet my ovaries on it.

This was a woman, a woman with a penis—a woman with size 34-C breasts and a penis, and I was about to be alone with her.

Maybe it was a shadow, I tried lying to myself, as I knocked on her dressing room door. *Maybe I'm so cock-obsessed, I'll start seeing them in trees.*

Now she was chattering away about the crisp, clear weather and how she somehow always ended up inside windowless stores on the most beautiful days.

She took off her coat, hung it on the hook, and faced the mirror, her back to me. She'd been telling the truth about the diabolical little zipper, and I reached out and pulled it down, revealing the back of an ivory silk bra. Her perfume was intoxicatingly vanilla.

"I can wait outside," I said politely.

As if.

"Look at us!" she said, pointing to the mirror. "We're practically twins. The only difference is that you're more beautiful."

"No, madam, you're more beautiful," I said faintly. "Not to mention being way younger."

"Well, you're way more polite," she said, with a delicious laugh. "I can't remember the last time someone addressed me as 'madam.'" Suddenly she reached behind her, grabbed my hand, and drew it around to the bulge. "But wouldn't 'sir' be more appropriate?"

Her hard cock nudged me through the black skirt.

I staggered backwards onto the built-in bench.

"Don't be frightened, sweetheart," she said. "Every girl should have one."

She released her skirt and stood before me, revealing her secret.

It was blue.

Bright blue.

It was blue, and it was rubber or silicone or something, and it was six inches long, and it was sticking straight out from the cunningly slit blue bikini panties to which it was attached.

"A better color for *us*, wouldn't you say?"

I nodded and nodded. I might never talk again.

"Meet the mayor," she said. "Won't you shake hands?"

My hand was already shaking, but what to do?

It was blue and it was rubber and it was attached to a woman, but it was a *cock*. And I have never been rude to a cock.

I gave the mayor my hand.

She moaned. I moaned.

And suddenly I was on my knees, and my tongue was all over her blueness, and my lips were playing wild music on it, and beneath my layers of tailored gray, my pussy was pulsing in tempo.

Her hands were everywhere at once—on her tits and in my hair, and then she was fumbling inside the bikini and suddenly I heard a soft whir, and her hips started thrashing, and I realized she'd ignited some kind of tricky little gizmo pressed against her clit.

Did I say I wasn't clitocentric? Mine felt so blood-rich and hot, I thought it might set off the smoke detectors. I wanted that blue rubber cock to nuzzle it and push me over the edge. I hiked up my skirt and pulled down my panties in one swift motion.

She propped my ass on the bench, took Big Blue in her hand, and stroked it just once across my clit, and I came so wildly I would have brought the store guards running with my screams if she hadn't swallowed them with her kisses.

"I don't know about you," she murmured, "but for me, the best fuck in the world is the one right after I come."

"You know everything about me," I somehow managed to say, and the next thing I knew she was pulling a condom out of her bra, ripping open the foil, and rolling it over her cock.

She put her thing inside me, and my Kegels squeezed and released until I came in places I didn't know I had. As I vibrated around her in concentric waves, I knew she was imprinting me forever. My first blue cock. Would anything else on earth ever feel this good?

And the truly crazy thing is she came too, with her eyes rolling back in her head just like dear old Lewis. As she slid down the condom and wrapped it in a tissue, I'd have sworn it was full of come.

She kissed me once, very sweetly, then glanced at her watch and frowned. I guess that goes with having a cock, never mind if you also have a pussy and tits.

"I have to meet my husband," she said. "He's down on two buying a suit."

She pulled a drawstring bag from her ladylike purse and dropped her panties and the gizmos into it. Then she handed it to me. "Washable," she said. "Sometimes it takes a cock to get a cock. Happy hunting, sweetheart. Now if you'll excuse me . . . I feel too naked for company."

I had to agree. I've never seen anything more exposed-looking than her soft mound of ginger hair. The same color as my snatch hair, of course.

I turned my back, pulled up my panties, and left the dressing room clutching my prize.

I was still working on normalizing my breathing when she came out of the dressing room and approached my counter. She handed me the mud-brown sweater.

"I should have listened to you," she said, in a Mrs. Everyshopper voice. "Really not my color. But the fit was perfect."

"Beyond perfect, if I may say so."

"Thanks for your help," she said.

"You're welcome, madam. Please come again."

"I did."

As she threaded her way past outerwear toward the elevator, I was stricken with a sense of loss. I knew I'd never see her again. And then, salvation: I remembered that I had an important part of her in my own purse now.

Five thirty arrived without further excitement. I closed out the register. I waved goodnight to my colleague and descended into the basement, where the staff restrooms and lockers are.

I pushed open a door and was greeted by whoops of laughter. I'd gone into the men's room!

"Now if I'd gone into the women's room, you'd be screaming lawsuit," one of the fellows called out good-naturedly.

"Yeah, yeah . . . and we'd win! Sorry, guys. Long day."

This time I went into the right bathroom, noted that it was empty, quickly washed and dried my cock at one of the sinks, went into a stall, and pulled on the magic panties. Tentatively I touched my new appendage. Gee, what would happen if I tried peeing standing up?

Enough excitement for one day. I tucked my prick between my legs and adjusted the panties over it. Nobody would guess my secret.

My manager was filling out reports as I headed toward the street door. "Hey, we missed you," he said. "How did you do upstairs?"

"Dullsville. You owe me, baby."

I'm usually buttoned-down with him, and he looked surprised. "Is that so?"

"Yup," I said. "And I expect you to go to bat for me and get me transferred up to men's suits. I've worked hard for you, and I deserve that. But meanwhile—" I glanced at my watch, "it's martini time. Enough with the paperwork. I want to buy you a drink. Don't break my heart."

He gave me two thumbs-up. "Well, okay! That's too good an offer to refuse, even if you're only making nice because you want something. Correct me if I'm mistaken, but haven't you been refusing to go out for a drink with me ever since you started working here?"

"Woman's prerogative to change her mind," I said.

My cock seemed to nudge me as I uttered the words. I bit back a giggle.

It was going to be an interesting night.

DOLORES PARK

Dale Chase

"Nice butt," says my bench companion.

I do not know him, and though his assessment of the young runner is accurate, I am annoyed at the intrusion. "Good package," I counter because it seems important to reply, even as doing so, to him, like this, two old men on a park bench, ruins things.

"Yum," he says, and I turn to see he is gray and tanned and lined. My mirror image. "I'm Jimmy," he adds, extending a hand.

My pause reveals my disdain for older men clinging to childish names. "Karl," I tell him. His grip is gentle, near flimsy.

"I know, Jimmy at my age, right?" he says with a grin. "But it's my given name, honestly. My brothers are Bobby and Jacky. Apparently the folks thought it cute."

"Mine were German. Hard consonants."

"Such a beautiful spot," he says as another morsel jogs by. We are on a bench in San Francisco's Dolores Park, ogling young men of the Castro while masked as two harmless old men. "The scenery is delightful," Jimmy adds.

"That it is."

"I'm new here," he offers. "Gave up a house in Berkeley to take a flat over here. I do enjoy the energy."

"And the scenery," I add, as two young hunks amble by, one in jeans and no shirt, the other in shorts and muscle tee. Both are stunning, one olive-skinned, one fair.

"One each," says Jimmy, as we enjoy the retreating butts.

"If only," I sigh, immediately regretting both the statement and the sigh because they sound hopeless or at least resigned, and I am neither.

"Torture," Jimmy says. "Visual masochism. Just one more young cock."

"One?"

He laughs. "Okay, and one after that. And maybe one after that one and, oh, who am I kidding? I want them all, rampant young dicks going at me until I cannot walk."

I let this sit between us because I can see them lined up, erection city, but in my scenario they turn and bend and I fuck them standing, moving down the line. In fantasy I can keep it up for hours and come a dozen times. As Jimmy lingers in his imagination, I tell him my dream and find that while I like sharing it, I hate hearing it.

Jimmy takes in my vision, and I see he's playing it off his own. We are quiet awhile. A hetero couple pushing a stroller goes by, then a female roller skater and a fat child on a tricycle followed by a thin and efficient woman I'd guess to be the nanny. When the parade breaks, Jimmy announces somewhat wistfully, "My lover was forty-six," as if nothing more need be said.

I cringe because my Don was forty-five. For a moment the urge to tell all rushes up like some putrid bile begging expulsion, but I swallow it down. Jimmy exercises no such restraint.

"He's really the reason I'm over here. Mitch was his name. Fourteen years together, bought a beautiful Craftsman house, had it all, but, well, you know how it is. The funny thing is, I think he broke up with me not because I grew older, but because he did."

I have no reply. I stare at the beautiful view. Our bench is on a hillside, and there are people and dogs frolicking below, while beyond, greater San Francisco reminds me of a larger world. I know Jimmy expects comment on his outpouring, but this is impossible. *Get up, get off this goddamn bench, get out of here!* I shout inside because the last thing I want, the very last thing, is the wisdom of age. I want to forget about relationships and ages and who is getting older, because it is a fact that young men stay young and old men stay old, and that is why they leave you. I shift on the bench, deciding which direction to flee, until a young punk saunters toward us. Shirtless, barefoot, black pants riding low and not revealing any boxers, he is somewhat a mess: bleary eyed, stubbled, hair an unkempt dark riot. He looks like a used-up waif, somebody to be taken home and bathed and pampered and fucked. I envision a persistent cock spurting come up his tawny chest.

Jimmy draws an audible breath and reaches over to squeeze my hand. I look at him and see him mouth, "I want that," as the boy reaches us.

I don't respond to Jimmy. I look at the boy, who glances my way and offers a sneer I know all too well, a mix of "here I am," and "don't you wish," but I don't care because my dick is filling. When the boy is in front of us, he steps on something and raises a foot to brush it off. Once righted, he adjusts his package while facing us, then saunters on.

"I may cream," Jimmy says, leaning against me.

"You wish," I snap because my dick is awake. The kid wouldn't be able to walk when I was finished.

"Well, he certainly gets the prize," Jimmy says when the boy is gone.

"And what prize is that?" I ask, holding back a sarcastic, *You?*

As if he can hear the unspoken mock, Jimmy says, "A man can dream."

And there we are again, two old men on a bench. The sun is high now, rare for a San Francisco summer. I am too warm, but unlike most men my age, I will not throw off the shirt covering a less than perfect body. Sweat trickles down my back and into my crack. I shift on the bench, think on going home, but don't move.

"Don was forty-five," I hear myself say. "He left me six months ago."

"How long were you together?"

"Eight years and four months. Pure bliss. I mean, I was old when we met which made it worse, you know. It's not like my aging could have surprised him."

"Was it for someone else?" Jimmy asks.

"Of course. A forty-something pastry chef. They have a place over on Eighteenth. I see them around sometimes."

Just then a young man, maybe thirty, runs up, and in pursuit runs a similar one. "Ethan," he calls, but the first one doesn't stop. "Ethan, please," he begs as they rush on.

"What do they know?" Jimmy asks when their chase has gone. "Babies."

"Some slight," I offer. "Looked at someone wrong or forgot to call."

"How simple it was."

"Was it?" I ask, then quickly add, "No, never mind. I do not want to go there. Life is the here and now." I stand. "I am going down to Twin Peaks for a drink. Care to join me?"

"I have a better idea," Jimmy says.

I wait. He smiles.

"Okay," he continues. "Let me make you lunch at my place. It's two blocks over."

As we walk there, I tell myself it's the heat that's undone me. Jimmy tells me as we go along that the flat is small so he sold most of his furniture. "Kept the best pieces," he says. He rambles a bit, and I wonder if it's nervousness because I too feel a growing apprehension. I mean, I don't do this. Not men my age. Never my age. It's the heat and this damnable sweat, like my body started without me.

He has the ground floor of a Victorian, somewhat dowdy inside, little updating, but there's a deck off the back and a lush garden. "This is why I took it," Jimmy says, offering wine as I stand on the deck in the shade from an old oak tree.

"Gorgeous," I tell him, happily distracted.

"Now, Karl, are you hungry?" Jimmy asks.

"Actually no. I'm hot from too much sun and I'm all sweaty."

"How about a shower?"

I turn to face him. He wears a loose, short-sleeved blue shirt, which means the body underneath is neither thin nor firm. Like my own. "Sure," I say.

The bathroom looks to have been updated in the fifties, a tub-shower combo done up in aqua tile. "I know," Jimmy says before I can comment, "but the water pressure is good." He sets out a towel. "Enjoy," he adds, and he departs but leaves the door open. I am both relieved and offended. Is he put off by thoughts of us?

I strip and get under a wonderful spray, forgetting all as I wash away the sweat.

"Karl?" I hear in a singsong.

"Yes?" I sing back.

"Would you like company, or are you otherwise engaged?"

I can't help but chuckle. I pull aside the shower curtain to see him standing naked, working a fine cock. His body is no surprise, thick but not fat, gray hair across his chest, formidable thighs. *All okay*, I think. I am sixty-seven, and Jimmy has to be around that. We are excused our flab. I motion for him to join me.

We are surprisingly awkward until Jimmy says, "There's a young man inside us both," as he reaches down to tug my cock. As I bask in his touch, I put my mouth to his and find his lips soft and welcoming, tongue eager. This awakens me as much as the pull below. I reach around and get my hands onto his butt, begin to squeeze, at which he moans. He is soft and too fleshy, but there are no bad butts. Soon I have a finger in his crack and he is spreading for me. When I get into his pucker, he says, "Bed would be better."

"Good idea."

We release one another, hop out of the shower and towel dry, then hurry to his room where a walnut sleigh bed awaits. Jimmy throws back the covers, falls onto his back, and opens his arms. I hesitate because this is new, and I want to tell him, but it reeks of insult so I simply crawl onto him. Our dicks stiffen between us, and I thrill to the encounter. Time and numbers are erased with the feel of a cock against mine. I begin to ride Jimmy and choke back a cry as it's the first contact since Don, and I am grateful. I kiss Jimmy, who runs his hands over my back, kneading until I finally rasp, "Condom."

He retrieves necessities from the nightstand. While I suit up, he lies back and raises his legs. I glance at a quivering pucker.

Once sheathed and greased, I climb into position, look down at his thick gray patch and the hard cock sprouted from its midst. Then further, to my own poised for entry. I guide myself in to the root, which Jimmy takes hold of. "Fuck me," he says.

Though I've done nothing since Don left, there is no urgency, and maybe there is some good that comes with age. Absent the rush of youth, I am free to enjoy Jimmy. I set to thrusting easily at first, leg and butt muscles awakening to complain about new activity. Jimmy swoons as I do him. He is most animated in a quiet sort of way, arms waving, hands fluttering, head lolling on the pillow, all of it in a fluid motion. "Heavenly," he says after a while. "I am transported."

He works his dick intermittently, and I enjoy the show, especially as he issues drops of precome and smears them down his shaft. I keep a steady thrust, not quite driven as yet. I take note of this because before, with Don, with others, the drive was all. Now I seem to have shifted to a lower gear, but it doesn't matter because I know it will be there when I am ready, and I am not yet ready. I want to be inside Jimmy for a good while. I want a good, long fuck, one that is more than just getting off. I want to know this man in the best way and later on, the worst.

After a good while, Jimmy's swoon begins to turn. His jaw stiffens, his breathing picks up, and he works himself in earnest. This rouses me from my indulgence, balls swelling with the stir.

"Make me come," Jimmy says.

"With pleasure."

I ease his legs up onto my shoulders and pick up the pace, ramming now, which gets a series of yeses out of him. And as I begin to feel my own rise, I see Jimmy start to come, his juice spurting up onto his stomach. The sight drives me over. I manage a "now me" before it hits, and I grimace and pound and push as I unload. Sweat flies as every muscle in my body seizes with the effort but mercifully spares me any crimps or cramps. I hear grunts and groans throughout, mine I suppose, but really I do not know. I'm that far gone.

Soon as I'm done, I pull out and collapse beside Jimmy. Heavy breathing is not adequate to describe the aftermath.

"Geezer ward," Jimmy says when he can speak.

"Beats the morgue," I manage.

We are quiet as we settle, and in this blissful period, I consider that I have now fucked an old man. I look at Jimmy, who raises his eyebrows and grins. He knows what I'm thinking, probably because he's thinking it, too. I roll onto my side to face him, and he does the same. We simply look for a while. Then I slide a hand onto his bottom.

"Nice butt," I say.

INVITATION TO LUNCH

Donna George Storey

WATCHING

She waits for him in their bed, naked, the blankets pulled up to her chin. She closes her eyes and takes a deep breath. The air rushes through her chest and pools in her belly, feeding the tiny flame between her legs.

When she inhales again, the air sinks all the way to her pussy, pushing out the lips. On the exhalation, her secret muscles flutter in anticipation. She can never predict exactly what will happen when he comes, but she knows it will be good.

The creak of his office chair, the steady tap of footsteps in the hall. She feels his presence in the room and opens her eyes. She smiles at the sight of him—fair Celtic features and smooth skin that seems all the more youthful in contrast to his silver hair, which has gotten him offers of senior discounts since his early forties. He smiles back, with that special twinkle he reserves for "lunchtime."

She watches as he unbuckles his belt and starts to unbutton his shirt. She's always liked to watch him undress, as if he's peeling away the public male self—daunting and untouchable—to reveal the part of him that is vulnerable, desiring, hers.

She still gets a secret thrill from admiring his big shoulders and arms, his sturdy legs that seem made for a kilt. His waist is a bit wider than it was when they met twenty-seven years ago, not that he ever had the surreal abs of the romance novel model. Which is why she feels a special pride for how well he wears his years.

He strikes a muscle-man pose to acknowledge her appreciative gaze, then, laughing, dives under the covers with her. His skin is cool, but deliciously soft. He snuggles against her, considerately rubbing his hands against his thighs before he touches her.

"Ah, you're so warm," he says.

Their limbs weave together in the way they love, his arm across her chest, her leg sandwiched between his. They share news of the morning, exchange a few private jokes. Why not take it slow? Today they have a full hour before they have to return to their computers and conference calls.

Soon they fall into silence.

He places his palm on her belly and takes a slow breath, as he always does at the beginning.

Again she closes her eyes and thinks of the times he held his hand to the hill of her stomach to feel the babies kicking and rolling inside. Then her mind takes a more fanciful turn, as if this capable, tireless hand that pleases her so well has the power to conjure up, layer by layer, all of their past pleasures dormant in her flesh. She remembers her gratitude that first night they were together, when she took the risk of telling him she didn't come easily during intercourse. He listened thoughtfully and asked her to help him please her. She remembers the months when they spent whole weekends in bed, reluctantly dressing only to refuel at their favorite pancake house, one of the few restaurants in the suburban college town that stayed open after 10:00 PM. As if leafing through a precious antique book, she sees their couplings in exotic hotels in Japan and Vienna and Napa, and best of all in their own bed when the rain beat against the windows and made them hold each other closer. Sometimes the memories are bittersweet—sex after they'd quarreled or when she'd healed enough after childbirth and felt like a virgin all over again.

Sex with him is truly like fine old wine, each year adding more complexity and mystery.

She turns to him. Their lips meet, tongues dance. Her mouth floods with the taste of him, male and foreign, yet profoundly familiar. She tries to name the flavors, as you do with wine—dried cherries, leather, Cabernet?—then abandons the effort. The answer is simple: His kiss tastes of sex and sweet history.

He cups her breast. His fingers tweak the nipple. The sensation surges straight to her pussy. He caresses her with easy skill, as a jazz musician might play a favorite standard, adding in a few flourishes and surprises. Only when she begins to squirm and moan does he roll on top and kiss her again. She loves the weight of him, his sturdy arms embracing her. She opens her legs and rhythmically pushes her mons up into his solid abdomen. When he starts to tongue her nipples, her moans go into overdrive. Still he patiently sucks until she thinks she might lose her mind.

Finally he rolls off to her right, the "sex side," and dips his hand between her legs. He knows how to play her there, too, rubbing gently at first in the groove to the right of her clit. Sometimes he'll spank her, just so, knowing a wave of pleasure will follow the sting. But today, because they have time, he scoots down between her thighs to feast. The blankets fall away, but she is very warm now, and she doesn't mind him seeing her in broad daylight. Although her strawberry blond hair is no longer her natural color, she is actually trimmer than she was in her thirties, thanks to daily walks and yoga. After years of struggle, she and her body are finally friends.

She gasps when he tastes her. His tongue is softer than his finger. She relaxes, cruising in the liquid buzz. Now and then, he'll ask her to come on his face, but it's not her favorite way. She likes him inside best, old-fashioned as it is.

As if sensing her unspoken thought, he pulls away, his breath tickling her vulva. "Look at that pretty pink pussy all spread wide," he murmurs. "They see you all naked and exposed. They're touching themselves as they watch, because they know how much you like to show off."

Her body tenses as if she's been slapped. Suddenly they are not alone in the room. The bed is surrounded by glittering eyes. An entire hockey team of horny college boys taking a lesson in how to please a woman from the coach's wife. Decadent oil sheik playboys paying a novice prostitute handsomely for an intimate show. Or her favorite standby, an elite businessman offering the sexual charms of his comely secretary to two entranced, drooling clients.

Of course he knows all about her fantasies. Now and then he'll dress up in his gray pin-stripe suit, which he never actually wears to work anymore, so she can clutch at the stiff wool jacket as he makes love to her on the desk, his hard cock protruding from the fly. In the tiny part of her brain that's still capable of rational thought, she makes a note to ask for the suit the next time they have an evening alone.

But they don't really need costumes or salivating strangers. Words are enough. His husky voice compliments her swollen wetness, her diamond-hard clit. He begins to strum her and she arches up, spreading her legs wider still.

"Please," she begs. "Fuck me now."

"Do you want to be on top so they can see your tits hanging down and your back get all flushed when you come?"

"Yes, yes, and . . . " The words freeze in her throat, but she forces herself past the embarrassment to speak, "and they can watch your cock going in and out of my hole."

"That's right, they'll watch my cock pumping in and out of your tight, pink twat."

She loves that silky voice, urging her on to greater depravity, ever approving of her "wickedness."

He lies back against the pillows. Kneeling, she takes his rigid cock in her fist. She teases the sensitive spot beneath the tip with her tongue, gives the shaft wet-lipped kisses. His breath comes faster. She takes him in her mouth slowly and begins to "milk" him as she does with her pussy, gentle contractions and releases with the soft walls of her cheeks. He makes a musical sound in his throat. His cock swells between her lips, satin wrapped around steel.

He touches her shoulder, his sign he is ready. He likes to be inside her, too. She sits up, straddles him, slides down onto his slick cock. Yes, the strangers are still watching. In this position her ass cheeks are obscenely spread for everyone to see her most private secrets. A few of the watching men take their cell phones out to film the lewd scene.

A simple touch will drive her over the edge. Will he make her beg for it this time?

While he flicks her nipple with one hand, the other trails down her back.

So, he won't make her beg, but he may extract another price.

His fingers reach her buttocks, draw leisurely circles on the globes, creep slowly toward the tender valley. She yelps when he touches her there. Unfazed, he tickles the ring of muscle. She lets out a low wail of pleasure.

"You like this, don't you?" As if he doesn't know the answer, gleaned from reading her erotic stories with a careful eye as to how to translate them into bedroom games.

"No," she chokes out. "It's dirty and bad."

"You do like it," he insists, "tell them you like it or I'll stop."

How could she ever admit such a thing to these faceless voyeurs? Yet she's so aroused now, if he stops, she'll surely expire from frustration. She has no choice but to stammer out the truth. "I . . . I like it. Oh, god. I like it when you play with me there."

"Oh, you are bad. You are such a sinful girl." His finger begins to strum her anus, like a second clit.

The word "sinful" makes her pussy clench like a fist. Backsliding Catholic that she is, she finds sex hotter under the threat of hellfire. He takes her nipple in the furnace of his mouth and begins to tap-tap-tap her devil's door in earnest.

She bucks into him desperately. The pulsing ball of fire in her belly throbs and bursts, rolling up her spine, exploding in a groan. Her skull shatters as she somersaults through the starry sky behind her eyelids and plummets back to earth. This was a good one, a great, big, full-body come. As she rides the last wave, he eases up on the stimulation, knowing her breasts and clit are exquisitely sensitive after orgasm.

Then he begins to move, thrusting his hips up into her, grabbing her ass cheeks hard. Her pussy tingles with each thrust, a sweet echo of pleasure. All of her senses are heightened as she savors the tension in his thighs, the chug of his breath, the quickening rhythm of his hips. She enjoys this almost as much as her own climax.

"Come inside me, my love," she whispers, and he does, with a ghostly tenor cry.

She collapses onto him. "That was amazing," "Wow." The words tumble out from both of them, as if this were the first time, a new revelation of how good they can be together, which, in a way, it always is. She rises up on her elbows, reaches for the tissues. Their eyes lock. He looks especially handsome after they make love, green eyes glowing, cheeks flushed.

After wiping up, they weave their limbs together and float, deeply satisfied.

No eyes watch them now.

SPEAKING

I have a confession to make. The erotic scene you just read is lifted straight from a recent "lunch" on a day my husband worked from home. By admitting this is memoir and not a fanciful fiction, I know I've broken an erotic taboo in our culture, where media expressions of sexual behavior are limited to people in their twenties with perfect bodies. Everyone knows if you are over fifty, you're allowed to pine wistfully for the sexual gymnastics of your youth or stumble through an arthritic imitation of coupling with the help of pharmaceuticals, but if you happen to have enjoyable sex in real life, heaven forbid with your own spouse, the least you can do for propriety's sake is keep this information to yourself, thank you very much.

Mature sex is silenced and erased from view in our society, but the truth is that I am happier and more comfortable with my sensual life now than ever before. A good part of this has to do with the fact I no longer much care what anyone else thinks. I care about how I *feel* and my partner's pleasure. By stark contrast, in my younger, officially "fuckable" days, I was rarely alone with my lovers. Unwelcome eyes of judgment and endlessly critical voices were always right there in bed with me.

Those voices told me my body was never as perfect as a supermodel's, I never came as fast as porn stars, and my curiosity about sex and acting out fantasies might please my boyfriend at night, but threaten him the next day. Even after I met my husband—perhaps especially because I wanted to be "good" in his eyes—I played it safe and let him take the lead with any new techniques or positions. Only when I started writing and publishing erotica in my mid-thirties did I find the perfect way to explore and express my own new desires. Thus I discovered my greatest turn-on of all: to arouse him with the stories I create from my limitless imagination.

After twenty-five years of practice in bed—and why can't we admit practice makes perfect with sex as with any other skill?— my husband and I are not only attuned to each other's physical responses, but we also have a new awareness of the spiritual connection sex brings. Each time we make love is like a renewal of our vows.

I wouldn't have had the courage to tell the truth about my sexual experiences back when I was seen as a sex object. But now that I am a subject, it's a story I very much want to share.

BEING

As an erotica writer, I've come to believe that our sexual fantasies have a valuable subtext that may not always be obvious at first blush. The scene that opens this memoir might suggest I harbor a desire to have sex in front of strangers. Nothing would dampen my libido more quickly in real life. Ever since I can remember, however, I have yearned to have my sexuality accepted and appreciated by others. Saying dirty words in bed is titillating, but it also satisfies a deeper need to speak honestly about my desire, something I was forbidden to do as a "nice girl." Older sex is very sexy. In fact, enriched as it is by experience, wisdom, and spirituality, it is the apotheosis of the human erotic spirit. Wouldn't we all, both young and old, gain by celebrating the possibility of enjoying sexual intimacy for as long as we live?

I don't know what the future will bring, but today, as my husband and I embark on our sixth decade, I'm happy to say that the only voices in our bedroom are ours, whispering encouragement. Now the only eyes watching are his and mine and occasionally a team of horny hockey players—strictly by invitation only.

OTHER PEOPLE'S STUFF

Susan St. Aubin

I'm wearing her fancy underthings, a "her" I've never met, though I've been through her dresser. That's where I found these black panties edged in pink lace with a hole where the crotch should be, and a real silk black camisole small enough to cling to my breasts, which sag slightly now in a way that makes them seem fuller.

I kneel over my husband's mouth and let his soft gums suck my clit, which thickens until it feels as big as a cock. Now he always removes his dentures for me. I imagine I can fill his soft-as-a-cunt mouth as I slide my swollen little man in and out, pounding until I come. Then he flips me onto my back, my cunt soft and smooth as only an older woman's can be, slick with the juices of his cunt-mouth, and he rocks his cock gently back and forth until he erupts inside me.

❈ ❈ ❈

How did we get here? One day a year ago, when our sex life had declined to rare Saturday mornings, he rolled off me and got out of bed.

"We make love like zombies," he said. "Always the same, as if we're staggering through it."

"But it works, Jaz," I protested. "We both come."

"Blind mechanics, Marge," he said. "We're sleepwalking. If you're going through the motions without any emotion, what's the point?"

My heart contracted. Hell, my cunt contracted. "Bastard," I muttered at his retreating backside as he walked out of the bedroom. We're both fairly fit for being in our late sixties, but even so, his skinny butt drooped.

Jaz was right. He used to live up to his nickname, but now his rhythm was irregular, and I admit I did nothing to shock it back to what it had been. Our lives seemed frozen. The luxury of Saturday morning sex was exciting when the kids first left home, but soon it became routine. He was always too tired at night, and even after we retired, when we could have fucked anytime, we seemed stuck on the occasional Saturday morning. My creativity went into the yard, where I grew prize-winning roses, instead of cultivating our personal garden.

"I'm more bored than you are," I called after him. "Mornings aren't my best time. What's the matter with Wednesday afternoons? Or evenings instead of the news?"

But he couldn't hear me from the bathroom with the shower already on.

※ ※ ※

Jaz brought a pile of advertisements to the breakfast table.

"Two estate sales in San Francisco," he said, "then we could go up to Santa Rosa for more, hitting one in Novato and another in Petaluma on the way."

That's what excites him now, I thought. *Estate sales.*

We're the post-modern hunter-gatherers. Every weekend we head out to sales all over the Bay Area. What have these people who've died or moved to small apartments left behind that we can use for the few years of relative health and freedom remaining to us? It's other people's stuff we want, as well as a taste of other people's lives. We grab kitchen implements we've never heard of (mushroom slicers! nutmeg graters!) and books we regret having given away. We go through closets for clothes we could never have afforded, and garages for nearly new tools we'll use no more than their original owners did. We leave with stacks of cashmere and tweed, as well as brand-new skill saws and shop benches, all sold for a fraction of their value.

Later that Saturday I wandered through a four-bedroom home that was stripped almost bare, with sheer white curtains covering dusty windows. There were no books, no clothes in the closets, no dishes in the kitchen, nothing but empty shelves and bulky antique chests I had no use for. The place was picked clean, as if the sale had been going on for weeks. Jaz went to the garage to see what might be left.

I found a small notebook stuffed in the back of a drawer in an oak highboy in the dining room, with nothing written in it except for one line on the first page: "If it were legal to suck my own boobs, I would." The handwriting was round and young, the ink faded, the pages yellowed. Through the windows, I saw weeds five feet high and several cactuses—all that remained in a neglected backyard. The swimming pool was covered in algae.

I wondered about the girl who had wanted to suck her own breasts and then kept this otherwise empty diary for decades. I was intrigued to imagine the possibility, or impossibility. What had stopped her from trying? Certainly there'd never been a law against it. I popped the notebook into my cloth shopping bag, but there was nothing else for me here.

I stepped into the hall, opening a door to find a staircase blocked by a single black and yellow plastic strip. I ducked under it and went down the stairs, which curved to reveal, standing at the bottom, a tall, white-haired man with a white goatee, his arms folded, who glared as if he were policing forbidden sections of the house.

"Oh," I said with feigned innocence, "are we not supposed to go downstairs?"

His dark eyes, black turtleneck, and stern face didn't seem particularly friendly, and yet he held out one hand, motioning me forward. When I reached the bottom, he seemed less threatening. "Those who need to come down are always welcome," he said with a smile.

He took my hand and led me into a corridor filled with closed doors, which reminded me of the funeral home where Jaz's mother had been laid out. I shivered although the basement was warm.

He opened one door and switched on a light to reveal a bed covered with a white and green bedspread. Immaculate white curtains embroidered with green shamrocks draped the windows, which looked out on a painted backdrop of a cottage garden in early spring, with crocuses and primroses just starting to bloom. One of the walls had white wallpaper covered in shamrocks to match the curtains, while the rest were the pale green of early leaves.

"In here, we can be on the verge of spring," he whispered.

When I didn't respond, he closed that door and continued down the hall. Behind the next door was the Valentine room, all pink and red with white ruffled curtains and, behind the windows, long stemmed red and pink tulips and white roses. "A bit clichéd, don't you think?" he asked with a laugh. "And yet, this was her favorite room." He sighed as he turned off the light, gently shut the door, and took my hand again.

The next room was Christmas, red and white striped drapes, bare trees covered in snow outside the windows, and red and green cushions on the bed. In one corner a blow-up Santa smiled, plastic arms outstretched.

"Dirty old man," my companion laughed. The bed was invitingly turned down, revealing red flannel sheets. "No?" he asked, then switched off the light when I shrugged.

In the next room, the light was dim, revealing a shadowy scene of walls painted black with zombies lurking outside the windows. On a bed canopied in decaying gray lace, a vampire doll lay on top of a blond doll in a long white dress, his mouth on her neck.

"Unappetizing, yet strangely exciting. As you know, this is what we come to, some sooner than others." He shut that door.

The last room was decorated for a party, with strings of blue and silver crepe paper draped across the ceiling and a bucket of ice holding a champagne bottle on a table near the bed, with two glasses waiting to be filled. The silver shades at the windows were pulled down.

"The perfect room for marking a new beginning," he announced as he walked inside.

I entered for a closer look. The champagne bottle was an empty prop, resting on plastic ice cubes, and the glasses looked a bit dim. When he sat on the bed, a cloud of dust rose.

I sneezed.

"I've been waiting for the right woman for this room," he explained.

When he turned off the light, it was so dark I couldn't see a thing.

"We always kept these bedrooms ready, like private theaters for our own play." His voice seemed to echo in the darkness. "Let the curtain rise."

He turned on the light. I found he'd removed the bedspread and most of his clothes, leaving on a pair of shiny black underpants. He lay down on the bed and patted the place beside him.

I hesitated.

"You can take your clothes off," he said. "No one is allowed downstairs unless I invite them."

Did he stay down here all day seducing women? I ought to have been offended, but instead I felt myself swell inside, I felt my clit twitch. He didn't even know my name, and I had no desire to know his.

"Anyone could walk under that tape, just like I did," I retorted.

"No," he said. "Obedient people never do. Only women who need me come down while their men haunt the garage."

I hesitated. Since I hadn't expected anything like this to happen, my underwear wasn't the best—plain white waist-high cotton undies beneath my jeans, and a yellowish bra held together with a safety pin under my white cotton T-shirt and sweater.

"Help yourself to whatever is in her dresser," the man offered. "You look about the right size."

I opened the top drawer and found a pile of brightly colored silk underthings: panties, camisoles, vests edged in lace. The next drawer held cheaper underwear of creative design: crotchless panties, tank tops with holes so your tits could hang out, a low-cut pushup bra in black and white stripes, the tips decorated with red bows. Under that was a drawer devoted to black leather: underwear, vests, armbands, and a pair of suede leggings. The last drawer held a variety of men's underpants of leather or silk, tank tops in all colors, and leather vests.

I chose red silk panties and a matching bra, which I felt would go well with my shoulder-length silver hair. Nothing ages a woman faster than short, dyed hair, no matter what stylists tell you.

The man looked me up and down as I took off my clothes and removed my sad underpinnings.

"Your skin, your hair," he murmured, "look finer than any silk. Come here, just as you are."

Again I hesitated. No fear of pregnancy, of course, but what about the diseases this seducer might have picked up? I didn't want to die any sooner that I had to, or have any more discomfort than my knees and back were already starting to give me. And lube! I couldn't function anymore without plenty of lube.

He slipped off his underpants, opened the drawer of the bedside table, and produced several condoms and sample packages of various lubricants. I slid the red silk things into my shopping bag, lay down beside him, and closed my eyes, my heart pounding with fear and desire. I felt his hands going over my skin, his fingers reading the braille of roughness along the backs of my arms.

"You are amazingly well constructed," he said. "There's evidence of too much sun on exposed areas, leaving a coarseness to the skin, but," he added, stroking my ass, "the hidden parts are the silkiest I've ever felt."

Something in his tone made me wonder if he was a retired physician.

I could feel his cock hardening between my thighs as we lay on our sides, his fingers drumming on my behind. There was a pause, then his moistened hand slipped across to my cunt, massaging it with lubricant, gently poking a finger inside, then two, a pause for more lube, then three, sliding around, tapping, until I caught my breath.

He blew my hair off one ear, tracing his tongue along the lobe. He had his wet thumb on my clit by then, rubbing to match the rhythm of his fingers inside.

He wasn't hurried like Jaz often was. He seemed to know when I was aroused and when he needed to change the pace. It was almost as if he were inside my body, reading cues only I could feel. His hand might have been mine, and when I felt my cunt throb and clamp on his fingers, they were part of me.

"Your turn," I said after we'd rested a minute, his softening cock pressed to my ass while he stroked my hair. I sat up, took that thing in my hand, lifting it to my mouth, glistening it with my spit, then rolling it between my hands like a bread dough that magically grew firmer. When he handed me a rubber, I opened the package with my teeth, sliding it onto his smooth wood. Jaz had been less firm lately, his cock falling sideways like a floppy zombie. Maybe there was more I should have done, like I was doing to this man now as I played his instrument with my mouth as if it were a flute.

He put his hands on my head, pushing me gently away. "I need your silky insides," he said.

He squished the contents of one of the lube samples into me, then slid his cock inside. I didn't have to stuff him in, like I often did with Jaz. He moved carefully back and forth, pressing against the underside of my clit, until, unbelievably, I felt a pulsation so faint I hardly knew what it was. I concentrated until it grew solid enough to make my cunt clamp down on him. He shouted as his fluid shot into me, so hot it burned, a sensation that faded as he pulled out.

"The smoothest yet," he said, his hand on my breast.

I reached into my bag beside the bed and pulled out the notebook. He took it eagerly, reading the girl's note about sucking her boobs, and then laughed out loud. "Even then, she knew what she wanted."

He turned the book over in his hand and paged through it, but there was nothing more. "She never kept diaries; she was too busy living. I never saw this one."

"Is that her handwriting?" I guessed she was his wife.

"Childish, of course, but similar. Yes, I'd say it's hers. She always did have a taste for the unusual. Legal," he snorted. "Funny, what kids think. They discover sex and it feels so good they figure there must be laws against it."

He sat up and began to lick one of my breasts. I sighed. "Did she ever suck her own?"

"Hers were smaller than these," he said, fondling my tits with both hands. "I don't know if she could have done it. We never talked about it."

"Mine were smaller when I was young, before I had three kids."

"She was just forty when she passed. We had no children."

"Boobs do seem to sag with age," I explained.

"'Grow' would be a nicer term." He lifted one breast toward my mouth. I stretched out my tongue until I could just reach my nipple, which to my surprise tasted almost as salty as a cock.

I sucked my tongue back in my mouth. "I don't want to strain it," I said. "Imagine explaining a sprained tongue to your doctor."

"You'd be surprised how often people do come to doctors with sprained tongues." He put my nipple in his mouth, swirling his tongue around it while I massaged his puffy tits with my fingers. We lay down on the bed, drifting pleasurably until he said, "You'll have to forgive me. I'm very tired," and he closed his eyes. "Take whatever you want from the drawers. Tell them there's no charge."

I thought of Jaz then, and I longed to get back to him and share my experience. I filled my bag with things he might like: crotchless panties and old-fashioned garter belts; pushup bras and silk camisoles. I took a few of the man's silk bikinis, imagining how good they'd look on Jaz.

I realized this man had no intention of leaving his basement. When everything upstairs was gone, he would wait in these rooms for women like me, lured by the promise of valuable stuff, but instead finding a renewed interest in sex. I tossed my worn underwear in the trash can, put on the red silk panties and bra and then the rest of my clothes. I left the notebook on the pillow beside the man's head and let myself out of the room, softly closing the door behind me.

Upstairs, Jaz was standing by the cashier at the card table in the living room. "Where were you?" he asked. I was surprised he'd missed me.

The young man who was taking money added, "He was very worried."

I smiled at both of them. "I had a little nap in an empty room downstairs." I showed the cashier my bag. "I was told there'd be no charge."

The young man winked. "Have a good day."

"Let's go home," I said to Jaz as we walked out the front door. "I can't wait to show you what I found."

He raised his eyebrows. I felt like all my days and nights were going to be good for the rest of my life.

LADY BELLA

I.G. Frederick

Lady Bella arrived at the sprawling campground in a dirty white panel truck driven by her slave's pet. The engine's hoarse rattle echoed through the woods as the truck worked its way down the single-lane dirt road. Half a dozen naked males followed the dust cloud.

Steven sprinted across the grass, beating his competition to the designated campsite. He arrived, panting, in time to open the passenger door before Lady Bella removed her seatbelt.

"Good afternoon, Ma'am." He dropped to his knees, back straight in presentation pose with knees open and hands palm up, on his thighs. "How may I earn the honor of serving you this weekend?"

Lady Bella swung her long legs out and braced one hand against Steven's head while she lowered her Teva-clad feet to the ground, then slowly pushed herself out of the truck. By now, the others knelt in a half circle around her. Almost six feet tall, she wore a piece of blue and lavender rayon wrapped around her lean figure from just above her knees to where it was tied above her breasts. A wide-brimmed straw hat covered the thick bun of her hair. Wisps the color of iron had pulled free to float around her face. Except for the gray hair and a few wrinkles around her eyes, she didn't look older than her early fifties, although some claimed she had to be in her late sixties.

She stuck one foot in front of Steven's bowed face.

"Oh, thank you, Ma'am." He touched his lips to her dusty skin before she pulled it away and offered it to Dennis and Ray.

"That's all I need, for now, boys. The rest of you can check in later in the weekend, if you'd like. I may require additional service."

She marched off toward the check-in table under the covered picnic area. Her slave, Lyssa, extracted herself from the middle of the truck's bench seat, and Lyssa's pet, Roger, opened the back. Steven, Dennis, and Ray jumped up to help him unload the camping equipment, ignoring the others who wandered away with heads hung low.

It took the four males almost two hours to set up Lady Bella's campsite, erecting a family-sized dome tent, a small pup tent, an open pavilion, and a canopy. The Lady's furnishings included a queen-size blow-up bed, a six-foot overstuffed sofa, half a dozen carpets, and a fully equipped kitchen.

When Lady Bella strode back into her camp, she smiled. "Nice work boys." She kicked off her sandals and stepped into the carpeted pavilion. Turning her head, she looked from one to the other. All dropped to their knees. "Who wants to wash this road dust off my feet?"

"Oh, please, Ma'am. Allow me." Steven didn't wait for an answer. He grabbed a basin from the kitchen and ran to the water spigot where the road met the grass of the field, returning to find Lady Bella stretched out on her sofa. Lyssa handed him two towels, and he stepped out of his own shoes before entering the pavilion.

"Thank you, Ma'am." He knelt, draping the larger towel over his shoulder, and dunked the smaller one in the basin. Wringing it out, he wiped the dust from Lady Bella's feet, admiring the perfect symmetry of her toes. She kept her nails short, but nicely shaped; unpolished, but buffed to a natural shine.

Steven cleaned every speck from between her toes, dried each foot with the larger towel, then massaged the balls of her feet with his thumbs. Lady Bella sighed and he smiled. He rubbed the length of both soles, kissed each toe one by one, then, whimpering in ecstasy, licked the silky soft skin on top of her foot all the way to her ankle. Her feet still tasted a little earthy. That helped ground him and kept him from slipping too far into subspace.

Lady Bella allowed him to suck on her toes and lick her feet until the clang of the metal triangle in the picnic area interrupted him. Although she withdrew her feet from his embrace, she didn't rise. Steven offered his arm and braced himself so she could use him to pull herself upright. Her dark brown eyes looked him up and down, and he sat back so his ass rested on his heels, keeping his back straight so his belly wouldn't bulge.

"Not bad." She ran one long finger along the underside of his engorged cock. "You like CBT, boy?"

"Yes, Ma'am. Thank you, Ma'am." He'd only tried cock and ball torture once. He wasn't sure he liked it at all.

"You've served well this afternoon. I'll play with you first after dinner."

"Oh, thank you so very much, Ma'am." Steven couldn't help grinning. Ever since he'd met Lady Bella, he'd longed to kiss her feet and feel her lash. But she was surrounded by boys vying for her attention at every event. Steven had signed up for this leather camp as soon as he learned Lady Bella held court here.

He followed her to the covered cement pad filled with a dozen long picnic tables, then ran back to his car to retrieve the cupcakes he'd made for the potluck. When he returned, Lady Bella sat with several other Dommes. Steven found room for his cupcakes before approaching her.

"Ma'am," he pointed at the empty plate in front of her, "may I have the honor of filling that for you?"

She gifted him with a smile that dimpled her cheeks and brightened her eyes. "I like to try just a taste of all the different dishes."

He filled Lady Bella's plate from the table crowded with casseroles, salads, vegetables, fruits, and breads. Steven noticed only three of his cupcakes remained on the separate dessert table, so he grabbed one and set it with the plate in front of her. "I'll get you a selection of desserts, Ma'am, but my cupcakes are disappearing, and I wanted to give you a chance to try one." He wasn't sure if she'd heard him; she was laughing at a story one of the other Dommes shared about a misbehaving sub.

After serving Lady Bella dessert and making a plate for himself, he looked over the crowded tables. Folks wore leather, latex, denim, or nothing at all. Several women and one man wore the sarongs that Lady Bella sold from her pavilion, but none looked as regal as she did in them. How could he consider himself worthy of her service? Still, he chose a seat where he could see when Lady Bella rose so he could quickly extricate himself.

After the welcoming speeches, he spotted Roger wheeling the wardrobe trunk Lady Bella used as a toy chest past the picnic area toward the dungeon set up among the trees. Steven rushed to stand behind Lady Bella, his hands behind his back to make his pecs look more respectable. At fifty, he worked out three times a week and kept his figure trim. He could still fit into his Navy uniform, if he held his breath.

Lyssa knelt besides Lady Bella, who planted one hand on the girl's shoulder and rubbed her own back with her other hand. She slowly extricated her legs from under the table and rose to her feet.

"I want to do a CBT scene with this boy," she nodded in Steven's direction. "Go get it set up."

"Yes, Mistress. Thank you, Mistress." Lyssa dashed off toward the dungeon.

Lady Bella turned to Steven. "I'm going to use the privy. I recommend you do so as well." One corner of her mouth rose, and a wicked glint lit her eyes. "Meet me in the dungeon."

Strings of colored lights hanging from the trees defined the dungeon, which included three St. Andrews crosses, an A-frame bondage rack, two spanking benches, four massage tables, and a suspension frame. Hissing propane lanterns lit the play stations. At least two of the trees were also in use for bondage. Steven shuddered at the thought of rough bark pressing into naked flesh.

He found Lyssa and Roger standing by a massage table near the fire pit. Several drawers had been removed from the trunk and now sat on top of it.

"Do you prefer being bound during a CBT scene?" Lady Bella's husky voice whispered in his ear.

"Yes, Ma'am, at least my wrists and ankles."

"Are you a squirmer?"

Steven bowed his head and held his breath. "I'm afraid so, Ma'am."

Lady Bella laughed. "What are you afraid of, boy? I like squirmers. I want to see you suffer. Stoic doesn't ring my chimes."

Steven grinned.

"Any medical conditions?"

"No, Ma'am."

"Limits?" Lady Bella patted the massage table, and Steven boosted himself up onto it.

"Haven't figured that out yet, Ma'am. Only done CBT once before."

Lady Bella held out her hand, and Lyssa put a leather cuff across the palm. "High or low pain threshold?" She fastened that cuff around one of his wrists and the subsequent cuffs Lyssa handed her around his other wrist and both ankles.

"I think I can take a fair amount."

Lady Bella nodded. He lay on his back, and she clipped the cuffs to tie points on the table. His breathing quickened. The thought of Lady Bella touching his cock, even to hurt it, made him stiffen.

She drew one finger along the length of him. "Nice."

Lyssa held one of the drawers near Lady Bella's elbow, just high enough so Steven couldn't see what was inside. Lady Bella extracted a mesh bag of plastic clothespins. Steven trembled. With gentle fingers, she moved aside his cock, which became rock hard at her touch, and pulled the skin of his scrotum away from his balls. One by one she attached clothespins. They pinched a bit, but he knew the worst was yet to come. She ran a hand over the ends, teasing him with pain, but the lustful gleam in her eye only made him want more. He could take anything to see that delightfully evil smile on her handsome face.

She reached into the drawer again and extracted a mini whip with a dozen plastic tails. With two fingers, she held his glans while she swatted his shaft. Gradually her strokes became hard enough to sting, and he wiggled his ass, pushing into her hand.

She leaned down, the cloth covering her breasts brushing his chest, and whispered in his ear.

"You like that, boy?"

"Hurts. So. Good." He gasped for breath. "Ma'am."

She grabbed his earlobe between her teeth and bit down. At first, he barely noticed, but she slowly increased her grip until he squirmed again. Without releasing his ear, she ran her hands across the clothespins. He moaned and squirmed. She rewarded him with a firm slap, bouncing his cock off his belly. He had to clench his ass cheeks to get himself under control. The last thing he wanted to do was spoil this opportunity by coming without permission.

Lady Bella released his ear and reached into the drawer again. This time she extracted a giant hair clip. She closed it gently around his cock. Plastic nubs that bit into his flesh lined the interior. She pulled out a metal handle attached to a small, rolling pinwheel of sharp little points. His eyes widened.

"Never had a Wartenberg wheel used on you before, boy?"

He managed to turn his head from one side to the other, his eyes never leaving the spikes.

She ran it up his forearm. Prickly, but not painful. On his cock, though?

Lady Bella tilted her head. He nodded, but then closed his eyes. She held him upright with the clip and ran the wheel the length of the narrow gap where the teeth didn't meet. The sound from his throat might have been a scream if he could have gotten enough air into his lungs. He became aware of a wondrous fragrance emanating from Lady Bella. Realizing that she was turned on by his suffering made him want more.

He pushed his hips up again, and she ran the wheel crosswise between the clip's teeth. He squeaked. Lifting his head, he was surprised to see no blood spilling from a hundred tiny holes in his cock. It only felt as if she'd punctured his skin. Her lips were parted and her breathing came in short, heavy gasps.

She dropped his cock and wheeled the spikes up toward his chest, pausing before the metal reached his nipple. He clenched his teeth. Her entire face lit up in anticipation. When the metal touched his sensitive nip, he screamed. She leaned over, bit one nipple while running the spikes over the other. Steven squirmed, the pain traveling from his chest to his cock. He needed to come worse than anytime since he jizzed in his pants when Mandy Lester knocked her pencil off her desk and leaned over in front of him, exposing the biggest cleavage in high school. But his hands were still attached to the table and a hair clip imprisoned his cock, so he could only wriggle in exquisite agony.

Lady Bella lifted her head from his chest and in his mind's eye, he saw blood on her lips. She put one hand against his cheek and he turned his face into it, reveling in the intimacy. "More?" she asked.

"Yes, Ma'am, please." His voice emerged in a hoarse whisper.

She reached into the drawer yet again. He recognized the white ceramic piece in her hand as a ginger grater, but couldn't imagine why it was in her toy chest. She ran one hand over the clothespins, reminding him how much they would hurt whenever she finally took them off, and she removed the clip. He whimpered. She dragged his engorged cock over the white grater and he screamed.

He lifted his head and peered down at his wounded member in the lantern light, expecting to see a raw, bloody mess. It still stood upright against her hand, engorged but intact.

Lady Bella tilted her head to one side. "Did that hurt, boy?"

He nodded.

"Want me to kiss it better?"

His eyes opened wide, the look in her eyes making him fear even the touch of her lips. But he nodded again.

"Can I bite it?"

Steven didn't want her to bite his cock, but in order to do so, she would have to wrap her lips around it. And biting would keep him from coming, which he knew would destroy any hope of gaining Lady Bella's long-term favor. Slowly, he brought his chin down to his chest and lifted it again. He watched, mesmerized as she planted soft lips against the side of his ravaged cock. She dragged her lips to his glans and took him in her mouth. He moaned. When he felt her teeth pressing into his flesh, the moan became a groan. Afraid to move his torso, visions of her biting through and blood spurting all over flashing through his mind, he clenched his fists and gritted his teeth.

She moved her mouth further down, again pressing her teeth into his sensitive flesh. Gently, hard, harder. When she'd bitten him seven times and worked her way halfway down his cock, she closed her lips around him and drew back up. He had to press his fingernails into his palms to avoid coming in her mouth.

Lady Bella licked her lips. "Such a good boy." She pulled off the first clothespin and he cried out as blood flowed back into the pinched flesh. By the time she had removed them all, they were both panting. She pressed her lips against his forehead. "You've been a very good boy. I think you deserve a special reward. She unclipped his wrists and ankles from the table but didn't remove the cuffs. Roger stepped forward and helped him sit up. Steven felt woozy.

Lady Bella used Roger's shoulder to ease herself up next to Steven. Much to his delight, she wrapped her arms around him and his face rested against the heated flesh of her bosom. He wondered if that was his reward. Tentatively, he stuck his tongue out and ran it the length of her breast, searching for her nipple. The cloth fell away, and he wrapped his lips around her nipple, teasing it with his tongue. Lady Bella sighed. She opened her legs, and her arousal penetrated his nostrils.

Was it an invitation? Did he dare? She'd promised him a reward. Without releasing her nipple, he pushed his hips off the table and positioned himself in front of her. Lifting her breasts away from her chest, he kissed his way down, until he found her sparse, gray pubic hair. He lowered himself to his knees and covered the inside of her thighs with kisses. Her skin tasted of salt and lavender soap. He couldn't see much in the lantern light, but he didn't need his eyes to find what he sought.

Her taste reminded him of rich French vanilla, and he couldn't get enough of it. He almost got discouraged when it seemed to take forever to get her off, but then she grabbed his hair and pressed him tighter against her lips. He licked, sucked, and licked until she shuddered. He latched onto her clit and tongued and sucked on it at the same time. Lady Bella shook all over. She released his head to grab the sides of the table. He continued until she put one foot on his shoulder and pushed him back.

"Thank you so very much for the honor, Ma'am." He sat back on his heels, aware he couldn't rise to his feet if he needed to.

"Believe me, boy, the pleasure was all mine. I have two more playdates scheduled this evening, but I think I'll keep you for later. Are you available for the weekend?"

Steven leaned forward and planted a kiss on each of Lady Bella's feet. "Yes, Ma'am. There's nothing I could possibly enjoy more."

Lady Bella reached for Roger's arm, and he helped her to her feet. She kissed Steven on the forehead. "Take him back to my pavilion. Make sure he has water and something to eat."

"Yes, Mistress." Roger put one elbow under each of Steven's pits and pulled him to his feet. He kept his shoulder under Steven's arm and helped him walk back toward the Lady's campsite.

"You must be good, dude. Never known her to pick a playmate to keep for the weekend on Friday night. She likes to keep her options open."

Steven could only grin. He hoped she would keep him for longer than just a weekend, but it was a start.

HAND JOBS

Kate Dominic

I didn't like winter anymore. The snow still painted brilliant whitecaps on the mountains. The wind blew clear and brisk. A lifetime of hard work let me afford trendy cashmere sweaters. But this only disguised my futile search for warmth. The bottom line was that even in sunny Southern California, winter was cold, and these days, cold on my hands just plain sucked.

For ten years now, I'd "worked around" the repetitive stress injury that drove me from the mainstream corporate world. Voice-activated software and the freedom of being my own boss let me control the pacing and schedules of the contracts I took on, to the point where my consulting firm had stayed competitive despite what were physically some really crappy days. Tendinitis. Tenosynovitis. Insert every tunnel-passing-through-the-wrist syndrome. Since I was the only one in the day-to-day trenches of my office, who was to know that my fucking hands and arms really didn't work very well at all anymore?

I was grouchy today. I'd been grouchy for a very long time. This winter, shortly after my fifty-sixth birthday, arthritis set in to my knuckles. The doctor said this was "to be expected" given my age and injuries. Whatever. It still sucked. The colder the weather, the more I ached. Older homes around here don't have central heat, and the wall heater in my living room doesn't throw heat far enough to warm the office. When it's a balmy 58 degrees outside for the Rose Bowl, that's also the temperature at my desk.

Typing with gloves on was my latest trade-off in the battle to maximize my hand use. My husband had gotten me a pair of butter-soft leather fingerless gloves for Christmas. I knew I'd make the deadlines for tomorrow's end-of-the-month reports with no problem.

It wasn't even housework at the end of the day that was irritating me. Twenty paces down the hall from my desk, I had enough ergonomically correct wonder gadgets to cook everything from French toast to gourmet dinners whenever I was in the mood. There were remotes galore. Hell, the appliances were so talented the house almost cleaned itself!

My problem had to do with bedtime. My husband was a hunk. Gorgeous blue eyes. Shoulders out to here that looked great in a leather jacket and a butt that showed how a man was meant to wear jeans. Jeff was smart and sexy, and he had a great sense of humor. Even though we'd been married since before I was disabled, I had trouble accepting that my trashed paws were no biggie to him. Okay, so I still had a few insecurities about my "hidden" disability.

The thing was, Jeff loved hand jobs. Fast ones, slow ones, tight or loose. And he loved his hand jobs wet. He was good with our using pretty much anything but hot sauce for lube. I had more kinds of hand lotion than a boutique on the nightstand by our bed. Unfortunately, the bedroom was even farther away from the heater than the office was. So, the 58 degrees on the thermometer outside the window at bedtime meant I was shivering in my sexiest flannel nightgown even with the space heater on.

Jeff had had that look in his eye all night. He'd been touching and nuzzling me. He was all about mutual satisfaction. He'd plied me with banana cream pie with whipping cream. Subtlety was so not his strong suit! He was wearing a soft new sweatshirt that emphasized his shoulders and the flannel lounge pants I'd gotten him last Valentine's Day. Several times this evening, I'd caught him unconsciously stroking himself through that warm, soft cotton. And he couldn't keep his hands off my breasts, something I'd encouraged by not wearing a bra.

My fingers were itching to touch him. I so wanted to stroke him long enough, and sexily enough, to really get him off. But between the swelling in my knuckles and the bone-deep ache in my wrists, my hands hurt badly. There was no way I was going to be able take my gloves off without being so miserable that Jeff would pick up on it. But, this afternoon, I'd come up with a plan.

Despite how nervous I was with the whole idea, I was going to try to start us both on track for a total glove fetish.

The trick was going to be in the timing. Thanks to the local thrift store, I was now the proud owner of an assortment of gloves. I'd laid out several pairs on the nightstand: an elbow-length pair in navy blue velvet; a retro, lacy white dress-up pair; fur-lined leather driving gloves that had been in the clearance bin because one entire palm was split open; some plain, pink knit ones; and three sizes of non-latex hospital gloves, because I wasn't sure which ones would fit for what I needed. The LED on the bedroom space heater said the room was now 64 degrees. I was just turning on the flameless candles when Jeff walked through the door.

"What's this?" he laughed, eyeing the nightstand and the turned-down bed. His hand drifted to rub his crotch again. His cock was already heavily tenting the front.

"My hands are cold," I purred, stroking my icy knuckle lightly down his cheek. His eyes instantly looked concerned.

"Damn, babe! Your hands *are* cold!" He tucked them under his arms. "Better?"

Oh, his smile made me hot and tingly in all the right places!

"Much," I smiled, carefully extracting my hands. "But I was thinking the way to keep them warm all night might be to wear gloves to bed." I looked meaningfully at the nightstand, then reached over and flipped the top off my favorite rose-scented lotion. "If that's okay with you."

I could almost see the wheels turning. He rubbed the front of his pants again. A wet spot appeared, and he swallowed hard.

"That could be okay." His voice was suddenly hoarse. He looked from the nightstand to the bed, then back to me. "What do you want me to do?"

"Lie down on the bed with enough clothes off for me to get to your cock."

In a flash, he was buck-naked except for his socks. The covers were at the bottom of the bed, and Jeff was lying in the middle of the sheets with his hands behind his head and his legs spread.

"Will this do?" he grinned. His cock waved over his belly like a thick burgundy flagpole. His tiny nipples were pebbled in the silvered dark fur of his chest.

"You'll freeze!" I laughed.

"I don't think so." His balls were pulled up close, but his voice held enough heat to warm the whole room 10 degrees. "I just need a little bit of friction." He clenched his groin muscles, making his cock dance. I giggled as a thin web of precum leaked down to his belly.

"Friction. Hmm." I brushed the back of my hand over his shaft. He gasped, his balls moving closer as he shivered. I smiled down at him. "Velvet would make nice friction. Keep your hands under your head."

His eyes followed my every movement as I slowly pulled the velvet gloves on in a reverse striptease. Inch by inch, I drew the dark blue gloves up to my elbows. Then I carefully worked my fingers all the way down, sliding the fabric carefully until each fingertip hit the base. Several times, Jeff's arms twitched, like he wanted to reach down to stroke himself. But each time, he caught himself and did nothing but watch.

I could feel my fingers thawing inside the velvet. In no time at all, the gloves were toasty warm. I reached out with just my index finger and drew the tip slowly up the length of Jeff's shaft. He gasped and arched his hips.

"I see you like that." I stroked in lazy patterns all over his turgid flesh. His shudders told me how much he was enjoying it. But his precum was getting my gloves damp. That wasn't the texture I wanted him feeling right now. I told him so, so he knew what was coming when I leaned down and delicately swiped my tongue over the head of his cock.

He groaned as I licked up the salty stream and blew him dry. Then I took his cock in a loose grip and pumped slowly up and down. I deliberately kept my movements erratic, twisting and turning until he was trembling. Twice more I washed and dried the weeping head. His moans were so intense I swore I felt them all the way to my pussy. I leaned down and gave his cockhead one quick final kiss.

"You know, love, I think my hands are actually getting a bit hot. I'm going to switch to something cooler."

Jeff's eyes were like magnets as he watched me peel off the velvet gloves. I laid them on the nightstand and drew on the lacy white gloves, once more taking my time working the fingers all the way into place.

I'd been surprised at how scratchy the lacy gloves were. Not on the inside—that was comfortably neutral. The outside, though, had a roughness that was completely at odds with the delicate feminine look of the lace—much like some of the summer negligees I wore to catch Jeff's eye, even though we both slept nude when it was hot. He quirked an eyebrow at me. I smiled innocently.

"You have such beautiful, manly nipples, sweetheart."

His indrawn breath told me he knew what was coming. I rubbed his nipples between my fingers, murmuring sweet, soft, very dirty descriptions of what I was going to do to him. Then I leaned over and licked his nipples.

He stiffened and moaned. I wasn't sure how much was anticipation and how much sensation, so I took my time getting his nipples nice and wet. Then I took the tips in my lacy fingers, and I rubbed very, very gently.

"Fuck!" He threw his head back, closing his eyes and panting as his cock jutted up. He was trembling beneath me, but I didn't stop. Eventually, he relaxed back into the bed, his breath shaky as he looked down at where my fingers were still rubbing his now tender, pink nipples.

"I'm going to rub your cock, too."

He groaned, his gaze glued to my fingers as I slowly trailed one lace-covered hand over his chest and down his belly. My touch was getting rougher. Then the white lace of my glove stroked firmly over the deep red skin of his thoroughly engorged cock.

"Stop!" Jeff grabbed my wrist, gently but firmly holding me still as he panted like he'd run a marathon. I waited, my hand frozen on his cock while he caught his breath. Finally he let go, dropped his hand, and slid it back under his head.

"Sorry," he smiled, though I could see he was anything but. "I was too close."

I tapped his cock, trying my best to look stern. "See that it doesn't happen again. Um, until I make it happen."

His cock twitched against me, hard. "Yes, ma'am!"

I trailed my finger up his shaft, lingering on the head as his precum soaked my lacy fingertip. An unexpected shiver ran through me as his eyes widened. I was really enjoying this! So I started to rub.

It had been a long time since my hands had done exactly what I wanted. I kept one hand on his nipple and one on his cock. It wasn't long at all before he was once again on the brink. So, I stopped again. The only problem with all this teasing was that by now, I was so horny I was ready to throw off all my clothes—and the damn gloves—and jump his bones!

On the other hand, I was having so much fun. Jeff's eyes were glazed with desire. I took my time with the fur-lined leather glove, turning the torn one mostly inside out so I could use both sensations to soothe the skin I'd sensitized with the lace. But we were both getting too worked up to last much longer. I skipped teasing him with the knitted glove and went straight to the surgical one—in my usual size. My hands were warm enough that I didn't need to double layer, or maybe I was just too turned on to care.

I squirted lotion in my palm, the sweet rose scent filling my nostrils as I rubbed my hands together just enough to warm the lube. Then I took Jeff's cock in a sturdy two-handed grip and pulled slowly up.

"Fuck! Fuck! Fuck!" His low growl made my pussy clench. Filthy incoherence is always a positive sign at that point in our lovemaking.

I varied my grip just enough to keep him from coming until he was writhing on the bed. Then with no warning, I tightened one hand, cupped his balls in the other, and touched him in the ways I knew he loved best. Jeff bucked up, shouting as his cock spurted streams of musky, hot semen all over my hands and his belly and the bed. The first shot was so hard, it landed on his nipple. By then my hands ached, and my wrist felt like someone had shoved a knife into it, but oh! I felt good!

As soon as he could breathe, Jeff hauled me down beside him, yanked off my nightgown, and used his strong, powerful fingers to make me feel even better. He rubbed my clit and fucked me with his fingers in ways my own couldn't anymore, and he didn't stop until I'd had three orgasms and was lying in a boneless puddle in his arms. Then before I could get cold, he hopped out of bed, shut off the space heater, and pulled the covers up over both of us.

"I love you, babe," he murmured, turning off the candles and hauling me back into his arms. He stilled, then snuggled closer.

"Damn, my nipples are tender!" A moment later, he laughed. "I think I like it!"

Gloves, I thought. As soon as I'd sent off the next day's reports, I was going back to the thrift store and buying every damn pair of gloves I could find. I was still smiling as I let myself drift off to sleep.

SMOOTH AND SLIPPERY

Doug Harrison

I'm shaving my torso in the shower. A few nicks, a little blood, but, hey, that comes with the territory. Warm water and aftercare with isopropyl pads and dabs of Neosporin mend all. The stubborn safety razor jams, grasping strands of my masculinity, but I persist. My boyfriend and neighbor, Jim, slated to arrive early afternoon after walking his yappy dog, likes me smooth. Says I look sexy. But I refuse to shave my legs. Looks goofy, like I'm a drag queen or am impersonating a much younger, proficient triathlete.

It's a very close shave. I feel no stubble as I slide my fingers around my firm pecs. And, I must admit, I'm excited by the smooth hardness. All right, I'm caressing myself. So what? I don't yank on my penis, well, not too much—that's Jim's job. He wants me naked when I fling the front door open, but he always arrives a few minutes early, a direct affront to my perennial procrastination and frequent attempts to tease with an outlandishly skimpy outfit.

No aftershave, no underarm deodorant. I reek of raw manliness, masculinity personified.

I know I sound a tad bit smart-ass, like a teenage boy, but that side of me emerges despite my technical PhD and career. It's my boyish charm, so I'm told, that hangs around, unlike my hair.

I've cleaned out—that's boy talk for douched—so Jim can fuck me silly. And I'll return the favor. Equal strokes for equal folks.

But we're not equal, at least not in age. He's twenty years younger than my seventy-two. Why do I attract younger men? Do they crave daddy figures? Well, that's a question for those who slump into therapists' chairs. I welcome guys of any age who rove my way, which repeatedly leads to satisfactory couplings. Perhaps my gold earring—left side, of course—and my gold nose ring hint that there's still a spark of life and concomitant joy in me.

The nose ring is always a conversation opener: "Did that hurt?"

"No."

Raised eyebrows.

"There's a sweet spot in there. A good piercer can find it."

"Oh."

Of course, I've always taken care of myself: diet, running, hiking, weight lifting, the works. So, I'm buffed, but now must settle for long walks. A good example of a solid foundation combined with HIV loss of body fat. Shuck my shirt, and folks gasp. Jim is forever complimenting me on my body, almost to the point of embarrassment. But we're intellectually compatible. At last, someone to share tech talk on this sparsely populated lava rock. Plus, Jim is also HIV positive. We compare our pill regimens like two old ladies evaluating recipes. It's important if I want to drink his piss. Don't want discordant medication sloshing around in my stomach. So he waits until after we play to gulp his handful of capsules and tablets.

Except for Viagra, Levitra, or Cialis—you choose—and we're hard. A young man's assistant and an old man's savior. My natural erections are almost hard enough and persist almost long enough, but insurance leads to assurance. Pop the pill, and I feel a body flush—a legal high. Soon it settles in one place and I'm ready for action. But not today—I have a surprise in mind.

Yes, my body isn't what it used to be, but I'm not waiting for mature resignation like the Marschallin in *Der Rosenkavalier*. My cock doesn't thwap against my belly when I think about sex, gawk at porn, or ogle sexy men and women. I jerk off once or twice a week, not my youthful two to five times a day. But I still curl, thrust, and parry my tongue like a pro. I open and relax my throat and massage a humongous cock like Jim's with supple throat muscles. I circular breathe like an operatic diva when necessary.

A few special toys are arrayed for Jim as an invitation, perhaps a challenge. I've included the inevitable butt plug. It's *de rigueur* that he shove one up my ass before I fuck him. Feels *so* good, like I'm being fingered while I plow him. And he'll bring his own toys. Always wants to surprise me. A cock cage here, nipple clamps there. My nipples have gained in size and sensitivity over the years. Play partners are attracted to them, perhaps because of my six-gauge, one-inch diameter, stainless steel nipple rings, and they all delight in coaxing moans of pleasure with gentle caresses and gasps of pain with pinching and pulling.

I'm well rested. My age and the HIV meds undermine my once-youthful vigor. I manage about three or four hours of work a day, perhaps push it a bit more with coffee. If it's hard labor, like yard work, I'm sedentary the next day. A heavy date requires a slow day beforehand and a preparatory nap.

Not like when I was a youthful stud—work all day, drive an hour or so into the big city for a hot date, get home late, and work like hell at my technical job in Silicon Valley the next day. No sweat—all in stride.

I don't come very often these days, and my infrequent spurts provoke bellows that carry through the jungle and must disturb the local mongooses, doves, and wild pigs. But it's great fun trying to squirt, almost like having multiple orgasms since I sidle up to completion, retreat, and repeat.

But all this is physical. What's most important is empathy, passion to compassion. What are my feelings about myself, about my partner, about us? Not only about what we do, or how we go about it, but why we interact. What's unique? Is it more than another playdate? If so, why? Not analysis, mind you, but synthesis. A reaching out that is reciprocated on, dare I say, a spiritual level. A coupling of kindred spirits sowed on trust, nurtured with experience, and expanded with friendship that sometimes develops into love: greeting each other with a warm embrace and basking in the cocoon of a serene and tender afterglow.

There's the doorbell. No time to choose and tempt with an appropriate costume. Damn!

"Aloha, Jim."

"Hi guy—you're wearing a towel!" He lowers the brown bags he's carrying and reaches an eager hand for me.

"At least come inside before you yank it off!"

"Yeah, I'll put these groceries in the kitchen—before I undress us."

Jim slips out of his sandals—customary in Hawaii, although I have yet to figure out why—what's a little dirt and dust, for Christ's sake? He steps inside, plops two brown bags on the kitchen counter, puts a few items in the fridge and something in the freezer—dessert, I hope. He shimmies out of his shirt, drops his shorts, and stands there, arms on hips, dick, as usual, already hard. A polished, stainless steel cock ring, perverted craftsmanship at its finest, captures both sac and dick. He moves into a funnel of sunlight, and the band sparkles like a large wedding ring.

He's a painter, creative with a sharp eye for color, form, and texture, whereas I can't even draw a half-ass smiley face, despite, or because of, my technical knowledge of colorimetry. His eyes avert the piles of books and papers roosting on the dining room table and kitchen counter. I apologize for the clutter, but he grins, flings his arms out, palms up, and says that he's here to see me, not the house.

He smiles. I smile. He throws my towel onto his heap of clothing. We clutch each other, our erections pushing belly to belly, his rock-hard, mine semi-rigid. Shall I kneel or bend over?

I rest my palms on Jim's shoulders. "Off to the bedroom?" I ask with a wink. He nods, and I grab his hand. I lead him down the long hallway, our arms swinging like two kids heading to the playground, which, in a sense, we are. I stop and ogle his dick.

"Fuck bench, bed, or rug?" I ask. "Guest's choice."

"Lean over the bed," he orders.

We move into the bedroom, where Jack, my large, orange tiger tabby, is curled in a tight ball on his neatly folded rainbow beach blanket on the far side of the king-size bed, paws covering his snout. I lean over the bed, firmly plant my feet, reach behind me, and spread my cheeks. Jack opens one eye. Sometimes he watches my solo adventures as I meander across the bedroom, following my bobbing dick, but not tonight. He yawns and resumes his siesta as only a cat can.

Jim kneels and runs a finger around my hole. "Nice, as usual," he states. "Good shave job." I groan. He explores deeper with his tongue, spits into the tunnel, and tongue fucks me. "Christ," I gurgle. I squirm, he slurps, and we settle into gentle kisses, slow licks, and moans of pleasure.

He stands, slaps my ass, leans against me, butt to butt. *Must be donning a condom and lube,* I think, judging by the vibrations. He grabs my hips, and I feel his dick probing. But not for long. He shoves its fat head in, and I receive it with a loud groan. Not a yelp, mind you.

"Ready for me, eh, slut?" he teases and again slaps my ass. "Feels great," he adds as he pushes his entire cock in.

"Sure does, as usual, Sir!" I respond.

He laughs and begins a slow, gentle piston motion. I purr. The bed shakes a tad, and Jack looks over. Jim gets serious, real serious, and screws me like it's our last time together. He knocks the breath from me. I clutch the sheets and yell. "Fuck, oh fuck, yes, yes, yes, do me, oh do me, thank you Sir, oh fuck, fuck, yes, yes, yes!" I bite the bedspread. Jack saunters over, rubs his Maine coon cat jowl against my cheek, a cat's way of claiming its territory. One of his fangs is chipped, and he drools on my chin. He licks my forehead, his feline agility compensating for my oscillations. "Scram," I shout and push him away. He retreats to his blanket, assumes a sphinx posture, and watches us like a movie critic. I'm almost embarrassed by being scrutinized by a neutered tomcat.

Jim howls, a mixture of laughter and pre-orgasmic shrieks.

"I'm coming," he roars. I clutch his dick with my sphincter and feel his shudders as he surges into me.

"Wow," he groans and flops onto my back. "Double wow!"

I synchronize my breathing with his until he slithers off my back, his slippery journey lubricated by our mixture of sweat. We sit on the edge of the bed, feet dangling over the edge, and I mop his brow with a small white towel, the usual cum rag. I hand it to him and he heads for the bathroom, dick dangling between his legs, supporting a cum-filled condom.

"Take your time," I say. He nods. I head for my office.

Two suitcases, hard black plastic with metal corners and hinges, are tucked in the closet. They contained electrician's tools, judging by the lift-up inserts with sleeves for screwdrivers and pliers. One now holds my electrical toys, the other my pumping equipment.

I haven't pumped my dick in ages. I washed the largest clear plastic cylinder with the morning dishes. It's ten inches long, two inches internal diameter, one end sealed with flat plastic that contains an air coupling, the other end open with curled edges. My smoothly shaved crotch aids and abets a tight vacuum seal. I join a small bronze hand-held pump similar to a bicycle tire pump to the cylinder with clear plastic tubing.

The preparations excite me, and I'm semi-rigid as I slide my dick into the cylinder and push on the far end with the four fingers of my left hand. I grasp the pump between my left thumb and index finger, and I pump with my right hand. The seal is immediate, and the tube presses into my crotch. My cock is reasonably large, so I'm told, but it's great to see my hard-on pulse and swell as its length increases about an inch and its girth fills the chamber. I pump until the plunger is immobile, and I tie off my dick by looping a leather thong several times around the base and secure it with a tight double knot. I uncouple the pump, click the air release, and, presto, a long, fat, very hard dick, without prayers or pills.

I return to the bedroom and lean against the bedpost, assuming a casual pose and a shit-eatin' grin. Jim returns, halts, and gasps.

"Holy shit!" he bellows.

"Your turn to get fucked," I announce as I fondle my beer can dick.

"You're not gonna stick that thing in me," he states, although his eyes say otherwise.

"Don't be a sissy," I sass back. "Onto the bed with you."

Jim forgets to mark me with a butt plug, crawls onto the bed, and looks over his shoulder at my crotch. I slowly and adroitly roll a condom over my dick and smear it with lube.

"On your back!" I order. I place a pillow under his hips, kneel, and pull his legs over my shoulders. I massage the perimeter of his hole and slide one finger in, then two, then three. I look into his eyes and smile. I massage his prostate and nod. He shudders. I ease my dick in. All the way. I pause, savoring the sensation of our pelvic kiss. I pull my shaft out, pause, lingering as his sphincter grabs my dickhead. I reenter halfway, pushing gently to the left, to the right, up, down, an explorer in an eager cave. I increase the intensity and depth of my thrusts, and he grabs his dick, hard despite the pounding he's taking. I feel my orgasm approaching, its ferocity not to be denied. I lean over and bite his lip.

"Together," I whisper, and seal his mouth with mine.

We arch our backs and erupt, our muffled grunts and screams flowing between us. Spittle slides from the edges of our harlequin smiles.

I pull out and rest on my haunches as our breathing returns partway to normal, and I untie my cock bondage. I trot to the bathroom and clean up as Jim rests, then stand in the doorway and gaze at him.

"Let's relax a bit," I suggest.

"Sounds good."

I move a clutter of books and pens from the far side of the bed to the floor. We stretch out on our backs, shoulders and knees touching, and link hands. Jack pounces onto the bed and curls up, perhaps drawn to our serenity.

"I want you to see this," I say and raise my head. It's late afternoon, and sunlight streams over the bedroom onto a stately Ohia tree, the largest on the property. The side facing us glows a deep yellow that tapers to dark gray on both sides of the column.

Jim gazes, his eyes running up and down the trunk, and focuses trancelike on one spot. I savor his appreciation. He looks at me.

"A perfect moment," he whispers.

Dinner can wait. We kiss and drift into sleep.

TONY TEMPO

Tsaurah Litzky

I never thought I'd end up like this, in the Crescendo Home for Aged and Indigent Musicians—I, Tony Tempo, once known as the trumpet king of swing. I'm heading towards that last command performance, watching *Jeopardy* with a bunch of lonely old wankers in the common room of a converted Victorian mansion in Baldwin, Long Island.

I thought I'd spend my old age with my darling Clara, my wife of forty-five years. I was sure she'd outlive me, me with my daily pack of Pall Malls and nightly half-bottle of Jack, but then she up and died. An embolism, the doctor called it, a bubble of blood, burst in her brain. He said it didn't hurt her; she just saw red, and then she was gone forever.

I had hoped we'd head south when I retired, move to Florida. After she kicked the bucket, I didn't retire. I hung on, kept touring, kept playing my trumpet, but wherever I was, whatever song

I was playing, she was always on my mind. A couple of years ago, I had this stroke, and I lost all the feeling and movement in my right leg. Now I'm an old gimp on a walker. At least I can still play my trumpet; at least I still got my memories.

I used to imagine Clara and me in Florida. We'd buy a nice condominium by the sea. In the evenings we'd have dinner in a fancy restaurant, then walk on the beach holding hands. After that, we'd go home and make love. Clara was always so hot for me; we partied every night until the day she died.

I'd lie in bed on top of the covers stripped to my birthday suit while Clara was taking her shower. She'd come out of the bathroom naked, my Venus rising from the sea. She was voluptuous, a va-va-voom girl. She would wiggle slowly towards me, doing a dance older than time.

She'd lick her lips, moisten them, and then bend over my belly and take me in her mouth.

Clara loved to smoke my pipe, as she called it. She had this trick, something she did with her head, twisting it round and round in a corkscrew motion when she had her tongue on me. It got me so worked up I was about to explode. She usually stopped to let me calm down before that happened.

How I miss her. There are no women here except for the nurses, and they treat us like babies. For example, Miss Pouty, when she knocks on my door every day at 3:00 PM, she says the same thing. Her voice is loud and syrupy, oozing with heartburn. "Would Tony like a little snacky-poo?" What I'd really like is a snacky-poo on some poontang, but I don't tell her that. I decide to have a little fun with her. When she knocks, I hobble over and open the door. I make as much of a gallant bow as I can manage.

"Good afternoon, lovely Miss Pouty," I say.

She draws back, surprised. She doesn't seem pleased. I've deviated from the script, our routine. "Would Mr. Tony like a little snacky-poo?" she asks, but now her saccharine voice has a sharp edge. I give her what I hope is a winning smile; too bad I don't have my dentures in.

"I'd rather snack on your lovely lips," I answer. She steps back, nearly drops the tray. Her complexion turns from pale gray to angry orange. "What's the matter with you?" she sputters. "You're too old to even think about such things. You're obviously showing symptoms of dementia. Try any funny stuff, buster, and I'll fix you so you won't even be able to change your own diapers." She slams the door, and I hear her clumping away down the hall. I don't even wear diapers, and she has hurt my feelings. So much for a little innocent flirtation.

I feel shaky, totter back across the room, sink down on my bed. She may think that all I have left between my legs is a skinny straw to piss through. Little does she know my sleep is filled with dreams of Clara. Every morning I wake up with my hand holding a hard-on the size of a one-pound salami, a poor boy.

A couple of nights after the Miss Pouty incident, I'm feeling low. I imagine Clara lying beside me without a stitch on. All she is wearing is the black leather mask she puts on when she wants me to take her in the ass. There is a loud knock. It must be ten o'clock, time for my nighttime meds. I hope it isn't grouchy Miss Pouty.

"Come in," I call.

"May I switch on the light?" a sweet voice, certainly not Miss Pouty's, asks hesitantly.

"Sure," I say. The lights go on, and standing in my doorway is a little woman with a nice face.

She cuts a trim figure in her nurse's uniform, first nurse I'd seen around here who has a waist. "I'm your new night nurse, Mary," she says. "May I come in?"

"Yes, ma'am," I answer, and I sit straight up in bed. She smiles at me as she steps into the room. She has a grin that would melt a snowman's heart.

"According to my chart, you're Tempo, Tony Tempo." Her big eyes take in the pictures, the framed album covers on the wall.

Those big eyes grow even wider. "You're *the* Tony Tempo," she says, her voice rising, "who played with the Harvest Moon Orchestra and with Bucky Bernstein's Big Band! You made the record, *Trumpet Solos for Love*. My father had all your records but he loved that one best. Oh, Mr. Tempo, I can't believe I'm actually meeting you."

"Call me Tony," I say. Her glance falls on my walker.

"Mr. T—I mean, Tony, I see from your chart that you had a stroke. Do you still play the trumpet?"

"I do," I told her. "Maybe I'll play a tune for you."

"Could you play 'Begin the Beguine'?" she asks. "That's my favorite." That was Clara's favorite too.

"No problem, I'd be delighted," I say.

"Right now?" she asks hopefully. Then she looks at her watch and frowns. "I forgot," she says. "Head nurse told me you are not supposed to play music after ten o'clock. Some of the other residents are sleeping by then."

The stiffy between my legs is perking up. I puddle the blanket over my legs so she won't see. "Don't worry," I tell her, "I hope to perform for you soon."

"I look forward to that," she says as she hands me my pills.

"When are you coming back?" I ask her before she leaves.

"Tomorrow night," she answers, then she clicks off the light and goes out the door.

❉ ❉ ❉

The next night by eight o'clock, I'm freshly shaved. What is left of my hair is parted on one side and neatly combed. My trumpet is in its usual place, resting in the case on top of the dresser.

At eight thirty, there's a knock on the door.

"Come in," I say.

"Good evening, Tony," she greets me, "I came to you first. It's still early enough for you to play me a song." She looks like a sunny day. I know I am being an idiot. Why should a pretty woman like her be interested in an old fart like me? Is she just trying to be nice, or is she genuinely interested in the music? It doesn't matter. I am just happy to see her.

"I was hoping you might show up early, because I had the same idea. Sit down, make yourself comfortable," I tell her.

She sits down on the bed and puts the tray of pills beside her. I notice she isn't wearing a wedding ring. "Tell me, Mary," I ask as I unlatch the case, "How come you're working nights? Don't you have a family?"

"My husband and I split up years ago," she says. "My son is still in school and busy with his friends. I like working nights. It keeps me from being lonely."

"I agree. It's hard to be alone. My wife's gone ten years. I miss her all the time. There are pictures of her on the wall behind you."

Mary turns her head and takes a look. "She's so pretty," she says.

"You're pretty too," I respond. Did I imagine it, or did her face tinge with pink?

She looks up at me expectantly. I pick up the trumpet, put the mouthpiece in, and start to blow. The notes come out, perfect, golden.

I can hear Ella's singing, *and down by the shore, an orchestra's playing and even the palms seem to be swaying . . . and there we are swearing to love forever, and promising never, never to part . . . what rapture serene, to begin the beguine.* I never played better. A woman can sure bring out the best music in a man. Playing for Mary, I almost feel like a kid again. Her mouth is half open, her eyes half shut. She seems enthralled. When I am done, she claps her hands.

"Oh, Tony, you sound even better than on the record," she says. "It's been so long since I've heard live music. Play another for me?"

"With great pleasure," I tell her. "I'll take requests from the audience."

"Hmmn," she says. "Let me think." She leans back, crosses her legs. They are very shapely, even in their shiny white nurses' hose and clunky nurses' oxfords. "How about 'Loverman'?" she asks, batting her thick, dark eyelashes.

I nearly drop my horn. Can she be flirting with me? I try to be cool, control the sudden shaking in my fingers. "This one is dedicated to Mary," I say, as if we were in a big nightclub. Once again, each note is perfect. The melody floats in the air like a kiss. This time Mary doesn't clap. She jumps up, puts her arms around me, and gives me a big, soft smooch on the cheek. She smells of rubbing alcohol and Dentyne.

"Tony, when you play, it makes me so happy. It makes me feel like dancing," she whispers against my shoulder.

"Dancing tomorrow night," I tell her.

"Okay," she says. "I'll try to come early again."

That next night I am ready and waiting for her by seven thirty. I even put on some Old Spice cologne from a bottle that must have been sitting in my bathroom cabinet for two years. Finally she knocks, and my heart races back and forth like a metronome.

Get a grip, I tell myself, *or you will welcome her with a heart attack.* I take a couple of deep breaths.

"Come in," I call.

"Hi," Mary says, as she steps into the room. "How are you tonight, Tony?"

I decide to go for broke. "Right as rain, now that you're here, Mary," I tell her.

She giggles. "You make me feel so special," she says.

"You are special," I answer. "Come sit down on the bed and we'll chat awhile."

She sits down on the bed and puts the medicine tray beside her like she did the night before. She is pale, has dark circles under her eyes. "You look a little beat. You working too hard?" I ask.

"No," she says. "It's kind of you to be concerned. It's my son. He's fallen in with a bad crowd. I don't know what to do."

"I hope you don't mind me giving you some advice?" I ask. "You need to sit down with him and talk to him straight. Tell him he only lives once, and if he starts to screw up, it's hard to get back on track. How old is he?"

"Twenty," she says. I'm surprised. I thought her kid would still be in grade school.

"When did you have him, when you were fifteen?" Her face perks up a little.

"I'm fifty-two now, Tony," she tells me. I had thought she was in her early forties.

"Well then," I say. "You're just the right age for me." She doesn't say yes; she doesn't say no. She suddenly leans over and kisses me right on the mouth, a lingering kiss full of promises. I kiss her back. I am glad I still remember how to do it. When her lips part, I slide my tongue in. The wood is growing up so high between my legs I'm afraid I'll poke her in her generous bosom. Then she starts sucking on my tongue, and I stop being frightened of anything.

"I'm feeling so much better," Mary says when we pull apart.

The way I am sitting, my knee pushes against the walker standing next to the bed. "I know I promised you dancing, Mary," I tell her, trying to keep any hint of bitterness out of my voice, "but even with this contraption, I don't know if I could manage a two-step."

"I don't care. You're still an attractive man, Tony." She puts her hand on the inside of my thigh, and her fingers brush against my cohones. She strokes lightly. I want to leap on her and take her right then, but she pulls her hand away. "I better go," she sighs. "I'm already late." She gives me a quick kiss and is gone.

I feel like I'm dancing in the clouds. Can this really be happening? Maybe Mary is some demented fantasy born out of my loneliness. Maybe I've finally gone over the bend. But I don't care because she makes me feel like springtime. I pick up my trumpet and play "The red, red robin is bob, bob, bobbin' along" until my next-door neighbor Reuben, a nonagenarian xylophone player, starts pounding on the wall.

I put away the trumpet, switch off the lights, and go to bed. Soon I'm in the limbo land between sleeping and waking. Clara and Mary are lying on either side of me. Mary has her hand delicately over my dick. Clara's head is curled on my shoulder. I hear a faint knocking at the door. I stumble up, nearly fall, before I grab my walker and make it to the door. It's Mary. I move aside to let her in. She closes the door and puts a finger to her lips.

She pushes me back till I am sitting on the bed. She unbuttons her uniform and lets it fall to the floor. Her skin is so white she gleams in the darkness like a giant pearl. She is wearing a simple black bra and a black pair of those newfangled thong panties. I can make out wisps of curly hair escaping the silky triangle at her vulva. This turns me on so much, my pecker rises up like a periscope. Mary must sense it, because quicker than I can say *Hallelujah*, she kneels between my legs, frees it from my pants. She takes it between her full lips into her juicy mouth. She sucks gently on my cockhead as she circles my pole with her hand and starts pumping. Her movements are syncopated so as her head moves up and down on me her hand does the same.

I am impressed. Mary seems to have had considerable experience.

I can feel the heat of her breasts moving on my shins. I reach down, unhook her bra, and pull it off. I lift one tit in each hand and start tracing my fingers up to the nipple and back. She seems to like this because she starts blowing me even harder. She starts tickling the little hole on the top of my cock with her tongue, and miraculously I'm young again, I'm Rambo, I'm unstoppable. I start to come and come and come into her mouth like a mighty warrior. Right away, I feel embarrassed. I should have pulled out before the moment of truth. I don't know if she likes to swallow like Clara did. But Mary downs my come like it is good, fresh milk.

When I am drained, Mary raises herself and sits beside me, my visiting goddess. I put my arm around her. She nestles closer. "I enjoyed that," she says. "It makes me very wet." She puts her hand over me. I am still half hard, and with the touch of her palm my prick jumps up again all fine and frisky. She pulls off her panties. I pull off my pajama top; she pulls off the bottoms. She straddles me, and I put my hands on her hips and help her slide up and down until we make the bedsprings sing "Begin the Beguine."

After she leaves, I feel the sheet, still warm where she was lying beside me. I don't know what will happen with this surprising new romance, but one thing I know for sure: Right now, I'm the happiest old horn dog in the world.

✱ *A slightly different version of "Tony Tempo" was published in* Tasting Him: Oral Sex Stories, *edited by Rachael Kramer Bussel.*

BETTER THAN VIBRATORS

Cheri Crystal

"Jean . . . ahhh, wait . . . higher, no . . . lower, right, oh God, yes, oh sweetie, yeah, just like that, only softer. Not that soft, ahhhh, yes, better, just purrrrfect, don't stop . . . don't ever stop."

"Okay, but I'll have to quit my day job," I quipped.

"Good, oh yeah, feels very good." Louise was the vocal type from the moment I'd met her in the student union thirty-five years ago. She was the university ringleader of gay rights before it was cool to be out. With her charisma, she inspired confidence in her convictions. Crowds gathered to listen whether they agreed with her or not. I hung on her every word as much then as I did now; it didn't matter if she was orating from a podium or orchestrating her next orgasm.

She murmured in sync with her gyrating hips as if singing to her favorite tune. It brought me back to our youth when we had high hopes and boundless energy to accomplish whatever cause or desire we set our minds to. It's funny how goals change with age. For instance, aiming to remember where you left your grocery list and wondering if you wrote one out in the first place. At fifty-three I could kick myself for taking good health for granted during my youth. All the abuse like smoking, drinking, overeating, and not sleeping enough came back to haunt me.

An aging body took a lot fewer punches to be out for the count. What in the world would I be like at eighty-three? If I lived that long. I didn't dare say that to Louise. She was six years my senior and fitter than me by a mile. I went through menopause before she'd even started. After my heart attack, the sheer terror of another one landed me on anti-anxiety drugs. Between a significant drop in estrogen, libido-altering drugs, and crappy genes, I was borderline diabetic, and my bones were thinning too. Calcium supplements weren't as bad as the special diet and exercise routine. What would be next?

If it weren't for Louise's chorus of love cries, I could really wallow in self-pity, but I love all her sounds, scents, nooks, and crannies. Her idiosyncrasies, the ones only I know, like how she often talks in her sleep and has no recollection of it in the morning, or my absolute favorite: her hum. The first time she went down on me, we were in my dorm room during a school day. She was a grad student with a free schedule until the afternoon. I was a naughty freshman and had skipped class. I was really getting into what her luscious lips and tongue were doing when I heard what sounded like the fridge on the fritz. The hum grew louder. You'd have thought I would have felt some extra vibrations on my nether regions, but I was a total dork when it came to Louise and longed to impress her no matter what. The hum totally distracted me because I worried we were about to have a short in the plug or something.

I can still picture Louise with her rosy blush over pale skin. As her bright blue eyes darkened with desire, her lips parted in puzzlement at my sudden shift. Her full firm breasts and large pink nipples, slim waist, ample hips, and especially her neat golden-brown triangle at the apex of her long lean legs drew me in more than any other woman I'd ever seen. She sat statuesquely as I quickly scanned the room for the source of the hum. When I glanced back in her direction, Louise wore a bemused, yet seductive, smile as she lured me over. We laughed until we cried after I learned it was Louise humming down there and not some faulty wiring.

I relived that memory often but was brought back to the earth when my hand had gone numb, courtesy of carpal tunnel syndrome, during my reverie. Louise nudged me with her knee.

"Jean, faster, yes, good, ahhh, perfect." It amazed me how she could concentrate on coming while carrying on a conversation, but Louise was an accomplished multitasker even in the throes of passion. While I couldn't speak and even held my breath to the point of passing out before letting go, my girl could do both and still whistle "The Star Spangled Banner" in a pinch.

Her body thrummed beneath me, our collective heat scorched the sheets. Louise was an inferno. I moved my legs out from under my butt to shake out the pins and needles. Choosing a supine position for the grand finale that was sure to happen any day now, I rested my head in the crook of my left arm while taking her to the pinnacle of orgasmic pleasure without interrupting my signature hand job to suit her needs. I added a few new ministrations for spice and was rewarded with melodious moans of carnality.

After ten minutes or so, I asked, "Are you getting closer?" I hoped I sounded inquisitive, not impatient, just wanting to judge the pressure she needed to achieve and sustain her bliss.

"Yes, no, well, soon . . . I think." Her bodacious bottom pounded the mattress like a meat cleaver rendering tough meat tender. Somehow I found this image hot. Don't ask why, I just did. Maybe I was missing red meat or maybe I was getting horny too, because just then my clit twitched. It had been a while since I'd had even a minute stirring down there, but Louise saved my libido from certain death.

"Please, don't stop, please, don't stop," she repeated. With several fingers luxuriating inside, I pumped her tightened depths and my thumb worked magic on her clitoris. I willed my hand not to cramp. Sometimes my body parts behaved older than my actual age. Still, I would rather go into rigor mortis than not satisfy the love of my life. I'd do anything for Louise.

The clock struck twelve. Most nights we zonked out in front of the television before 10:00 PM. How did we ever manage to stay awake until the first rays of sun flitted across the horizon during some rally or mountain retreat back then? And now it was hard to find the stamina for a short sex session, let alone a marathon.

"Oh God, I'm coming, yes, now—"

I slowed my thumb over her folds, added more lube, and paid particular attention where she needed it most. Rubbing, gliding, and palpating, I didn't stop until her breath caught, her hips slowed, and she clenched my fingers inside only to push me out and suck me back in the closer she got.

"Ohhh, so good," she moaned, writhing atop the sheets. I had her right where I wanted her. I was dripping with anticipation as sweet now as the first time I summoned up the courage to plant my first kiss on her porcelain cheek, cold and bright red against the steam of my hot breath during a white winter's day my freshman year.

"Slow down, babe, enjoy it." My voice was raspy, my throat as tight as my pussy, matching the squeeze her pussy had on my fingers.

"Yes, that's it, Jean, Jean, Jean!"

Pushing sixty, Louise took longer to come, but when she finally did, her orgasms soared above the charts.

I milked it for all it was worth.

"Oh, Jean! You're my hero. That was the best orgasm I've ever had."

I removed my fingers slowly, not wanting to, but knowing I couldn't really stay there all night, and leaned in to kiss her lips.

"I love watching you come," I said. "But they can't all be the best ever."

I basked in her radiant glow, threading my fingers in her silken, silver-white hair, clasping her head with my palm. I brought her closer so that my lips could merge with hers. One more succulent kiss and I'd let her sleep. She had other ideas.

"Your turn. Move over and let me in," she teased, squeezing my tits until my nipples responded.

"You can pay me back tomorrow . . . with interest," I said, no longer able to stifle a yawn.

"At this rate I'll have to take out a second mortgage to settle my debt," she joked, but I detected her disappointment. I tried to convince her that her orgasm was good enough to satisfy us both, but she wouldn't buy it.

"I'm exhausted. Tomorrow, I promise. Night, babe. Love you."

She turned away. "Love you too." With her back to me, we fell asleep in each other's arms with me spooning her smooth, bare behind.

❀ ❀ ❀

While I put on a pot of coffee, toasted whole wheat bread, and set the table, Louise whipped up egg white omelets and sliced fresh orange wedges. Soon we had a nutritious, hot breakfast on the table, a huge difference compared to grabbing donuts or Danishes and washing them down with Cokes on our way out, unconcerned about clogged arteries, empty calories, and the battle of the bulge. These days we made a conscious effort to allow ample time for a decent breakfast, and I really looked forward to it.

I peered into her vibrant blue eyes, running the tip of my index finger along the high arch of her eyebrow and down along her nose, and finally tracing her full lips before planting a pre-breakfast kiss.

"Every time I think I love you the most, I fall in love with you all over again," I said. "You're more beautiful every day."

"And you are as wonderful for my ego as ever." She lifted her mug in a toast. We clinked and sipped the brew. "Oh, yum. Nothing like the first cup. It's sensational."

"It's decaf. Nothing like making you come. Now that's sensational."

"You always say that, but no fair, you didn't let me play. What's up?"

"It was late." I took a huge mouthful to avoid speaking.

"That never stopped you before."

"I've never been this old and on heart drugs before."

"While that's true, isn't it possible you're just scared to get back on the horse, so to speak?"

"Maybe. I know I used to be an insatiable, howling horn dog. To tell you the truth, I'm scared shitless of another heart attack."

"Your doctor said sex would be okay. You just need to let go and see that it will be all right."

"I don't know if I can. My heart sounds so loud—it's scary."

"I know. I have an idea how to get past that. This weekend we're going shopping."

I groaned, loudly. She knew how much I hated shopping. Shopping was her idea of fun.

"Not the kind you're thinking of. I'm talking about toy shopping."

"What for? I have a vibrator . . . somewhere."

"You mean the one we almost left the store without paying for over twenty years ago because we were too embarrassed to buy it from that cute baby dyke?"

"Yeah, what's the problem?"

"Even if it still worked, it was made of hard plastic and was the most unimaginative contraption ever. I think we should at least explore a few new options. Come on, play."

I smirked. "Yes, dear," I said, and she gave me her most award-winning, pearly-white smile, the kind of smile that surpassed her prominent cheekbones and crinkled the tiny lines on the outsides of her big blue eyes. She had me at the smile, but her captivating eyes turned me to mush.

❈ ❈ ❈

Louise and I took the Long Island Rail Road into Penn Station early enough to walk to Babeland when it opened.

"Ohhh, Jean, will you look at this! Surely we'll find something to get you out of your slump."

"Shhh, not so loud." I cringed. "Too late." A guy who looked barely old enough to shave and skinny enough to fit inside one leg of my Levi's with room to spare sauntered over with plenty of time to hear Louise's every word. "Great," I mumbled.

"May I assist you ladies today?" My faint blush turned scarlet, but he didn't seem to notice.

"Yes, young man, my partner and I have no idea where to start." Louise gazed at all the gadgets with a flourish.

If I could have blinked myself away from there, I would have even gladly gone to Hades wearing a snowsuit. That's about how hot I felt anyway. Louise walked right over to the vibrators and snatched the brightest one off the shelf. "This looks interesting," she said. The assistant honed in and began his sales pitch.

"Good choice. This rabbit model is very popular. It has a well-placed clit-teaser that's activated by the smooth vibrating penetrator." He turned it on full speed to demonstrate.

"Kill me now," I whispered under my breath.

"Its ultra-soft silicone is durable and waterproof and delivers discreet pleasure to all the right places. It has ten speeds, two are pulsating, and it's fully rechargeable."

"No batteries to run out. That sounds perfect," Louise enthused. "We'll take two."

"Two?" I gasped.

"Which colors do you like?" she asked.

"Why are we getting two?"

"Coming contests. We can have an orgasm race! Winner gets special favors."

I blushed beyond recognition after she freely shared our secrets in front of an infant store clerk.

"Blue and purple, please," Louise instructed him.

After we had paid for our merchandise, I needed more than dry tuna on rye. "Let's get some pizza and beer and go to hell with ourselves," I suggested. "It's a treat day after all, isn't it?"

"Yes, you will be rewarded for being such a good sport, but only if you go right back on your diet. You were really adorable in there."

"Gee, thanks. And you were bold." Too bold, but whatever.

After suffering low-fat pizza and salad with fresh lemon and pepper, I enjoyed real ale for a change and had another. It tasted like heaven. I had a nice buzz on the way home. The moment we entered the foyer, Louise attacked me. She chucked her blouse, skirt, and shoes and helped me out of my shirt, pants, and boots. We were naked before we even had washed the vibrators.

Louise grabbed the purple one, impatient to get started. "You first."

"Oh no you don't. This was all your idea."

"You promised."

I chuckled. "Your memory is too good."

"Lie down."

With my head resting in my hands, I watched and waited as she lubed up what she dubbed "the purple penetrator." I tried not to laugh as she fiddled with the buttons, biting her bottom lip. It soon started. A low hum filled the room.

The silicone was slick and cool against my heated core, which invigorated my clit like a live wire. I started to swell. In figure eights she danced the wand around my clit and teased my opening. If I could have spoken I would have urged her inside.

"Wow, this is great," she said. Each time she eased the vibrator away to change the setting, my butt shot up off the mattress.

The hum grew louder still. "This is such fun," she gushed. "How did we ever live without it?"

"Please Louise, you're killing me here," I croaked, growing desperate.

"Hold on a sec." She poured lube onto the blue vibrator and fired it up against herself. Before I could protest again, she pumped the long end of the purple penetrator deep inside me while playing my bursting clit with the shorter tip. I whimpered. If this was heaven, Louise took me higher. With her other hand, she used the "blue bliss" on herself.

"Love this!" How she wasn't distracted doing us both simultaneously was mind-boggling. She even increased the speed a couple of times.

I was totally lost in reaching my climax. We moaned, writhed, and sighed in unison. She moved frantically, then sporadically. I squeezed her hand as a guide, and she accidentally increased the speed higher still. But we couldn't stop now. The need was too great.

When we reached the pinnacle, even Louise was speechless for a second. I could tell she was as close as I was, and rather than rush it, I let her lead. The moment she started, I was sure to follow.

The pressure mounted, my heightened arousal fueled by her love cries, a resurgence of desire, and one uncontrollable vibrator that extinguished negative thoughts. My mind zoomed in on one thing, and it had the most desirable effect.

"Oh, Jean, your clit is huge, but . . . please wait . . . for . . . me," she panted.

I was close to exploding but insisted Louise come first. She held two vibrators and my rapt attention. I repositioned my hips to move the toy off my clit, which helped me focus on Louise, but not by much.

Thankfully she didn't make me wait much longer when she shouted, "I'm, oh God, com . . . ing, now, oh God!" Her body jerked with each spasm and her hands shook, knocking the vibrator off my clit. But I was already too far gone to stop the orgasm that hit me hard and fast.

I surged, shuddered, and stilled; euphoria set in. My heart resumed a normal rhythm, and all fears of another infarction vanished. The vibrator didn't give me much choice whether to come or not. I just did, and it was exactly what I needed. With all the love I had, I squeezed Louise tight. I was grateful to be alive and lucky to have her. I was reminded of how sweet and freeing it was to let go, and that while life is tenuous, it isn't to be wasted. My recent reluctance proved unfounded; I was back in action and planned to take advantage.

"That was one wicked orgasm!" Louise said.

"*Two* wicked orgasms," I corrected, and she beamed.

"Vibrators are nice, but do it the old-fashioned way next time."

AFTER TWENTY-EIGHT YEARS

Dorothy Freed

My husband, Dave, and I had a playroom date last night at seven o'clock. We arranged it beforehand, to be sure to have the entire evening reserved for pleasure. Dave told me what to wear, and I shyly said, "Yes, Sir," which set the erotic tone for the evening.

I was almost ready at five before seven, and I checked my appearance in the bathroom mirror before joining him. My hair was still damp from the shower. My lips were freshly painted, and I'd accented my large hazel eyes with a touch of green shadow. I wore a knee-length, low-cut black dress with tiny rhinestone buttons—and the black crotchless panty hose Dave bought for me when we were in Paris, years ago. What fun we had trying them out in our hotel room. We were up half the night.

Not bad, I decided, for a girl of sixty-seven, and with an appreciative nod to my mirror image, I headed down the hall to the playroom. Dave had thoughtfully turned up the heat. The air in the house felt warm to my almost-naked skin. I entered the room and closed the door behind me, smiling in anticipation of our encounter.

The playroom blinds were closed, the lights were low, the shadows were deep, and a candle flickered. Dave was there already; he sat, white bearded, bare to the waist—the lord of the land. The room was transformed into a dark, mysterious place, where secret desires could be spoken and shared.

"Come here," he commanded, and his stern tone excited me. I obeyed and stood before him in my provocative clothing, hands clasped behind my back, posing for him. In that moment I forgot that my hair was the color of silver, and that my body bore witness to the passage of time and forces of gravity.

I felt ultra-female and completely desirable.

My lover agreed. I saw how he looked at me, eating me up with his eyes. He'd laid out an array of sexual condiments: lubricants, dildos, an anal plug, a blindfold, my Hitachi Magic Wand, and my favorite small rubber whip. Hot little currents of excitement raced over my skin.

"Kneel," Dave ordered, and I eased myself, very carefully, to my creaky knees, onto the pillow Dave had set down for me. The act of my kneeling before him was our private moment of power exchange—not to mention being a highly convenient position for me to go down on him, for as long as my knees would allow.

"Whose woman are you?" he demanded to know. Leaning forward, he toyed with the buttons of my dress, slowly unfastening them, baring my breasts. Smiling, he stroked my face and neck with his fingertips and kissed me lightly on the mouth. Without warning he grabbed two fistfuls of my hair and pulled them—almost, but not quite, to the point of pain—while staring intently into my eyes. Releasing me, his white chest hairs brushed my nipples as his arms went around me and we hugged. I melted against him, breathing him in, loving the smell of him.

"I'm yours, Dave," I said honestly, gazing up into his eyes and thinking, *The man's seventy. He still makes my pulse quicken.*

My strongest sexual arousal has always been triggered by fantasies of male dominance and female submission—of being taken, swept away, made to give up control. When Dave and I met twenty-eight years ago through a relationship ad, I discovered not only that he was single, gainfully employed, and open to long-term commitment, as I'd requested, but also that there was sexual chemistry galore between us from the start. I liked the bold way he looked at me, with his dark, deep-set eyes, and the way he gave me his full attention when I spoke. We were so turned on to each other immediately that we took turns revealing our erotic turn-ons—they were compatible in both nature and intensity. Our first date was so passionate that it went on all night.

I was a bit of a swinger in my thirties and was hooked on sexual variety, but once I discovered BDSM in my forties with

Dave—a safe, sane man I loved—sexual fulfillment reached whole new levels of physical and emotional satisfaction. Together we went all out with our fantasy life, creating an erotic, red-lighted, toy-filled playroom in a back bedroom of our suburban home, where we felt safe and free to explore.

We also became active members of the San Francisco BDSM community. We attended play parties and other social events, where we met people like ourselves, who were drawn to the intensity of erotic power exchange. We sometimes played with others in our early years together, mostly at parties. Now and then we'd have a couple over, or go to their place. Dave and I were primarily monogamous, and our play, although highly arousing, even to orgasm, most often didn't include sex with our partners.

❊ ❊ ❊

Whoever said our brains are our primary sex organs certainly got that one right. Dave and I have continued to enjoy each other and our playroom, and we have an active sex life all these years later—although we have had to dial back a number of our more athletic efforts to accommodate our physical challenges. Yes, I once swung from the rafters. No, I no longer do.

Dave suffers from the narrowing of his spinal canal, which over time has restricted his range of motion and has impaired his sense of balance to the point where he uses a cane when he walks. Supporting himself on his hands and knees while on top of me in bed no longer works for him—and sitting astride him no longer works well for me—so we often have sex in the black leather sling that hangs from the playroom ceiling.

"Lie back," he ordered after lifting me into the sling. I was naked now, except for red, fleece-line cuffs on my wrists and ankles. "Raise your arms and legs. Spread them wide. Hold that pose."

"Yes, Dave," I responded, as a flush of arousal spread over me. I felt deliciously vulnerable in the sling, so wantonly exposed.

He positioned me carefully—using snap hooks to secure my wrist and ankle cuffs to the chains supporting the sling—so that my tender, exposed openings protruded slightly over its edge.

"I never tire of seeing you this way," Dave said, once I was arranged to his satisfaction. I blushed under his gaze. "You're so accessible, my darling—and hot, beyond belief."

He ran his hands over me, slapping my inner thighs, first with his hand, then with the small rubber whip that stung so delightfully, heating my bottom and making me quiver with excitement.

Placing a chair before the sling, he sat, feasting his eyes on me. Pulling me closer he began kissing my inner thighs and silvery Venus mound—lapping at my swollen labia, massaging carefully around my clit with the flat of his tongue.

"My God, you know how to make me feel good," I whispered. Closing my eyes I went with the feelings. My breathing quickened. I felt like I was floating. Dave took his time pleasuring me, using lips and tongue and teeth. Slipping his fingers beneath my ass cheeks, he teased my puckered rear opening. The exquisite sensations heightened my arousal. I moaned, muscles straining, feeling my blood pounding through my body as my orgasm built. I cried out with joy as it washed over me.

"That's my girl," Dave murmured, stroking me, his hands warm on my flesh, until my breathing quieted. I opened my eyes. He sat up, looking pleased with himself. "Is your circulation okay?" he asked, standing to feel my hands and wrists.

"Fine for now, Sir," I said, smiling happily, shifting my weight in the sling.

Nodding, Dave reached for the lubricant. I moaned as his hands, slick with lube, massaged my vaginal lips. One, two, three fingers slid slowly inside me. Delving deeper, he massaged my g-spot. My eyes closed again.

Dave penetrated me from a standing position—holding the sling to keep his balance, and swinging me back and forth onto his penis. He filled me, taking my breath away. My vagina was relaxed and ready for him. I raised my hips to meet his thrusts. My second orgasm came more easily than the first.

Dave held me, stoking me gently, kissing each wrist and ankle as he uncuffed them. Later, he took his turn in the sling—no cuffs involved this time—while I went down on him, bringing him to orgasm with my hands and mouth.

I was highly sexual in my younger days, but not easily orgasmic—a huge source of frustration for me. My exciting erotic life with Dave that began in our forties was a dream-come-true for both of us. We spent our first ten years together in a state of high sexual excitement. I came easily and often. Life was a joy.

Then in my fifties, I went through menopause. I gained weight, had trouble sleeping, cried easily, and worst of all, lost most of my sexual desire. I mourned the loss of it, as something I loved that had died.

Thankfully, it returned, full tilt, in my sixties, along with my orgasms, and Dave and I are making the most of it.

As older people, our sexual responses are slower. We take longer to warm up and get going, and we tire more quickly. Dave, who has circulatory problems, uses Viagra to help him achieve and maintain an erection.

"I *love* being hard," he murmurs, with such deep appreciation. I do my utmost to prolong this pleasure for him—sucking and licking my way from the head of his penis down to his balls, and stroking him with my hands. Still, even with Viagra (and me), he sometimes loses his erection and becomes frustrated with his aging body.

Our BDSM play works in our favor here, by triggering our arousal. To us, erotic spanking, the use of restraints, and the use of nipple and labia clamps are delightfully intense forms of foreplay that, thankfully, still excite us both.

I have my own share of physical issues to work around: lack of lubrication, creaky knees, and a touchy right shoulder—not to mention the cushiony sandals with the metatarsal arch supports I wear for comfort these days, no matter how sexy I want to look. But physical challenges aside, I'm having every bit as much fun with my aging partner as I had years ago—more really, because we know each other's turn-ons so well now, and our level of trust is so high.

Once we became more accepting of our aging bodies and physical limitations, we relaxed into this new phase of our sexual life together, and we began exploring our current needs and desires.

Today, I am overjoyed and grateful. Not only have Dave and I made it through twenty-eight years together—we are still interested and actively engaged in giving and receiving pleasure. It's been years since we attended a play party or played with others. But our fiery beginning served us well. We keep ourselves aroused by drawing on a huge storehouse of hot memories. I think that for us, the erotic thrill we get from Dave's taking charge and my giving up control never grows old—even though we continue to do so.

MY NEW VAGINA

Audrienne Roberts Womack

I use to pride myself on how much Mother Nature hadn't let me down like so many of my aging sister friends. At fifty-eight, I still had that mind-set, even though at first it was just something to say to make my old ass feel as though I was as youthful as I thought I was. I needed convincing that I still saw myself as an ageless beauty, even though I knew good and damn well that my stretch marks were getting deeper and my jam had turned to jelly.

After my divorce, I thought I would never have sex again. After twenty-eight years of marriage and eight children, I thought my husband would be my partner for life—until he announced six years ago that he had found a younger, slimmer, and sexier version of me who he would like to settle down with to replace me. There had been no warning signs prior to his announcement.

My heart was broken for a long time, but after the smoke cleared and I realized that my ex-husband liked having sex with me more *after* we were divorced, I figured I could have the best of both worlds. I never had to worry about lonely nights and an empty bed, because I saw my ex more after the divorce than when we were married, now ain't that some shit!

When I eventually began to date again, my ex had the nerve to get jealous and forbid me to have sex with anyone but him, until I reminded him that we were no longer married. It took a while, a long while, before it registered that I was no longer his and that I could do what I damn well pleased.

I was getting too dependent on my ex-husband's lovemaking and our casual booty calls, and I needed a sexual diversion of my own. So in celebration of my new life as a single woman, I created a sexual bucket list and started to enjoy my sex life, right along with everything else in my life I needed to celebrate.

I loved to masturbate anytime and anyplace, so the first thing on my list was to join a masturbation club where I could get off in peace with other open, adventurous, and like-minded women and men. My club met every Wednesday night, and I always positioned myself next to the large, picture-frame window where club members could watch and enjoy.

I brought my favorite lube and a vast assortment of vibrators, and even though cameras were not allowed in the masturbation room, I still saw a camera or two slip in from time to time. I didn't mind—the diffuse lighting and the way we were positioned made it difficult to see who anybody was anyway. I enjoyed being watched, because I knew that everyone in the club was all about masturbation just as much as I was. We weren't there to judge or point fingers at otheres for trying to get their freak on.

It was a big sexual release, and after my divorce I needed something that would take my mind off of being kicked to the curb and then blindsided with divorce papers. One of my oldest and dearest friends went with me, and we also masturbated at my house or her house when her husband wasn't home. We stopped going to her house after we almost got caught when her husband came home earlier than expected. I was right in the middle of a killer orgasm when we heard her husband announce, "Honey, I'm home!"

I always wanted to go to a lesbian bar. I had never kissed a girl, and I wanted to try just one time, especially with the girly girl type I find to be so compelling. So that was next on my bucket list. Cautiously I ventured out in search of my one-night stand. It was easy finding a lesbian club, because they were all around, but it was harder trying to find one with women who didn't look young enough to be one of my daughters, but yet not so old they couldn't teach me something new.

I never considered myself bisexual or bi-curious or any of those new labels they have been using nowadays. I just wanted to kiss a woman, check it off my bucket list, and be on my way. It was all in the name of research.

When I entered the lesbian club, I felt like I had a big sign on my forehead that said ALIEN. Just as I was deflating my self-esteem and deciding to take my miserable, self-pitying, woe-is-me self home, this fancy chick—complete with butterfly tattoos, piercings, and spandex jeans—asked if I wanted to dance. She looked young enough to be carded, but she had a mature air about her that seemed both intriguing and innocent at the same time. I kindly took her up on her proposition. We danced just close enough for me to smell the Egyptian musk oil she was wearing. We had a couple of drinks and a good conversation. But I was starting to get tired and was ready to go home and relax.

Before making my grand exit, I announced that I had to use the ladies' room, and my companion decided she needed to go as well. I tried to enter my stall and close the door, but she quickly slipped in behind me. She looked me dead in my eyes and started to slip her hand in my pants and maneuvered down into my panties. I took her by the hand, opened my legs slightly, and guided her hand to the moist spot forming between my legs.

Her fingers were soft and purposeful as she played with my pubic hairs before entering me. One by one her fingers tugged and twisted the soft wet hairs that were now sticking to my body. First there was one finger, then two, then three, and then she alternated between the three keeping in sync to some invisible carnal beat. I was in tune with her every movement, riding her fingers with every stroke. It was the best hand job I had ever had, and she had barely started. The heat that was growing between my legs was seething. I had to bite my lip to keep from anyone overhearing us. I'm not sure if I led her on in some way or if this type of thing happened all the time in lesbian bars, but I felt that since I had come this far, I might as well go along with the program.

Her fingers went deep inside of me, fingering me and stroking my clit with one hand. I started to moan or groan or both, and with her other hand, she covered my mouth. As she stirred up the friction in my pants, my body started to gyrate to the beat of the music playing in the background. When she couldn't muffle my moans with her hand any longer, she removed her hand and stuck her tongue in my mouth. She kissed and licked my mouth until I came all over her hand.

When she finished, she went to wash her hands, licking her fingers first. I didn't know the correct protocol for dismissing myself after just being fingered in the bathroom, so I thanked her for an interesting evening, hugged her, exchanged numbers, and wobbled out of the bar. I needed a hot bath, aspirin, and sleep, before adding another well-deserved check to my bucket list.

The next item on my bucket list was delayed when my uterus decided to drop. After discussing my options with a specialist in urogynecology and reconstructive pelvic surgery, I scheduled an appointment for laparoscopic surgery, a repair procedure that in my case required a hysterectomy to remove my uterus.

Since both of my ovaries were healthy, I was able to keep them, which made me feel as though I still had my woman parts, regardless of being beyond childbearing years.

The doctor noticed that I had some vaginal tearing over the years, and so many babies left my vagina less tight and snug than it used to be. She would tighten up my vagina as an added bonus. My sex life would be better because my vagina would be tighter. Who would have thought that after all these years I finally would get the designer vagina that I had always wanted, all new and improved!

My ex-husband wanted to be the first to try out my new goods, but after thinking long and hard about it, I decided that he didn't deserve to be the first. Maybe the second or third, but certainly not the first.

Soon after, I bumped into Barry, a man about fifteen years younger than me. I have often stopped by my favorite happy hour spot to get a drink, flirt with a young man or two for the novelty of it, and go on my way. Barry was a little bolder that the other young men I had been meeting lately, though, and that began to make him more alluring.

Barry had flirted with me on and off over the years, but I never considered kissing him, let alone having sex with him, as he was so young. He was on the same community advisory board I was on, and I didn't mix business with pleasure, especially so close to home. But the more I kept bumping into him, the more he started to look kissable—and sexable.

One evening after an intense community meeting election, I gave Barry a ride home like I usually did. This time, when he invited me up for a beer, I took him up on it, since we had been celebrating our electoral success all evening anyway. After a few rounds of small talk, Barry began his usual flirtatious bantering, and I did my usual cougar moves, all in the name of fun, but something was obviously different this time.

Barry slowly walked up to me, placed his hand comfortably between my legs on my upper thigh, and whispered, "You gonna let me hit that tonight?" I gave him the green light to go further by stepping slowly into his grasp. By now his hand was softly but firmly positioned under my skirt, near the wet spot between my legs. He moved in closer beside me and slowly ran his hand further up my thigh. His hand felt good between my legs, just like it was meant to be there. I wanted to see how far this would go.

"If I were you, I wouldn't start anything I couldn't finish," I said, barely above a whisper and hoping he wouldn't stop.

Barry continued to run his hand up and down my thigh. As his hand slowly made its way to my wet spot, I pulled away from him, while I still had the strength to do so. "Why are you always doing that?" Barry asked with a smirk on his face. "You always pull away from me, and you know you want this." He was right. I did want it. I looked down at him. He was rubbing the biggest erection I had seen in a long, long time!

I decided, tonight would be Barry's lucky night. And mine.

I was too old for games and too horny for wasting any more time. He was an obedient young man and came to attention as quickly as the wood in his pants that was now saluting me at full mast. I liked what I saw: his thick, monstrous, bulging appendage that was hanging before me in full frontal view in all its glory. I certainly must have done something right to get so lucky! I think I may have looked as though I needed CPR because he asked me if anything was wrong. I reassured him that at that moment, all was right with the world!

It was a little awkward at first, because I started to feel insecure. I couldn't remember if I was wearing my thong or my granny panties, and I didn't remember if I still had that unsightly panty liner still attached. Did I even shave under my armpits or pluck the extra hairs under my neck? In the wrong light, my breasts looked like cow udders. In the right light, they looked like voluptuous torpedoes. Tonight they had a mind of their own and were hanging east and west, but heading south. I couldn't remember if I had shaved the gray hairs from my lollipop just in case it was going to get licked, like a lollipop should be licked.

Without warning, Barry grabbed me by my arm, which shook all the negative thoughts from my head. With my full consent, Barry began to pin me down like a hungry dog in heat. I didn't resist, because I like it rough and wild and I was glad to finally meet someone who was just as nasty as I was. I was sexually as hungry as Barry, and the heat was turned all the way up to a boil. I was matching his rhythm note for note and trying hard as hell not to miss a beat. As he started massaging my breast with one hand, his other hand attentively forced its way down my pants and didn't stop until he got to the cream-filled middle. On cue I used my free hand to ride horseback on his hand that was already buried deep inside me. I held it tight, making certain that he wouldn't remove it until I was ready for him to ease it out.

Before I could talk him into letting me take off my clothes, he had me facedown, with my pants around my ankles. Barry was both amiable and forceful, just the way I liked it.

Then I remembered my surgery and was scared to death, because I didn't know how he was going to feel inside of me. All I could think of was him busting my stitches and sending me running back to the hospital. Between heavy breathing and gasping for air, I informed Barry of my surgery, and he immediately asked, "Do you want me to stop?" I told him I didn't want him to stop. I just wanted him to be careful and take his time and pace himself for my sake.

When he tried to enter me, it was tight. So tight that I figured my doctor had sewn me up a little too much. Then I feared that Barry would feel like a battering ram trying to force his way into my tiny keyhole. However, Barry tuned in to my sensations. As soon as I became apprehensive, he stopped to check in with me. He went from forceful caveman to a gentle giant. He became patient and refined, taking his time inch by inch, until I had swallowed all of him and was moving in time with his rhythm once again.

He loved me long and hard. It was tasty. It was mouthwatering. It was finger-licking good. He filled me up from wall to wall. "Damn, that feels good," he would say between each sweaty stroke. Stroke by stroke he began to build momentum, but slowly

I was easing my way back into the driver's seat. As we began to pick up the pace, I began to get my old buzz back. Barry took my legs and spread them like a wishbone.

It felt as though I was outside of my body looking down at myself, and I liked what I saw, I liked how it felt, and I liked how my vagina was brand-new and tight. I turned off all the mind clutter. I moved when he moved and did what he did. I was a puppet on a string. I lost control. I was under his spell.

When it was over, it was over. I dressed, kissed him on the forehead, and left. He wasn't my husband, my man, or my boyfriend—just barely my friend—and I was fine with that. In fact, I loved that. I couldn't wait to get home and check this off my bucket list. Then I was going to soak in a hot tub of Epsom salts, pour some champagne, and celebrate my new and improved vagina—and all the years we had ahead of us!

TRAIN RIDE

Harris Tweed

I took the train to Salt Lake. Why not? Seventy years old. Hadn't made a journey by rail since I was sixteen going from Billings to Glasgow, Montana, to brand cattle on the highline for a football buddy's uncle. Now, fifty-four years later, I was going to Salt Lake to give a talk on noir fiction at the college. I'd worked on it while we steadily rumbled along out of Oakland, but once we started the climb through the Sierras east of Sacramento, I looked out my window more often.

I was gazing at a bend in the Truckee River when someone in the aisle brushed my arm passing by. I glanced up, expecting a conductor or steward, but saw instead a slender, gray-haired woman in a soft, wool dress.

She said, "Excuse me," and I nodded, and that was that, but after another page of editing, she returned to my mind. What a lovely smile, and her eyes held a liveliness that stirred me. Okay, who was she, and what was she doing on this train?

I felt like a teenager scoping girls in the bleachers at half-time. Planning my reconnaissance, I'd decided to feign a search for the dining car. I'd carry my briefcase like I was planning to work while eating. If I walked up-train, I'd find where she was sitting, get a better look, maybe even make direct contact. I might learn whether she was riding alone, whether she wore a ring, whether she passed her time memorizing the Bible, that sort of thing.

Turned out she was on the same side I was, up about twelve rows, aisle seat in front of a large woman who had obscured my vision. I slowed just before I reached her and bent, ostensibly, to straighten my cuff. Kneeling I could see a slender left wrist, sapphire-colored ring on her middle finger, the same pale gold as her thin chain bracelet. I could see that her silvery hair had a pleasant luster and that her shoulders were back, not hunched. All to the good. I rose and brushed her arm as I walked by, excused myself, and then pretended surprise to see it was the same person who had brushed me just minutes ago.

"Hello," I said. "I believe I zigged when I should have zagged."

She gave me that smile again, said nothing.

"Have you been to the dining car?" I asked, noticing that the seat next to her was vacant.

"No," she said, tolerating my intrusion. She glanced at the seat back directly in front of her as if its pocket might hold a map. Shook her head and smiled again. "I haven't. I don't even know if it's that direction."

"Forgive me if I'm being a bother, but I'm wondering if you'd like to join me and find out. We could have a quick cup of coffee or a bone-dry macchiato, hold the nutmeg."

She turned her attention up a notch, searching my eyes to decide whether I was teasing, or obnoxiously overconfident, or worse, maybe a perv of one of the myriad types.

"Sorry," I said, "mixed message. I was serious about having a coffee together. About the macchiato, not so much, unless that happens to be your favorite warm drink, in which case we should order two."

She glanced at the *Atlantic* magazine she was holding and then at my briefcase.

"I'm carrying this everywhere," I said. "A talk I'm working on. I couldn't afford to lose it."

She set the magazine beside her and fiddled with the top button of her dress, considering. She looked out the window but didn't seem to find anything interesting.

"Please," I said. "I've interrupted you. I'll go get a coffee and let you get back to your reading."

She brought her eyes back to mine. "No, I've read enough for the moment. A coffee would be fine."

I saw that in her fiddling with the button she'd wound up undoing it. As she stood, she undid another. Her skin was a light tan, and the V her top now made was fetching.

She caught me looking and colored slightly. "Shall we?" she asked.

My thoughts tumbled as we walked into the next car. And the next, and finally, the dining area. We chose a table for two on the far right corner, which, at least for the time being, had no close neighbors.

Our waiter came immediately, immaculate in black slacks and a short white jacket. He poured water, took our coffee order, and left, polite but businesslike.

"My name is Malcolm," I said, "and unfortunately people call me that. It's not a name that nicks well." That earned another smile.

"Last name?"

"Scrivner," I said. "Not a bad match for a man who's giving a talk on noir fiction."

"I rarely read any of that," she said. "I don't like the snappy patter."

"The detectives?"

"Yes, and the crooks in general." She unfolded her napkin and placed it in her lap. "Guess that dates me," she said. "They don't say crooks anymore, do they?"

I laughed. "Goons, goombahs, thugs, palookas . . . they don't say any of those much anymore. Noir seems to be moving away from crime and into everyman kinds of dilemmas. Road rage, drug use, accidental murder in the suburbs, kinship wars in Appalachian hollows."

Her eyes left mine and wandered again to the window. I was boring her. "And your name?" I asked, trying to win back her attention.

"Guess," she said, a bit of a twinkle.

"Desdemona."

She barked a laugh.

"One can hope," I said. "I've never met a Desdemona."

"You're a terrible guesser." She dabbed her mouth with her napkin though she'd had nothing to eat or drink.

"I am," I agreed. "One more try and you tell me."

She waited.

"Emily."

"The poet," she said. "I've always liked that name. No, Rachel. Rachel Ames. My maiden name," she said. "I took it back after my husband died."

"A terrible question popped into my mind," I said and waited.

"I usually love terrible questions. Ask it."

"Do you miss him?"

"That is a dangerous question, isn't it? He could have just passed; he could have been the love of my life and you would have . . . what do they say now? Killed the buzz?"

In that moment I think my heart actually leaped. Could a seventy-year-old heart still leap? I could barely put my socks on. Whatever, it was beating faster and I knew why. Buzz. She was feeling some kind of similar attraction, and yes, here came that shy blush and a lovely swallow.

"No one who knows me has ever accused me of being sensitive," I said. "Should I withdraw the question?"

"No . . . that's not something I've been asked before."

The waiter was at our table so soundlessly it seemed he materialized. He put the small, ceramic cream pitcher between us, followed by the sugar bowl with its slightly tarnished tongs. From his wooden tray he lifted nearly translucent porcelain cups atop saucers and centered each between our utensils. Finally an aromatic coffee was poured with neither a clink nor a drop spilled. He couldn't keep himself from brushing at a speck near the middle edge of the tablecloth. "I'll bring you a menu shortly," he said, "should you become hungry." He turned and strode toward the galley without a backward glance.

I found myself reluctant to break the spell by taking a sip.

"We should all be so professional," she looked after him.

"What was your work?" I would not have been surprised if she said minding a house. She could have been some wealthy person's trophy wife a few years ago.

"I started out a lawyer. Hated it. Became the publicity person for the San Francisco Opera. We had the best parties in the world at bars like Vesuvius, Tosca, the Tivoli. God, what a job."

"The opera work seems to fit your . . . elegance," I said. "But I'm surprised by the parties. You must not be as . . . uh, reserved as—"

"So you haven't realized I bumped you on purpose? The best man in the car? You thought I simply couldn't walk a straight line?"

I couldn't respond. I was that stunned. Before I recovered, she went on.

"No. I don't miss him. I got tired of him. All his rules. David had an opinion on everything and about how anything should be done. I gradually quit sharing daily events because I didn't want to hear his pronouncements. He could be generous. Very generous. And quite gracious in social situations. But at home . . . An opinionated prig. Is that too harsh?"

"Probably," I said, unable to squelch my laugh.

"Are you a prig?"

That caught me completely off guard. I had to think for a moment. A whig was a . . . an ancient politician? Something like that, and a prig was . . . well, I wasn't sure. Someone too straight-laced for his own good or anybody else's? Smug?

"God, I hope not," I said, laughing. "But I suppose a prig would say the same thing."

"There's nothing worse than a surreptitious prig," she said, narrowing her eyes, teasing.

"How about a man who's old enough to know better but foolish enough to remain amorous, and senile enough to believe he can still cut the mustard?"

"Are you referring to *my* mustard?" she asked, her eyes now positively merry.

"Metaphorically, I believe I am," I said, making sure I didn't look away.

"Well," she said, bringing her napkin from her lap and setting it next to her coffee, "perhaps we should walk to the vista car and make a metaphorical sandwich."

✻ ✻ ✻

I led the way, relieved that she couldn't see my face. I swear I could feel my blood chilling, and I was getting cold feet. That brought an unwilling smile that, even if she saw, she'd misinterpret, because my feet were the least of my problems. I was shriveling, damn it, and I could imagine the nerves in my groin flipping switches, turning out the lights, and getting ready to move energy toward my legs which would quickly need a power surge to start running.

What was the matter with me? What happened? She'd agreed too quickly and that started red lights flashing. So as I walked, I searched my emotional database. If she was agreeable, I might have to perform. I'm hearing Don Meredith sing, "Turn out the lights, the party's over." *Relax!* I *can* perform. Done it hundreds of times. But lately? Huh uh. If you want something done right, you better do it yourself. I'd done that in spades. But this woman was smart, funny, attractive. Rising to the occasion shouldn't be impossible.

What else? I could hardly let the thought surface. Could she be a man? I didn't for the life of me remember her throat or her wrists. Weren't they both delicate? But men were easy . . . do this kind of pickup thing in the drop of an eyelash. Do cross-dressers age like she has? Hard to imagine. And if he was an actual sex change, who the hell cares? One foot in the grave, shut your mouth. But that's ridiculous. So, what else? From my approach and flirting, what if she's expecting something I can't deliver.

A big dong. The lasting power of a machine. No. No way. She's older, experienced. She's not a Dallas cheer queen hoping to get schtupped by the goddamn quarterback.

So really, what was it? The answer arrived, and I was embarrassed. My thrill had been in the chase, such as it was. I wanted her to want me. A fucking confirmation. I don't mean that. A validation. Reassurance. If I had a tail it would be dragging so far between my legs she'd step on it. Pathetic. It damped me that she had set this rendezvous in motion. She wasn't after me. She was after *it*.

"Give me your hand," she said, narrowing the distance between us. "Lead me."

It wasn't as submissive as it sounded. We were getting ready to go between cars during a particularly rough area of track, and I had already begun tensing, preparatory to opening the door. The briefcase was a cumbersome mistake, and I tucked it under my arm before I reached back. Her warm fingers clasped mine. Delicate! If she was watching the back of my neck redden, I hoped she put it down to passion.

We jostled, I felt her breast brush my back while I widened my stance, navigated the short passage, and opened the vista-dome door. We had an immediate opportunity to climb stairs to the upper level. I took it. At least we would get a way from casual foot traffic.

Halfway up she said, "Just a minute," got a firm grasp on my shirt sleeve, and lifted one shoe and then the other, removing a wisp of silk and slipping it in my pocket.

Modest in a certain way, but unmistakable, and maybe the sexiest move I'd ever seen in public. Who was this woman?

I stumbled on the next step and cursed myself silently until we were seated in a cozy nook right at the top of the stairs— the only two seats facing toward the muted afternoon sun—I definitely wanted to hear a warning if we were going to have company. Well, we did have company: a younger couple, holding hands, examining the mountain scenery and whispering twenty feet from us in the out-facing middle section, and three people looking like they were in consultation perhaps fifty feet away at the head of the car. If she noticed them, and I believed she did, they were no deterrent.

Hip to hip, we angled and faced each other.

"You don't want to, do you?" she said, looking through my iris, past my cortex, and into my limbic system. "No grind for my bump? I'm disappointed."

Ouch. I heard the command "full speed ahead," but had no idea how to put it in play. "Of course I do. You're lovely. But I'm very . . . my arousal depends a little on uh, seeing."

Before I could savor my incredibly brilliant save, there was a flittering in my peripheral vision. I turned my head to find her holding a small lacy bra. She must have undone it while I was hypnotized.

She tucked it into a tiny purse and put that at her feet. "Girl scouts are prepared, too. I think our motto is 'when opportunity knocks, answer the door in your negligee.'" As she spoke, she was carefully opening more of her dress. When I noticed the buttons went all the way to the hem and realized that in a moment she would be practically naked, I could not smother a laugh.

That earned a knitted brow and features descending toward outrage.

I raised both hands to stop the slide. "I'm not laughing at you," I said, "really. Never. You are absolutely beautiful."

Her mouth had become thin, her cheeks hollowed.

"No. Please. I'll tell you exactly what I was thinking." I put my hand over my heart as if pledging honesty. "It hit me like a missile. I've wished for this particular moment my entire life. Most men have. I was thinking, 'I've gone to heaven,' and I don't even believe in heaven. It's one of those this-can't-be-happening things. Rachel, it's true. I don't deserve you, and I don't think you really want me. We shouldn't be doing this."

She leaned away until our hips no longer touched, her eyes still nailed into mine.

"That said, how about a little kiss?" I raised my eyebrows and gave her my best smile.

The ensuing silence brought an end to time. I could have driven to Chicago or read *War and Peace*. During the next seven or eight seconds, I understood relativity.

When her features almost imperceptibly softened, I gravitated forward with the stealth of a mime and, without hands, kissed her so lightly on the lips that I could feel molecules bonding. Later, at some point, the tip of her tongue ushered my thoughts

quietly out the huge windows to the snowy mountains and farther to the line of dark clouds on the northern horizon, farther
to Montana and the majorettes who set me on fire and burned
through my belt and my jeans and my skin until they finally
melted my spine and I was nothing but jelly moving slowly back
and forth until I was nothing at all.

AT THE WANE OF THE MOON

Bill Noble

When just the sliver of a moon was climbing through the oaks, Beth came home with a story to tell. She shed her thick crocheted sweater, slipped out of the old flowered dress, and draped her clothes helter-skelter over the bedside chair. She slid under the covers, pale as a wraith, to breathe a single word: "Tom."

The eighty-two-year-old man turned his face toward the slanting moonlight with an affectionate murmur. He kissed her papery fingers.

"Tom." She brushed his temple with her cool lips.

He opened his eyes suddenly. "Is everything all right?"

"Oh, yes," she whispered. "Oh, indeed yes."

She kissed his eyes shut again and pressed herself against his frailness. She slipped a hand over his belly to cup the bony crest of his hip. "I came down the canyon from my evening walk. It's such a warm night. I came down by Jason's. I . . . I watched Jason and Bianca make love. I sat on the hill for a long time, watching them."

"The kids who just moved in down at the corner?" His eyes fluttered wide again.

"The curtains were open. I came down through the woods past their house. I could see candles burning, and then Bianca walked in front of the window, just shining. You know, her breasts were so lovely in the candle glow, and Jason snatched her up from behind and kissed her."

"*Elizabeth*," he said. He always called her that when he disapproved. She laid a finger across his lips to shush him.

"Thomas," she teased. "They were beautiful, and it stirred me, so I watched. At my age I can watch if I want." He knew better than to argue.

She kissed along his collarbone, then let her mouth rest for a while over the pulse at the side of his neck. He sighed, and she began to stroke his chest and belly, tenderly and slowly. "We have such a sturdy neighbor," she said. "He's such a wonderful father and such a dear of a husband. I knew when they moved in they were a good pair." She traced fingertip circles around Tom's nipples until he sighed again and shifted closer against her. "I have to say, when he picked her up like that—oh, the way she looked at him after they kissed, Tom! But when he stood there with her in his arms like that, so strong and easy, and her perfect round bottom—well, I have to admit, I blushed a little. I almost looked away when his penis was bobbing around right under her . . . "

"Elizabeth," he said again, but she bent forward and put her lips over his nipple. Then she raised her head to look him in the eye. She gave him a peculiar little twinkle, kissed him on the nose, and disappeared under the covers. He sighed. "Beth, it must be terribly late. We need to sleep."

"Can you hear me all right down here?"

"Yes, Beth, but . . . "

"Then just listen. I want to tell you about it."

"Beth, I don't think . . . "

She began to brush her cheek and lips gently against his penis. "Well, he just stood there with her in his arms, right beside the bed. They kissed a bunch more—oh, for a long time—and then he began to lick her breast—you know, great, long strokes with the whole of his tongue, just the way I used to like you to lick *my* breasts. And his penis jumped every time he licked her. You know, it's curved up as if it was trying to look around. But, oh, Tom, she has the loveliest breasts. Were mine ever so beautiful, do you think, when I was twenty-eight?"

He began to stroke her back with his fingertips. He reached a hand to cradle the furrowed scar on her chest. A tear trailed down his cheek onto the pillow.

"Bianca grabbed hold of Jason and started to stroke him. Like this." She began a slow up-and-down with Tom's still-sleeping penis. "You should have seen the way his legs locked up and his butt clenched! He's a real stallion, Tom Maynard.

"Anyhow, Jason dumped her right on the bed. Then he threw her legs up over those big shoulders of his and just buried his face in her. She made the most amazing noise—I wouldn't know what to call it. Right through those double-paned windows and all."

"Beth, really . . . "

"Well, really, your proper self! You remember the things we used to do? Remember the time you took me skinny-dipping way up Slater Brook, and by the time we were through we could only find enough clothes lying around for one of us to get home with? I had to go in your pants and fetch you back another pair. Or the time we spent the weekend at the Brenners' and never got up till noon—oh, I'm sure we must have been forty then—and Dewey and Jill blushed all the way through lunch, and hardly spoke? Oh, Tom, we were a pair, weren't we?" She slipped her lips over the head of his penis and began to waltz little circles with her tongue. After a few minutes of silence, she took her mouth away to ask, "Does this still feel as good as you always used to tell me it did?"

"You're such a wanton woman. My penis thought it had already answered that question." A muffled chuckle came back from under the covers, and for some reason it was the chuckle that seemed to set him stiffening. He was torn between surprise and a sudden onset of delight.

Beth began to slurp and suck, waggling her face, clowning over him. Another laugh welled up, and he felt Beth's stomach begin to shake in silent accompaniment. He grew fully erect.

Beth wet her hands and stroked him vigorously. "Should I tell you what Bianca's climax was like?" He started to say something, but she continued, "It didn't take her long. Tom Maynard, you're as hard as a prize salami. I believe you're enjoying this!

"Anyhow, she just kept making those noises, but she started to shake, bouncing around on the bed. Jason had to wrap his arms round both her legs to hold her in place. I was afraid the poor boy was going to break a tooth trying to keep his mouth on her!" Tom reached between Beth's legs to pet her. She squealed a girlish little squeal and then lifted one leg to straddle him. He caught her rich, familiar scent and felt the fullness and heat of her engorgement. She stroked him hard and fast, then slowed to an almost painful delicacy. He felt the warmth of her lips on him again for a moment before she reverted to full hard stroking with her hands.

"Bianca left big red welts all down his back. And she threw her head back so far I was afraid she was going to break her neck. I'm surprised you didn't hear the commotion all the way over here. Her shaking just went on and on and on. You should have seen the way Jason was thrusting against the edge of the bed—but he never took his mouth off her. Shall I tell you what happened next, what Jason did?"

"Wait, Beth, wait."

"You want me to stop?" She was prepared to be outraged.

"No, no. Mercy, just for a minute. I want to do something." He sat up on the edge of the bed, trying to catch his breath. Beth had emerged from the covers and was watching him quizzically. After a moment he turned on the little bedside lamp and hobbled to the dresser. He rummaged through the bottom drawer and returned to the bed.

"What have you got, you mischievous man?"

Deadpan, he handed her a tube of lubricant. She grinned up at him.

"Tom Maynard, I believe I've had an effect on you! But what are you hiding behind your back?"

He laid a faded photograph on the sheets. She took him in her hand and stroked him toward hardness again, turning to look at the picture. "Tom! I didn't know you kept these!" The photo showed two strong young bodies coupling on a lawn next to a stately bed of iris. The picture was slightly askew. The tops of the couple's heads were cut off. "Oh, Tom! Do you remember how the camera kept falling down every time the shutter went off? And how hard it was to run back round and try to get inside me again before the thing fired? Oh, I didn't know you still had these! Do you remember," she laughed, "we had to find an ad in some sleazy magazine and mail the film all the way to Chicago?"

"You're a beautiful woman, Elizabeth Ann Maynard." He laid her down on the covers. He put a pillow on the floor to cushion his stiff knees and knelt between her legs. "It's my turn."

She held the picture, gazing alternately at it and at the disheveled snowy hair and familiar old head that pleasured her. She couldn't name the reason for the tears they brought. She tried to continue the story of Jason and Bianca, to give Tom something of the wonderful images that moved in her mind, of the run of muscle in Jason's haunches and down the length of his candlelit back, but the words trailed away. Her sounds, when she came to them, long after words had failed, told a story they both seemed to know well.

He moistened her with great tenderness, inside and out, and she lubricated him and brought him quickly to erection again, smiling. He entered her with a long, moaning exhalation while she held his face between her hands like an unexpected prize. They kissed in lazy delirium, first one moving, then the other. They anticipated one another's pleasure, knew when to give respite, when to take up the rhythm again. When he climaxed, her hands clutched his buttocks, pulling him deep into her. He held himself carefully inside long after they were through.

After a time, Tom turned out the lamp. She helped him lie next to her, side by side, as the moon's silver receded across the bedroom floor. Long after it had vanished, they turned and moved into one another's arms, breath and pulse flowing together through the deepening night.

❋ *A slightly different version of "At the Wane of the Moon" was the final story in the last issue of* Paramour *magazine in 1998, and was later republished online at* Clean Sheets *magazine.*

PEAS IN A POD

Maryn Blackburn

"I can't just drop everything at work." The double crease between Diane's brows deepens, and her pursed lips accentuate the little lines he will soon kiss smooth. "I'm not some booty call."

"Of course not." Russ takes her coat, his bare feet freshly appreciative of heated floors, the source of debate approaching argument during the renovation.

The empty wooden hanger is his secret reminder that Diane will come again, will hand off her coat, will do things outside either of their marriage beds. The sight of the hanger coupled with faint traces of her perfume rising from the coat's satin lining wakes his cock. "I only found out I had the place to myself a minute before I called." He hangs her coat.

"What happened?" She pours herself a scotch without offering him one.

"Logan Airport is snowed in, no flights until morning at the earliest. Apparently getting a hotel room was quite the coup."

"I can't stay overnight. Don't even ask. This is a dentist's appointment. I need to go back to work."

Wouldn't someone smell the scotch?

"I'm reading your mind again. It will be natural for me to come back smelling like toothpaste, if anyone gets that close. I brushed in the ladies' room before I left, too."

"Of course. Discretion is the only reason this works. Did you park at the mall?"

"Yes, and took a cab from the other end. With a Penney's bag." She gestures with the pointed toe of a black boot.

Russ opens his wallet and sets a twenty on the occasional table near the door, more than enough to cover the round trip. They no longer bicker about him reimbursing her costs. "I bought us something. Care to see?"

Scotch in hand, Diane trails him to the master suite. He turns at the open door to see her reaction: salt-and-pepper brows raised, her mouth a lipsticked O.

The mahogany chest at the foot of the bed glows red-gold with candlelight, the flames multiplied in the crystalline lube drooling down a purple butt plug. Matching satin ribbon surrounds the base in an artistic swirl before trailing to the floor.

He rests his hand on her sleeve, the way he reassures his mother-in-law when she is once again confused by the ordinary. "If you didn't want to expand your horizons, you'd be home with your husband, not here with me."

Diane nods. "Same as you. We're two peas in a pod."

"Exactly. This is not a part of my marriage, either—but I've always wanted to try it."

"I don't think I could possibly—"

"It's for me." The familiar shame engulfs him, heating his face and ears. It prevents him from looking into her eyes and speaking with the honesty they've promised.

"For you." Sly playfulness touches her voice. "I'm sure you remember how cute I think your ass is. If this is what you want, then by God, this is what you'll get."

He doesn't realize he's raised his shoulders until they drop with relief. "Thank you. I was thinking you might use the ribbon to tie my hands, so I can't interfere."

"I'm raping you with it?"

"No, merely making me take it. The usual rules apply. I say 'red,' you stop. Finish your drink first, if you like. Another?"

She upends the glass, swallows, and blinks comically. "No, one's enough."

"Set it on the chest, so I won't overlook it. You're adorable. You know that, right?"

"A reminder never hurts. Tie your hands how?"

"Like shoelaces, I suppose. In front." He offers his wrists. His forearms are bare, his watch removed, cuffs rolled in anticipation.

Diane bends forward, tipping her head to see through the proper part of her trifocals. It's oddly endearing, familiar, and she's no longer as self-conscious as she was when the glasses were a newly acquired symbol of her age.

The ribbon circling his paired wrists could be tighter, but her bow is pretty. "I feel positively gift wrapped."

"I don't usually put a bow on a present to myself," she says. "Which is what this is. I get to plug this nice little ass, and you can't stop me? Merry Christmas and happy birthday."

"Unbuckle my belt?" Russ raises his wrists for her access. The brass clinks merrily. He feels rather than hears the trousers' waistband released. The soft susurration of the zipper hisses in the charged stillness that has overtaken the room. His trousers fall, the belt buckle ringing like a bell. "I was thinking bent over the side of the bed."

She pushes down his underwear almost roughly. "The person who's tied up doesn't get to decide. Or think, for that matter."

Yes! He nods his assent and steps from the clothes overflowing his bare feet.

"On the bed, hands and knees."

Though he's lean, Russ is glad of his dress shirt hanging down, disguising his abs, which have yielded to six decades of gravity.

"No, knees and chest. Oh, yes, that's perfect. Let me get a good look at you. At it."

He should have had a scotch. His exposed vulnerability is more intense than the first time he undressed in front of another person. For a long moment neither speaks. The air in the room crackles with tension as she examines his most private spot.

"Very nice," she says. "A pretty color. If I'd known, I could have sold you a terrazzo that matches." Her boot heels tock on the floor her company installed.

She lifts the plug by its base, smoothes the lubricant's thick dribbles to cover more of the silicone, smiles, but not at him, and leaves his line of sight to stand behind him. "This looks pretty big," she murmurs. "And you don't."

"Slow and easy is what works," he says.

"You've done this before?"

"Never on the receiving end. You want steady, gentle pressure, giving it however long it takes."

When she touches it to his center, the coolness startles as his face heats anew. She presses, light yet insistent.

Russ can't believe he's doing this. The sexual fantasy of being invaded, the source of fifty years' shame, is about to become reality. His heart speeds up as the plug eases inside just a little.

This is intimate in a way that far exceeds thrusting himself balls-deep in this or that indifferent partner until he met one worth marrying. Not many years passed before there was one more sad entry on the list of indifferent partners. Russ tried to be a better husband, waited with patience for change that didn't come. Finally they'd talked it through, though it hurt them both, agreeing to remain beloved friends.

Friends who did not expect sex.

From one another, anyway. The job offer that brought them here changed everything. The money was excellent. Russ could leave the career he'd come to detest, instead renovating a glorious older building fallen on hard times. The job's grueling travel schedule let his marriage stay intact. They met their physical needs separately with complete discretion.

Alone here, Russ kept himself busy with designs, contractors, budgets, and decisions. He'd asked Diane, the manager of the best tile and flooring store he'd visited, if he might bring samples to the building to see how they looked in its light. She'd insisted he needed to see an area larger than a single tile. Might she arrive with four-foot sections to be delivered on a pallet, at his convenience? She could. A few days later, when she'd agreed the most expensive was not the best or even second-best choice, he'd liked her honesty and offered to make lunch for them both; the kitchen was done enough to be functional. She countered: She would stay only if he agreed to keep his mind open as she praised heated floors. And so it began.

Now Diane turns the plug from side to side, calling his attention to it. To her. "Am I doing a good job?"

"Oh, yes. So good. You're so good to me. For me."

"I am. A little more?" Diane does not wait for a reply but presses anew.

He never dreamed of heated floors, or that only a few weeks later the sight of a bare wooden hanger would harden him. For the first time in years, Russ dared to dream of this. Her hand, feathery light on his lower back, urges it down, his ass up. Russ complies, and the plug enters more deeply.

"This is hot." Diane's voice says she is, too.

Once again Diane's touch has changed him from a tired old man nobody wants to a silver-haired fox unapologetic about passing the age to draw his full Social Security benefits.

He rarely sees women like her, embracing her sixties, hair more silver than brown, clothing classic rather than current. How could other men miss the beauty of laugh lines and calm wisdom which added so much to any woman who wore them with dignity and pride at being herself? Diane didn't look terrific for her age—she looked terrific, period.

"Oh, my," she says. "More, and a little firmer, yes?"

It almost hurts, yet it does not. The rounded tip passes the cylinder of muscle to enter his rectum. The nerve endings there are more sensitive than his fingertips, or even the head of his cock with the foreskin pushed back.

His heart thumps in his chest. "Stop—but don't take it out."

The pressure leaves him. "Are you all right?"

"Fine. A little too good. I was thinking about you, and how this feels, and—well, I had fears my private party would be over before the guest of honor arrived, if you get my drift."

She laughs. "We have time yet, and you took your pill, obviously. Let whatever happens, happen."

Without asking, she pushes on the plug. He imagines her behind him, the frown of concentration, the good posture of a woman who's on her feet all day, the dark-skirted suit and low-heeled winter boots seeming severe. Russ pretends Diane will force it inside, no matter what, as so often happens in the fantasies.

"I wish you could see this," she says from far away. "You're opening right up. So big, and a little bigger, and bigger." For the first time, Diane gives the plug a sharp shove. "In it goes."

It splits him, or feels like it might, the slicing pain paralyzing. Only seconds later, though, it rolls back to a level he can endure.

"Hang on. I can tell that hurt, but it's already better."

"Yes, a little."

The pain Russ can withstand soon diminishes to a strong discomfort, then further de-escalates to a mild distress which excites. He's always marveled at a plug's effect, but at last he understands. It touches him in ways he's never imagined. "Oh, God . . . "

"Russ?"

"I'm fine, just fine. This is incredible."

"I thought it might be. I've seen you hard a lot of times, but you're weeping cum like some teenager."

He grins. "A good woman can do that to a person."

"So long as she's got a good plug. What do you say to standing up?"

"I say, 'Yes, ma'am.'" Moving with the plug inserted fully astonishes him. It rolls in place at the slightest movement, insisting he pay it attention.

"Slow and easy," Diane mimics his earlier words. "You know what your blood pressure medication does if you get up too fast."

Russ hasn't fainted, but he's made himself dizzy enough times to heed her warning. Straightening one leg produces an exquisite awareness of the silicone piercing him, amplified when the other foot finds the warm floor.

The center of his being has relocated.

He stands at the side of the bed, acutely conscious of the plug, more than the hard-on bobbing almost parallel to the floor. Russ puts his tied wrists behind his neck, a prisoner not of war but of sex. The ends of the ribbon tickle his back.

Diane moves downward, settling with care. Her arthritis is mild, she says, and the heat's effect on her knees far outweighs the discomfort from the hard surface.

Her tongue glides under his foreskin, his cock held steady by thumb and forefinger's light touch. At first his being uncut fascinated her. That she found it exotic flattered Russ, whose sophistication consisted of being born to parents recently immigrated to New York.

He suspects she's never traveled outside the United States, been with few men, hasn't even seen much porn. While some people sneer at such provincialism—hell, he's married to one who does—Russ finds her simplicity refreshing and honest.

Then her tongue drives all thought from his brain as it circles beneath the soft collar of skin, flicks the frenulum like a forefinger on the bass string of an acoustic guitar, moves onward, slower for the second lap.

He is only sensation, nothing more. A cock lightly toyed with by an expert mouth, an ass well-plugged, hands restrained, unable to stop any of it.

Her mouth accepts the head now, rolling it in her warmth and once almost-chewing. The resulting little tremor makes him clench on the plug. It hurts in a way that's wonderful.

She pulls back. The room air is cool where he is wet.

"You like the plug, don't you?"

"I do."

"I know. I think I like it in you." She plunges, taking most of his cock, and not gently. Her index and middle finger meet her thumb, wrapping the base, working as an extension of her hot mouth.

Diane's lipstick smears as she works him. Russ bought the rosy shade at the city's best department store. It matched her pussy, and the young saleswoman swore it did not stain lips or skin. "That's what I like about it," she said with a blush which implied much.

Russ carried it in his pocket for weeks, enjoying the small risk of being unable to explain it, before giving it to Diane. She wears it whenever they will be together, although he suspects it's a bit brighter than she might choose.

But her skin smudged pink arouses him, so graphic that its sexuality is obvious even after the act, the evidence clear. The color extends well beyond her mouth, he sees with a pleasant shudder which ends at the plug. It demands he acknowledge it holds him agape an inch or more.

Short nails scrabble at his lower buttocks, spreading him for the moment it takes one hand to grasp the plug and turn it. The sensation draws a gasp from him, another when it rotates the other direction. Her mouth engulfs him as she gives it a 360-degree crank, and it's over.

He comes, down her throat, his ass clamping the butt plug anew with each wave. The pain is superb and makes the orgasm last a long time.

"Wonderful, just wonderful," he says finally. "And now something for you, as soon as I get this out and wash it."

She swipes at her face with a tissue, removing the lipstick. "Anything I want?"

"Anything." Russ helps her to her feet, enjoying the role of courtly gentleman.

Her smile is devious, and very pretty. "Keep it in."

Though exhausted, his cock stirs, and his asshole nips sharply tight. "Whatever you want."

"I want . . . " The pause lingers too long. Diane is not groping for a word or a lost thought. She's afraid to say it.

She stands at the window, folding back one edge of the heavy drapes. The sky has gone an angry gray; snow before long. "I want you to buy one of those for me. Smaller, maybe, or just . . . " She doesn't finish, just hitches up her skirt.

Russ finds the end of the ribbon with his teeth and tugs, freeing his hands. His cock jerks when he sees she's not wearing panties. Untrimmed pussy fur in a moist curlicue at the front announces she's aroused. When his knees press the floor it hurts, but since his motion shifts the plug within his body, it claims the greater attention.

Then she's set one booted foot on the low window still and he's at her, lapping as if his life depends on it. She rocks her hips, thrusting her pussy at him and taking it almost away, the tip of his tongue batting her clit from side to side, back to front, then licking the oozing center of her again, his thumb finding the entrance, fucking her like an undersized cock while his front teeth nibble at her. He can tell when she's about to come, her reactions paused in the stillness of an imminent orgasm, and his index finger bores between her cheeks to tickle her tightly closed asshole, the one she wants him to plug next time, like his is plugged right now.

When Diane comes, he emits a weak spurt of what little cum his poor balls can muster in so short a time. It smears across the front of her boot. Without stopping to think, he bends to lick it off. The plug moves, and he presses his cheek to the damp leather, content to be plugged, pleased to be servile, however briefly.

"Whew!" she says, the word so wholesome it delights him.

"Whew indeed." He gets up stiffly. "What do you say to a little nap?"

"I really do need to get back to work." She pushes her skirt into place. "I wish I could stay." Her skirt has twisted.

"If they're giving out wishes, think big."

Her laugh is self-conscious. "Okay. I wish that Bill would sell the damned flooring business so we could both retire. Split the proceeds, file for divorce, and remain on good terms because he's a good man. Just like Mark is a good man."

"He is," Russ admits. "We're alike again. Peas in a pod. My wish would be that neither one of us has a husband."

ENDLESS PRAISE, TIMELESS LOVE

Linda Poelzl

I rush out to buzz Max in when the doorbell rings. He is my most regular, ardent, enthusiastic, and skillful lover. He knows my body well and how to bring me from boredom to ecstasy every time we make love.

Every week, his driver drops him off, and I wait at the top of the stairs and watch him climb up energetically, looking up at me with hungry eyes. When he reaches the top, he holds out his arms and cries, "Sweetheart, let me hug you!" I gently but quickly usher him in, not wanting to disturb the neighbors, and close the door before he can grab me. Once inside, he crushes me to his chest, then holds me at arm's length and studies my face intently as if he's seeing me for the first time. A litany of praises and compliments follows: "You are so beautiful! Your hair is shining. You have a beautiful figure! You feel so good in my arms! I missed you so much! I love you to no end! Let's make love right now!"

One might imagine this could get tiresome, but he is so fresh and present that it always makes me giggle and hug him. Besides, Max is eighty-two and I am fifty-nine, so to him, I am definitely a younger woman and a total babe! He is no typical eighty-two-year-old in his appearance, either. Almost completely bald, he keeps his head shaved but sports a salt-and-pepper beard and mustache, which I love to caress. He's slim, six feet tall, and wiry. An avid walker and swimmer, he's got a well-toned body and a nice, hairy chest. He likes to wear offbeat clothing, kind of like an aging hippie, although he's way beyond boomer age. He's got quite a collection of T-shirts with silly slogans. Today he's wearing a black one that reads, "A clear conscience is the sign of a bad memory." We both laugh at that one, since he's not the only one with memory issues.

Just like a typical guy years younger, Max is always ready to go before I am. "I am so horny," he whispers hoarsely into my ear. I smile, enjoying his eagerness, while I steer him toward my comfy recliner where we can cuddle for a while.

"I want to kiss you all over," he mumbles into my neck as his hands begin to roam.

"Max, I love your enthusiasm," I say, while I catch one hand wandering toward my breast, "but you know how I always need a little more time than you to get in the mood for sex. Remember our last conversation?"

"Yes, sweetheart. I will slow down, if you wish, but I want you so badly and I'm so excited!" I feel his excitement in his rapid breathing and the way he quivers as he hugs me tighter. He gives me about thirty seconds before he makes another request.

"There's something I want to do, and I hope you will allow me," he begins, rather formally.

"I'll bet I know what you're thinking about," I tease.

"I want to kiss you all over and lick your vagina!"

I gasp, feigning shock. "I'll let you, as long as you do it as long and as thoroughly as you did last week."

"We did it last week?"

"Yes, you kiss me all over every week."

"Really?" he exclaims, astounded that he made love to me orally last week, and that we can do it again today. "Can we do it now?"

"Soon, but first I want you to caress me through my clothes. You know that helps me get excited and wet for you."

"Yes, dear, I want to please you."

"I'll show you how." Still cuddled in the big leather chair, I drape one leg over his and guide his hand to my crotch, showing him how to slide his fingers over the slit between my lips. Even though it's through both my silky skirt and my lace panties, his touch starts to excite me slowly, the way I like it. I gently correct his movement when he veers from the target. We get into a zone, breathing and rocking in the chair, his hand beginning to arouse me more and more.

I like the feel of his touch stroking between my legs and the other hand cupping and caressing my breast, gently kneading and squeezing my nipple. I grope my way to Max's crotch and roll his soft cock between my thumb and fingers, eliciting some moans from him. His cock doesn't get really firm, but he loves when I touch and caress him and give him oral sex.

"Can we lie down now, sweetheart? I want to kiss you all over," he pleads, fervently kneading my breast.

"Yes, Max, but you lie down first. I want to undress for you." He instantly leaps from the chair, strips, and dives naked onto the futon. I put on some music and slowly strip for him. It's always the same, which doesn't matter. Max never gets bored.

He showers me with compliments as I undulate while inching up my camisole, exposing my breasts. "You are so beautiful! Your figure is divine." He sits up and tries to grab me.

I dance playfully out of reach. "Lie down and enjoy my dance. You'll get to touch me soon," I reply, shimmying my ass in his face, tantalizing him. He obeys, lying back and enjoying my show.

After my dance, he claps and holds his arms out for me. I crawl into them, and he starts busily kissing my neck and running his hands all over my body. "Slow down, Max, we've got plenty of time," I say, rolling onto my belly. "I love it when you kiss my neck and kiss and lick me down my back." That's all I need to say and he promptly obeys, flicking his tongue around my neck and shoulders, evoking shivers of pleasure. Slowly he works his way down to my ass. He loves rimming me, and although I don't return the favor, I always make sure I am squeaky clean and let him go at it. It gets me warmed up for what's next.

After a while, I roll onto my back, causing him to follow the trail from my ass to my pussy, but I have other plans.

"Max, you always suck my nipples so nicely. Come and suck them awhile."

Max grunts and crawls back up and starts licking and sucking.

"Oh, that's good," I drawl, my eyes rolling back with the pleasure. Then I'm distracted by his hand squeezing my thigh. Unfortunately, for my less sensitive nipples these days, the thigh-squeezing is too distracting. I prefer one clearly felt sensation at a time. Max has a hard time controlling his urges to touch and squeeze. After a while, I just nudge him down toward my pussy, where he is more than happy to go.

On my pussy, I have to ease him into action, because Max tends to just dive onto my clit (again, like a lot of guys). "Lighter, please, gently," I whisper, holding Max's head and pulling him back slightly from my pussy, encouraging him to flick his tongue over my clit and vaginal lips, rather than planting his face and mashing his tongue around. It takes a while to get it just right. Patience is the key, because he truly loves and lives to please me.

"Oh yes, that's it, Max. That's the spot," I moan, holding his head, keeping him where I want him. He begins to growl, which is both sexy and scary. He starts moving faster, licking my clit and then nibbling on my outer lips, growling again.

Some men say they love pussy, and they might spend a few minutes there and move on to something more interesting—to them—like fucking. Max *really* loves pussy, giving me an average of twenty to thirty minutes of undivided attention. He does have to stop here and there to adjust his neck or slide a pillow under my hips. Max spoils me, and I get to be a real "pillow queen." He'll lick me until I stop him.

But now I'm ready for him to stop and he's still lapping away. I place one hand on either side of his head and pull his face up. Our eyes meet.

"You pussy hound!" I call him. He loves it when I call him a pussy hound.

"Sweetheart, I could lick your pussy all day!"

"I know you could, but I am ready for the next act now," I say, reaching for my vibrator and my favorite bright pink dildo. Well-trained, Max cuddles up next to me and starts licking and sucking my right nipple, the more sensitive one that I like to save for the grand finale. I drip some Liquid Silk onto my dildo and lube it up.

"Let me help you with that," Max offers, reaching for the dildo.

"You can do it for my second orgasm," I answer, sliding the dildo into my pussy and pumping it slowly. I can feel my g-spot and vaginal tissues swelling from all of Max's attentions. This makes the dildo feel so good sliding into my cunt. I start pumping myself, getting the feel of rocking with the fucking sensation. Knowing the drill, Max hands me the Hitachi Magic Wand, which I apply to my clit. I imagine myself as a goddess with multiple arms. Thankfully, Max keeps up the sucking and licking on my nipple.

"Oh yeah, that's it," I moan, as I sail screaming into my first orgasm. These days, my orgasms can go on and on. They used to be stronger, but now they make up for it by being longer. I keep up the pumping and the vibrator and dear Max is faithfully, hungrily, slurping my nipple until I turn off the vibrator, remove the dildo, and gently stop him.

I let Max play with the dildo and suck my nipples for the second and third orgasms. He fucks me with the dildo just right this time, not too slow, not too fast, while avoiding the Hitachi's big head, which I'm holding against my clit—all at the same time! His dexterity and coordination are frankly amazing, as is his stamina.

Soon I am lying there spent, and Max is singing my praises. "You are an amazing woman! I have never known a woman like you. You are a goddess! I love you!" I rest for a while in his arms, letting his praises wash over me, as I catch my breath for our real grand finale.

"Move over, lover," I say, nudging Max to the other side of the bed. He quickly gets into position on his right side with a pillow under his head. I swing over so that my hips are perpendicular to his. We are ready for penetration.

But first I stroke Max's cock with some lube. He moans happily despite staying soft. I slide a cock ring onto him, which will help maintain any erection that happens. Then the condom.

"Sweetheart, we don't need that! I don't have any diseases and I don't ejaculate."

"I know, but it's one of our non-negotiables. We've talked about this before. Remember?" He doesn't, but doesn't care. As long as I keep going, he'll be happy.

I gently grab his cock and line up my vagina and "stuff" his soft cock into me. I wait a moment and squeeze my vaginal muscles.

"Oh, that feels exquisite!" Max exclaims, throwing his head back and gasping. Undeterred by the lack of a hard-on, he pumps away, slowly. I am awed by his sensitivity. Every time I even slightly squeeze my muscles, he gasps and bucks his body in ecstasy. "I'm in another world, sweetheart," he exclaims. I feel his cock slightly hardening inside me. What a man!

Sometimes, I am underwhelmed by all this fucking. My orgasms came and went earlier, and this is not too sensational for me, yet I enjoy his pleasure vicariously. However, today I feel subtle sensations in my vagina as Max thrusts. The sensations I've noticed could be compared to feeling our genitals stuck together, magnetized—as I've only experienced when practicing Tantra. Max even remarked on that, feeling like he couldn't pull away, even if he wanted to. When he thrusts gently, it's like a tidal pull on my vaginal lips, connecting me to a more oceanic field of experience, a place where penis and vagina ("lingam" and "yoni" in Sanskrit) connect. It's magical and primal, and has little to do with erections or not.

We rock together dreamily. There's no place to go, no goal to be reached. He's not going to ejaculate. We're just hanging out with the energy. We caress each other softly, as our breathing rhythm slows. I sigh with deep relaxation, cradled in Max's big arms. How pleasant it is to drift, just being here now with each other.

I feel my heart swell with love for this man I've been seeing almost weekly for nearly four years. I do sexual healing work, and he is my favorite client. He came to me originally through a referral from his psychiatrist. Max has Alzheimer's, and he was getting into trouble with some prostitutes who were extorting money from him. One thing that many people don't know about Alzheimer's is that the disease can have a disinhibiting effect on a person's libido. An aging man who may have left sex behind years ago suddenly becomes amorous, flirtatious, and sometimes sexually inappropriate, or gets taken advantage of by criminals. Max's doctor proposed seeing me as a way to provide a safe container for his sexuality and intimacy needs. It's worked very well for all of us. His family is delighted that he has a safe person to be with.

Max's doctor tells me that Max has more consistency and continuity in his relationship with me than with any other person, including his family. Maybe that is because our relationship is confined to our two-hour weekly sessions, which follow a fairly predictable routine. Yet, for Max, it is always new. He often doesn't remember what we did twenty minutes ago, asking me if we can make love after we've just finished. Although he has Alzheimer's, it doesn't seem to have any negative impact on our interactions. If anything, it keeps us both firmly, sensually, and bodily in the present moment. With Max, I am forever new, amazing, precious, beautiful. He is never bored. What a delicious gift—for both of us.

THE HOTEL LOUNGE

Skyler Karadan

*Beautiful young people are accidents of nature, but
beautiful old people are works of art.*

—Unknown, though often wrongly attributed to
Eleanor Roosevelt

The hotel lounge was crowded with conference attendees from
the civic center across the street. The air inside the bar smelled of
freshly reapplied perfume and damp wool overcoats due to the
snowy, wet weather. Thank God it was one of those blessed es-
tablishments lovingly referred to as "smoke free." I had stopped
in for a happy hour nightcap before retiring to my room to attend
to the final preparations of my presentation at the conference the
next day.

I spotted her sitting at the bar as I made my way through
the maze of tables. She sat surrounded by three or four younger

men, each vying for her attention and a chance to make the evening more interesting. Her mid-calf length black skirt was slit up the side and offered a generous view of her shapely thigh when she crossed one leg over the other. She seemed to be enjoying the attention she was getting from the horny young lads, but she gave me a warm smile when our eyes met briefly as I looked for an open space at the bar. Just as I reached the bar, the couple standing next to her walked away, leaving a gap that I quickly occupied.

"Kinda crowded, huh?" she asked as she turned away from her admirers to face me.

"Yeah," I responded. "Looks like the place to be."

"Anywhere inside is better than out there," she said. "Besides, it's kinda fun being in here with all these young professionals."

"I noticed you can draw a pretty good crowd," I said with a smile.

"Oh, yeah, right! I'm old enough to be their mother. Get 'em liquored up and anybody looks good," she said with a laugh.

"Well, I'm not 'liquored up,' and you look exquisite. Can I buy you another?" I asked.

"That would be very nice. Thank you," she said.

We stayed at the bar and chatted over a couple of drinks, her sitting and me standing, as there were no tables available. People continued to crowd into the comfortable setting of the warm hotel lounge. This was obviously a favorite spot among the local young professionals. As we talked, I found myself becoming increasingly infatuated, stimulated, and, yes, even aroused by this intoxicating beauty. Her brown-green eyes sparkled with youthful mischief, and the subtle, almost invisible laugh lines that embraced them hinted of a life of gleeful enjoyment. The lounge's overhead lights, although dimmed for effect, danced in the strands of the gray-streaked hair that caressed her face. As we watched the crowd, we talked about the joys of midlife. Yes, I said the "joys" of midlife, not the heartache. Our comfort with each other grew expansively, devoid of the all too common pretense that seems to choreograph the mating dance of the younger adults.

At one point, the crowd of patrons attempting to reach the bar to place their drink orders grew so that their jostling and bumping forced my crotch into her knee several times. My growing erection became obvious in my loose dress slacks. Leaning into me, she planted the wettest tongue-filled kiss on my lips I have ever experienced. As her tongue sought mine, I felt her hand wrap around my hardness and begin to stroke me through the silky thinness of my slacks. As I am not a believer in the confines of underwear, it felt as if there was nothing between her hand and me.

When we broke our kiss for air, I noticed that her nipples were so hard and erect they appeared to be straining to break free from the lacy swirls of her top. She must not be wearing a bra. Her seductive eyes never left mine as she reached between the panels of my open topcoat and slowly unzipped my slacks. Her tongue hungrily grazed her lips as I sprang through the unzipped opening, celebrating in my emancipation and anticipation! Precum was already running down the length of my shaft, bathing the hardest, longest erection I had enjoyed since my thirties. Glancing over my shoulder, I turned my back to the crowded lounge, not believing what was happening literally at the hands of this lustful vixen. As one hand was spreading my precum over my hardness, her other hand grabbed mine and pulled it under her skirt to her exposed, shaved vulva. Her clit was swollen hard, and, after discreetly depositing saliva onto my fingertips, I spread it liberally over her hot button with my thumb. She gasped loudly, squeezing her eyes shut while biting her bottom lip.

"You know," she said breathlessly into my ear, "it's getting really crowded in here. Why don't we continue our conversation up in your room?"

With the deftness of years of experience, she slid me back into my slacks and carefully zipped me up after giving me one more slow, steady stroke. *Thank God for overcoats,* I thought, for there was no other way I was going to make it all the way up to my room without my erection noticeably announcing our progress.

I paid for our drinks, and we made our way to an empty elevator, only to be forced to the back wall by a group of partyers getting on as the doors were shutting. As the elevator began its ascent, I felt my zipper once again open and a familiar hand reach in and pull me out. Conspicuously coating her palm with her saliva, she began to stroke me almost to oblivion. I wasn't going to be able to handle much more of this before shooting my load all over both of us. Finally the partyers exited on their floor with nary a glance back at us.

As soon as the elevator doors closed, I immediately dropped to my knees, raised her skirt to her waist, and dove into her sweet folds, first plunging my tongue as deeply as possible into her inviting entrance, and then sucking her clit hard between my lips while slipping a finger deep inside. As I continued to suck and lick her shaved lusciousness, her hips began to buck as she fell back against the elevator wall. She moaned as she grabbed the back of my head and forced my face deeper into her. The elevator bell announced our arrival at my floor. Quickly I pulled her skirt back down over her hips, stood up, and zipped my slacks closed as the elevator doors slid open.

We practically ran down the hall to my room. By the time we arrived at the door I had the key card out, and with a flick of my wrist we were falling through the doorway, clothes flying everywhere, and we landed in a lust-filled pile of nakedness and hungry gropes in the middle of the bed. She rolled me onto my back and, pinning my wrists to the bed with her hands, she began to slowly lower herself onto my throbbing shaft.

"I can't believe you're so wet," I gasped, as I felt myself slide effortlessly into her vaginal embrace.

"You mean, for a woman of my age?" she asked with a wicked little smile. "You can thank my hormone supplements. They do wonders for this kind of thing."

She was so tight she had to gently rock me into her. What a perfect fit! After our pelvic bones began kissing, it took just a few trips up and down my length to push us both over the threshold of explosive orgasmic bliss accompanied by our harmonic moans and screams.

Still feeling the aftershock of our sexual earthquake, she quickly dismounted from my still fully engorged penis. (Viagra be damned!) She positioned herself on her hands and knees, inviting me to enter again from behind. This amazing woman was not finished! The tattoo of two entwined snakes forming a heart at the top of her beautiful ass pointed the way.

This time gentle entry was unnecessary. As I plunged into her depths, she reached under and began feverishly rubbing her swollen clit and rocking back and forth on her knees to slam that amazing ass of hers into my crotch repeatedly. I wished I could look into her face but had to settle for watching those caressing snakes perform their own version of a mating dance. Again after only a few full-shaft thrusts, we both came with body-shuddering, mind-blowing orgasms. I didn't know that my middle-aged prostate could produce that much cum!

Spent, satiated, and in full sexual bliss, we found our way under the bed covers, folding into each other's arms, our bodies entangled. "You know," I whispered, "you could have had your choice of any of those young studs downstairs in the lounge."

"Oh, no," she said. "I'll choose a seasoned, beautiful artist over a beautiful accident of nature any day."

"This role-play thing is awesome!" I said. "Can we meet again next weekend?"

"Oh, I am so sorry," she said. "Did you forget? We're on grandparent duty next weekend. We're keeping the kids while Jack and Susan go away for a short trip, just the two of them."

"Should we turn them on to this role-play stuff?" I asked.

"No," she answered. "They're much too young to handle the vulnerability. We'll let them discover it later on their own."

"Rain check?" I asked.

"Absolutely," she answered with enthusiasm.

"God, I love my life with you," I said.

"And I with you, my dear," she responded in her sexy, sleepy voice, her head nestling into the soft, gray-white of my chest hair.

COMING FULL CIRCLE

Cela Winter

Annie turned slowly in front of the full-length mirror. She hadn't been able to decide between the blush-colored teddy or the lilac baby doll at the lingerie shop, so she'd bought both—a breathtaking extravagance. She justified it to herself that this was a special occasion, very special. Closing her eyes and unhooking her mind, she slid her palms down her body, imagining that it was Ben gliding the fabric over her curves, exploring the contrasts of flesh and silk.

There'd been a few dates, some gaspingly sweet kisses, touches, and then the preliminaries of intimacy—or rather attempts at them. For once, Annie wished she lived in a city where it was possible for two people to go about their private business without being noticed—and interrupted—by everyone.

But then, a few days ago, Ben said, "This isn't going to work out." She'd nearly cried, thinking he'd given up on wanting to see her that way—it was just too difficult. Then he asked her to go away for a long weekend, somewhere that kids, grandkids, friends, and neighbors couldn't get at them.

"I don't want this to be some kind of furtive, hurry-up fuck, Annie. I want to make love to you, *then* we can, uh, fuck. But I'm not the kid I once was, so . . . there'll be considerable downtime in between. That's why I want a weekend." He gave a grin and a one-shoulder shrug that utterly melted her heart. She agreed almost before he finished speaking, glad that the years of friendship, for lack of a better word, eliminated any pretense between them.

The words *make love . . . fuck . . . make love . . . fuck* swirled around in her brain all week. People kept asking her what she was smiling about. The smile was the least of it. Anticipation roamed over her like a lover's hands, startling her with its power. Her lips would tingle or her breasts ache with wanting, her sex felt full and heavy and . . . *ready* as she went through her busy days.

Had Ben known his words would affect her like that? She hoped so.

She held up the baby doll in front of her, eyeing it critically. Each lacy ensemble, not too sheer, concealed what she thought of as figure flaws but discouragingly revealed others.

"Why am I so anxious? It's *Ben*." She shook her head at her own foolishness.

He'd always been part of her life, her brother Stan's best friend, while Annie was the nuisance of a little sister, trying to tag along and yelling at them to wait up.

One day, there was a shift in her vision, and her brother's pal became a whole lot more than just a playmate. There was a tug of awareness, sidelong glances, and awkward flirting, then that unforgettable summer at the end of high school. She didn't consider herself the sentimental type, but she'd been very lucky with the men in her life. Every girl should have a first love like that.

What was that saying? Life is what happens while you're busy making other plans? Nursing school for her, an Army hitch for Ben. They got busy . . . and drifted apart.

Annie met Carl; Ben came back to their hometown with a fiancée, Nora. The following forty years were full—where *had* the time gone?—rewarding, hectic, as family and work always were, yet there remained that subtle pull between them, like the force that keeps two planetary bodies in orbit. Somehow, he just understood her in a way that Carl, as much as she loved him, never quite did. Stan, Nora, Carl, all were gone now, one way or another. The kids were grown, raising their own families.

Annie knew the talk and speculations about him from the other nurses at the hospital, typical small-town gossip. He dated sporadically but never seriously. The consensus was that he still carried a torch for his ex-wife, but Annie didn't think that was true, merely convenient. When asked, Ben would just say nonchalantly that he was too choosy for his own good.

He was so great all during Carl's final illness, the best of family friends, always nearby as she groped through the tangled exhaustion, rage, and bewilderment of loss. Once again, subtly, things between them changed. Self-doubt whispered in her brain that it had been a very long time since she'd been with a man, even Carl. How would she—Annie cut off the uncomfortable thought.

She'd been sad, of course, and lonesome, but it was more than that. Beyond loneliness or missing Carl or simply missing sex, it was *intimacy* she lacked, that intangible connection between herself and a man, the sense of completeness.

She knew that he was watching and waiting, letting her decide when she was ready. That was Ben Alderman's way. She watched and waited, too, letting his patience beautify her, basking in the heat growing between them.

At last. She was waiting by the door as he parked in the driveway. He looked so nice in khakis and a striped shirt instead of jeans or his work uniform. Annie was glad she had dressed up too, wearing the rose-colored wrap dress that was her nice outfit for warm weather. The silky teddy was like a soft breeze on her skin under her clothes. She reveled in her secret finery, a preparation of body and mind for the upcoming encounter.

"So . . . where are we going?" she asked as they turned onto the highway.

"Out to the lake. I got us a cabin . . . a very private cabin."

"Really? The lake and you didn't bring fishing gear?" she mocked lightly.

His face lit up. "No kidding? You want to fish?" He slowed the car and started to pull over, preparing to make a U-turn. "We can just head back to town and get the—"

Annie let out a squawk of protest before she saw the smile playing under his mustache and realized that he was teasing back. They laughed more than the joke warranted and held hands as they drove, taking the two-lane through farmlands and into the forest. The conversation faded away as they approached their destination and the atmosphere between them thickened. The sun was dropping behind the mountains, and the air was growing cooler as they parked.

The word "cabin" hadn't prepared her; she'd been thinking of a fisherman's camp, utilitarian and plain. So long as there was a comfortable bed and a lock on the door, she was fine with that. Ben bowed her in with a flourish. She entered a few paces, then stopped and turned in a full circle, exclaiming, peripherally aware of his pleased grin at her reaction.

The place was gorgeous, made of milled logs, with huge windows, an artfully rustic fireplace, and, in the room's ell, a vast bed.

"I had the fridge stocked with various things, or we can go out," he said hesitantly, after lighting the ready-laid fire. "There's the restaurant at the Lodge or—"

"The wining and dining can wait, Ben," she broke in. Her voice sounded rather far away to her ears.

"I . . . I just don't want you to think, you know . . . " His voice trailed away.

"I don't." *He sounds nervous.* She would have laughed, if she hadn't been feeling exactly the same. Taking a deep breath, she said softly, "This has been a long time coming, Ben. I think we both know what we want."

"Yes, but for me . . . it doesn't end here, Annie."

The simple candor banished her last pangs of anxiety. "Me neither." With a chuckle, she said, "So, now that we've declared that our intentions are honorable . . . "

She tugged at the tie of her dress and shrugged out of it, letting it fall to the floor. Feeling an intense gratitude for the kindliness of firelight, she stood before him, wearing only the blush-colored teddy and her high-heeled sandals.

The admiring glow in Ben's brown eyes turned hot and flinty. "You look like you did at seventeen." It wasn't true, but for once she didn't care.

He stepped nearer, then nearer still, stopping a hand's breadth away from her; the electric pulse of arousal that crossed the tiny air gap between them was as potent as any physical contact. Annie couldn't tear her eyes from his and felt her breath getting short, suddenly very aware of her nipples tightening. They hadn't even kissed yet.

Another step. He pressed her back against the smooth planks of the front door. She could feel the warmth of his skin through the crisp cotton of his shirt and the fragile fabric of the lingerie.

He remembered.

All these years and he remembered that she liked the pressure of his body just *that way*, the feeling of surrender that swept her from knees to collarbone when there was no place to go, when his sheer physical presence demanded all her attention. The lines of his body were hard against hers, and his hands were pressed to the door on either side of her head, while his lips and the tip of his nose barely ghosted over her hair and throat and jaw, inhaling the scent of her skin.

Feeling that she would choke on her own desire if they didn't move faster, Annie flung her arms around Ben's neck, landing her mouth on his and inviting his lips and tongue to engage.

Oh god! Not only the sensuality but also the sheer *relief* of finally kissing him, after the week—and longer—of yearning, made her giddy. His lips were still soft but firm, just like always, and their tongues and breaths mingled as naturally as if the last forty-something years had never happened.

For an instant, she was a girl again, in love for the first time, giving herself to the boy who had completely reordered her awareness of herself.

There was more now, though; a sense of deep, masculine power that called to her on an unexpected, fundamental level, surprising her with the strength of her response. Annie leaned her weight against his chest, slipping one leg between his. Strong hands stroked her hair and drifted down to caress the smoothness of her bare shoulders, then traveled farther, rounding the curve of her ass, pulling her tightly to him, against the thickness of his growing erection.

Without conscious command, her fingers began working the buttons of his shirt, desperate to lay skin against skin. She pulled his shirt free from his waistband and circled her arms around his naked back. His body was still fit, but somewhat thickened around the middle; she found that embracing his girth was both comforting and exciting. Still kissing leisurely, but with even greater intent, Ben walked backwards toward the bed, drawing her along, and sat down heavily, spreading his legs for her to stand between them.

He pulled at the ribbon laces and then parted the teddy. His hand curved and filled itself with a breast. The rumble in his throat as he squeezed and kneaded raised the heat that was seething deep in her source to an almost scorching level.

His other hand gripped her bottom, and he drew them both up onto the bed, rolling her onto her back and resting his weight on one elbow and forearm. He brushed his lips over hers, along her throat, then further down. Annie shivered at his hot breath as he traced a line around her nipple with his tongue, then fastened his mouth to her and began to suckle, softly at first, then more vigorously as she moaned and arched into him.

"Touch me," she pleaded.

His fingers deftly moved the lacy strip that formed the crotch of the teddy, gently exploring her lips before slipping between them. The delicacy of his stroke on her clit was too intense—she cried out and bucked into his hand, seeking a firmer pressure that would allow the sensations to build.

Another change. Far from the fumbling eagerness of a boy, his touch was now sure and intuitive, guided by her reactions.

Annie trembled as her excitement grew, and Ben responded with a gravelly hum, clasping her to him as the tempo of his fingers outpaced the pull of his mouth on her nipple. This sound of his arousal pushed her over the peak and she sobbed softly with the swirling, gripping waves of her release. He held her tenderly as her breathing slowed and the repletion of her climax was stirred by the growing need to return pleasure.

"We're not even naked yet!" Annie exclaimed with a gasping laugh. Her sandals had come off at some point, and Ben helped her out of the teddy, embellishing the process with kisses and nibbles. Perhaps she should have been more bashful, but it seemed pointless as her flesh burned for full contact. She undid his buckle and zipper then, and with a playful shove made him stand up off the bed. She eased his khakis over the swell of his cock, which bobbed heavily as it was freed. Ducking down, she rolled the flat of her tongue around the head, savoring the musky, salty tang and smiling to herself at his hiss and shudder.

Ben had changed and grown, learning along the way—so had she. Giving a smile full of promises, she leaned back and worked her way up on the bed, pulling him along with her till she felt the pillows' support behind her shoulders. With judicious shifts, she arranged him so that he straddled her upper body. Threading an arm through his thighs, Annie lifted herself to nuzzle the soft skin of his sac, inhaling the richly male scent of him. She lipped and licked her way down the length of his cock, searching out the spots that made him twitch and grunt, then revisiting them. She took him in deeply, guiding him to surge in and out of her mouth as she looked up and watched his expression change.

"Damn, woman! That's so good!" Ben gripped the headboard and gingerly extricated himself. Reaching over to the box of condoms on the nightstand, he made a few quick preparations and moved to settle between her legs.

"A-a-a-a-aaaahhh . . . " The soft sound poured from her throat, growing in volume as he rocked in slowly, filling her with his length and width. The intimacy she had craved was now shockingly immediate—she had forgotten the sensation of stretching and accommodating. Then the primal urge to respond to his rhythm took her over. As they moved together, all her senses were saturated with him, his smell and the scent of their bodies joined, his sweat-slick shoulders under her encircling arms, the coarse hairs of his legs against the smooth skin of her inner thighs, the huff of his breath.

He pulled back, tantalizing her, leaving only his cockhead inside her, moving just slightly, while she squirmed and whined beneath him, then he plunged into her, thrusting fast and deep. As she neared her orgasm, he pulled back yet again, teasing her till she was almost howling with frustration.

"Oh, god, *Ben!*" she cried out, weakly pummeling his back. "Ben, *please!*"

He shifted, sitting back on his heels and pulling her up onto his thighs. "I want to see your face when you come," he said gruffly. "I've thought about it so many times."

Annie felt a wave of dizzying arousal. What he could do to her with his words! She clamped her legs around his waist as he grasped her hips and began pounding into her. The top of her head was making contact with the headboard at each thrust, but she couldn't bring herself to care, so long as he kept up his possession of her body. His thumb sought out her clitoris, rolling it with ease in her silky wetness.

She was getting close. Her chest and face and throat were hot, and she knew the flush of her approaching climax was blossoming on her skin. Digging her fingers into his hips, she tried to drag him even farther inside her as she arched against him, while twisting pulses of sensation carried her away. From a distance, she heard herself cry out Ben's name, mixed with curses and endearments.

His thrusts grew wild and erratic. Fluttering open hazy eyes, she watched as he threw his head back and forced harsh groans through gritted teeth as he jolted his orgasm into her.

They lay together, sweaty limbs entangled, as gradually their hearts quieted and their breathing calmed. Ben stretched out one leg, then the other, and they both gave a little whimper as they became unjoined. He rolled onto his back with a happy mumble, and Annie snuggled into his side, finding that hollow in his shoulder where her head fit so naturally. She realized that not once since she'd shed her dress had worries about her age or appearance crossed her mind. She only knew that she felt beautiful, womanly, and sexy.

"That was . . . as good as I remembered."

"Better."

"Yeah . . . "

Afterglow.

Whispers, husky laughter, caresses that started out languid but grew in intent. At length, he propped himself up on an elbow to look down at her, smiling. "Remember how I said something about needing more downtime than I used to?"

"Um, yes . . . "

Warm lips pressed into her ear, murmuring, "Well, I've got something to prove."

The words created an anticipation that billowed from her inner core to her extremities. "And just what would that be?" Her heartbeat began picking up again.

The lips were replaced by his tongue, which began a meandering voyage down her neck, around her breasts, to her navel. Once there, Ben laid a hand on the curve of her belly and rested his chin on it, smiling up at her. "Some parts of me are just as good as they ever were . . . "

The downward journey recommenced.

GEORGE

Lorna Lee

I stared at the "submit" button on LastResortDateSite.web. Elvis appeared in my mind's eye, hips jutted out, and began to croon, "It's now or never . . . " as his hips gyrated in sync with the melody. "It's now," I said as I smiled at the memory of The King. I moved my cursor and hesitated over the button. One click, and then just sit back and wait while all the seventy-plus-or-minus-year-old studs within a fifty mile radius of my home read my profile and reply. Of course, how many of those studs would want a seventy-year-old hot mama remained to be seen.

My gal pals had tried various electronic dating sites, and their biggest complaint was that all the codgers came calling with a pocket full of Viagra. All they really wanted was to show my friends how young and virile they still were. Did I want a seventy-year-old who truly thought that with the help of a pill, he was still sixteen? I thought long and hard about clicking on the "submit" button after spending several minutes answering page after page of personality test questions. Elvis kept crooning in my mind; I clicked. My biggest fear was that I'd find some old man who wanted a nurse!

Exhausted, I went to bed. A bit away from the foot of my bed, he waited. My lover. George. As always, he sat on his cloth-draped stool, not quite facing me, not quite in profile, looking down his long aquiline nose at something only he could see. The only article of clothing he wore was on his head—a Greek fisherman's cap, bleached from years in the sun. His face wore a perpetual expression of patience and a neatly trimmed silver beard and mustache. Thin, his well-tanned skin covered ropes of muscle developed through years of fishing on the open seas. An old amulet of protection hung from a leather cord around his neck. He sat as he always sat, relaxed but ready for whatever would come his way, his right ankle on his left knee, both hands resting on his walking stick, held to his left side, toward me. This beautiful, tanned man did not even wear a tan line. Nude men seldom turn me on, but George was different, and he knew it. He never presented the full monty when the light was on—he waited for darkness and my wild fantasies. Strong, silent, with a touch of mystery, he never made demands.

"Ah, George, you are so patient. So caring. I wonder why I feel this compulsion to find someone else." As usual, George replied with just a hint of smile. He is truly one of the strong and silent types. I slipped into bed between the sheets, turned off the light, and pulled the blankets up to my chin. George soon slid in beside me.

His arms wrapped around me, his mouth found mine, and soon he shifted in the bed, pulling blankets and sheets off me, and moved his mouth down my body. I felt the warmth of his mouth on my breast, his teeth lightly nibbling my nipple; the coolness as his warm, wet mouth moved down my belly. I moaned in the promise of what would happen next.

He separated my legs, found my secret self with his hot, wet tongue. His tongue slid around my clit, which I've named Ethel, and over it, and too soon, I flooded with warmth. Maybe that's why I feel the need for a different lover? George always knows what I want, and goes right to it. There is no mystery with George, no long, drawn out foreplay. George is good for instant gratification, but Ethel never really has a chance to wake, to reach her full potential of enjoyment.

A short eternity later, I lay in my bed; the sheets and blankets back over me, neatly tucked in. I reached for George, but of course, he wasn't there. He had returned to the cloth-covered footstool near the foot of my bed. I rolled over into deep, satisfied sleep.

The next morning, I said nothing to George as I passed him on my way to the shower. I hurried through my ablutions, poured a cup of coffee, and with great expectations, turned on my computer.

I had winks from men two thousand miles away, winks from men who lived across two mountain passes, and a few winks from locals. I dated some of the locals. One thought primitive camping and hunting was the way to live. His first question when we met was, "Do you know how to gut a deer?" Another gentleman wanted to live in a sports bar, watching games and drinking beer. His major question for me: "Ya gonna bet on da Packers, right?" And then there was the survivalist who did time in the federal penitentiary for illegally possessing and selling weapons—some of which actually ended up in the commission of felonies, including murder. I despaired of ever finding a compatible man through LastResortDateSite or any other online site.

"Oh, George," I wailed in self-pity as I crawled into bed that night. "Is there a decent, intelligent, fun man out there who isn't already taken? Will I ever find him?" Shortly after I turned off the light, George slid between the sheets and pulled me to him. He stroked me, and as my sobs subsided, he kissed away my tears. His hands began to caress my breast. He nibbled my nipple, held that nipple in his mouth as his hand slid down my belly. He slowly caressed my Ethel until I could take no more. I called out, spasmed as my legs clamped shut, and then I fell into sleep.

The next morning, I received another wink. From Dave. In reading Dave's profile, I saw we matched 98 percent on our personality test. We shared the same religion, read the same books, belonged to the same political party, and he lived eight miles away—I winked back.

"George," I sighed that night as I crawled into bed, "is this going to be another letdown? Do smart, intelligent, and decent men use LastResortDateSite.web?"

There was no response from George, no slipping between the sheets to hold me. No love from my ever-faithful lover. I slept fitfully.

The next day, Dave and I set up a meeting.

Since we both love Thai food, we arranged to meet in a small Thai restaurant. I recognized Dave as soon as I entered the restaurant from his photo on LastResortDateSite. The photo didn't do justice to his height (a foot taller than me). Or his thick and wavy silver hair. Or his green-hazel eyes. Or his contagious smile. Or his intelligence or capability to carry on a conversation beyond hunting, survivalist philosophy, or pinochle. We ate lunch and talked for hours. We covered topics from death to physics to swimming pools.

"Oh. My. God. George, the man can think. On a variety of topics. And his jokes are funny. True, I don't melt when his hazel eyes focus on me, not like I did when the survivalist turned his ice blue eyes on me. But, when I looked Dave up in Google, the worst thing I could find about him is he used to run marathons. That night, George silently crawled between the sheets after I'd gone to sleep. I felt his hands explore my body and find my nerves, and after a while, I moaned, then called out, then dropped into deeper sleep. George again sat on his stool, guarding me.

❊ ❊ ❊

And then, the night arrived when Dave came to dinner—and stayed for dessert.

"Lorna, I need to tell you something. I'm impotent. I can't take Viagra because it interferes with the other medication I'm on. I can cuddle, and caress, but that's about all. Will that be all right?"

I leaned across the sofa cushion and kissed him for a long time. It was a sweet, chocolate-and-wine flavored kiss, unlike the ones from George, which actually are flat as a black-and-white photo.

Dave's hands reached for and cupped my face. The kiss lingered.

"Come," I said and stood to lead him down the hall to my room and my bed with freshly laundered sheets.

Dave stopped at the foot of my bed, and again held me in an embrace. He leaned down and gave me another long kiss as his tongue circled mine. He held me close with one arm as the other hand untied my wrap dress and dropped it to the floor. I managed to unbutton and remove his shirt and get his pants to the floor, next to my dress. He eased my bra and panties off. I eased his shorts down. There we stood, naked with all our wrinkles and gray hairs and extra flesh, shyly exposed to each other. Although neither young nor inexperienced, we were new to each other.

Dave's arm relaxed, and I fell back a bit. He caught me and chuckled, "I'll show you mine, if you'll show me yours."

We both laughed. A man who can actually laugh during sex is a treasure!

He lowered me to the bed and stretched out beside me. On his side, his elbow bent and his head above me, he caressed my body. His fingers traced meandering trails along my belly, my thighs, my breasts. I started to mirror the motions, to caress and explore his body. I felt the warmth of his chest beneath my hand, the smoothness of his belly, the roughness where my hand met hair.

"No," he said as my hand caressed his chest and moved down his belly. "Not tonight. Tonight is my treat." He moved my hand over my head. He spread my legs, and his hand lightly stroked the inside of my thighs. I felt ripples of warmth radiate out from his fingers. That warmth followed his fingers and moved deeper as those strong and gentle fingers moved from my thigh to between my legs. They caressed Ethel. I shivered with delight.

He shifted his body and knelt between my legs. His mouth pulled on my breast. One hand held and squeezed the other breast while his other hand tickled its way down my belly. A moan of anticipation escaped me.

His kisses and licks traveled from my nipples down my belly. My hands found his head, and I tangled his hair with my fingers. As his tongue reached my clit, Ethel woke. Truly woke. I held onto his head, my fingers grasping ever tighter. Unlike masturbating with George, this was the real thing. Pleasure like this had not happened to me, or to Ethel, in years. Dave's tongue caressed Ethel. First with hesitancy, then with ownership.

His mouth closed over her and pulled her into him. I moaned. I don't know how long his tongue stroked me—it felt like forever before I shuddered with a true orgasm, then moaned with a second. Then I pulled him up to lie next to me, for truly one can have too much of a good thing.

"Heaven," was all I could say. We held each other, teased each other, and grinned like we had just discovered sex for the first time.

The next morning, we woke still entwined in each other's embrace; I disentangled myself, padded off to the kitchen, and brought back coffee. We sat in bed and drank it. "Who's the nude dude?" Dave asked, pointing to the black-and-white photograph on the wall.

"Oh, I don't know his real name. I call him George. My girlfriend is a professional photographer, and she took it some years ago. I liked it and bought a print. Besides," I grinned, "I like having a man in my room."

"Really?" Dave smiled down at me. "We'll have to see what we can do about getting you a real man in your room. It is a little intimidating sharing you with another naked man."

Dave left after breakfast and the promise of more nights to come. I entered my bedroom, our bedroom, and moved the photo of George to the guest room. There he remains, sitting on the draped stool, still without a tan line, still handsome and virile as ever. Did I imagine it, or did he wink when I passed by?

IN THE MEANTIME

Miriam Kura

As I enjoy my late morning tea in the upstairs nook of my home, Andrew sleeps downstairs. We are in the middle of our periodic twenty-four-hour tryst.

Last night, in this same knotty pine sleeping nook, we lay on the bed and watched a movie while he slid his hand to my breasts to fondle them and awaken my desire. He explored all the ways his palm and fingers contour to my breasts and nipples, an absent-minded yet knowing move that thrills me every time. When the movie ended, I rolled over and faced him, wanting more. We spent an hour letting our fingers languorously glide over each other while we kissed, talked, and sighed our way through teasing touch.

I'm surprised that I'm ready for sex all the time, more than when I was a younger woman. Is this post-menopausal zest?

However, we waited until the next day to make full-on love. That way we could take advantage of Andrew's increased desire earlier in the day. We came downstairs to the king-size bed in my tiny bedroom and fell asleep spooning, his hand over my breast.

❊ ❊ ❊

I've come a long way with this man. *Finally*, we found a way that works for both of us; it's just not the way I expected. Seven years ago we fell deeply in love and had a two-year romance. He was sixty-one; I was fifty-three. I wanted a long-term romantic partner, but he was restless. Our breakup was amicable but wrenching, with infrequent contact for two years while we each healed our hearts.

During that time Andrew discovered the source of his restlessness. At his core he is a polyamorist. He longs for ethical love relationships with more than one woman at a time. Meanwhile, my dream died that Andrew might be my life partner. Eventually, I was able to move on, date other men again, and remain committed to my goal of finding my mate.

With this loss of intimate male companionship I felt impatient and petulant about my romantic life. Some women solve that problem through casual sex with men they recently met. But that's not in my DNA; I can only make love to a man I know well and trust. Then I heard about the practice of having a sex friend, someone you know well, to share nurturing touch while searching for a life partner. I couldn't think of anyone I knew until I realized that Andrew could be a great candidate. He seemed to be a short-cycle relationship person, so he wouldn't be looking for a commitment from me while not being able to give it himself. I already knew and trusted him because he had always been honest with me.

Emotionally, could this work? Sexperts said that it was ill advised to do this with an ex-lover. My friends told me they wouldn't be able to handle it. I wondered if I could and still look for a longtime, committed love. I wouldn't know unless I tried it.

Two years ago I sent an email to Andrew to broach the subject. We met and discussed whether it could work. He said, "A year ago I proposed something similar, and you nixed it right away. What's different about this?"

"I'm different than I was a year ago. Back then I still wasn't over you. Now that we're back to a friendship, I'm looking at this as an experiment. I know that we aren't meant to be mates, but I won't know if I can be sexual with you and stay on my goal of looking for my life partner unless I give it a try."

We talked about the terms. I proposed that we date other people but remain sexually monogamous with each other until either of us found someone we fell in love with. That's when I learned of Andrew's new realization about himself.

"I don't want to be monogamous. I'm finally coming into my own as a polyamorist. I'm not going to be monogamous with anyone anymore. If I fall in love, it will be with a lover I add to my other lovers, not one for whom I leave all others."

That was almost a deal breaker. I didn't feel safe about my sexual health if I was having sex with a man who had other partners. But, as is our custom, we kept talking until we had an arrangement that worked for both of us—we would engage in some sexual activities while he has other lovers. Then we would add more options if he has no other partners and is "accidentally monogamous" with me.

We are both free to date whomever we want, and we do. He has sex with whomever he wants. I want sex with only one man, and for now, that's him when I'm not seriously involved with someone else. The only way this works is that we are both quite sure that we are not each other's mates and don't have a long-term future together.

Thus began our episodic sexual visits. This is my current in-the-meantime arrangement until I find my life partner.

Now at one o'clock in the afternoon, I return downstairs to my bedroom, where Andrew reads the newspaper in bed, wearing his black satin boxer shorts. He hears me approach; the paper rattles as he pushes it aside to look up and smile.

He says, "I've prepared," code for the Levitra pill he took a half hour ago.

I spy the condom already opened and ready on the nightstand: We want to be sexy *and* safe. "So have I," I reply, taking my long sweater off to reveal my black camisole and lace underwear.

"Oooohh, that's sex-y-y. One minute I'm reading the paper, I look over at you, and the next second I'm amped for sex. You look sooo sexy in that."

I'm delighted to hear it. It's taken me a while to learn not to flinch when flaunting myself in front of him, to accept his compliments with grace. He gets a view of my ass when I bend over the iPod speakers to begin the "Afternoon Delight" playlist.

I crawl into bed. He pulls me toward him and caresses me with light sweeps over my arms and thighs. He stares at my lace underwear, and then pulls. "Let's get this off."

I slide my hand from the springy white hairs of his chest to the sleek black hair on his belly. My fingers slip underneath his waistband to graze his penis. I think, *I'm greedy for your skin on mine.* I push his underwear down.

Now that my thigh is between your legs, I dare you to resist such sweet enticement. His torso undulates against me in slow rhythmic waves. This begins that inevitable warmth between my legs, that urgency. He presses against me, igniting my desire for him.

Let's make sure we've arrived in the same place. Are you with me? When we were together as a couple, Andrew was just discovering an unreliable erection. It distracted him from enjoying sex. His anxiety made him less present and attentive, either rushing or not starting at all. There was little I could do to reassure him or help him to get with me in bed, just to enjoy what fun we could have.

Now Levitra helps enormously with these issues, but I still have the tendency each time to wonder if he'll relax into lovemaking.

It also helps *me* to slow myself down until we're in sync with each other. So I glide my hand back up his torso to his shoulder. I trace his collarbone with my fingers until I feel the bony knob at the end of it, a place I like to alight when I'm feeling the strength of my desire.

He says, "I love the feel of your soft skin, so different from mine." He pulls my camisole aside to cup my breast and wake my nipple. Andrew finds my breasts endlessly fascinating. They fit within his palm. He lingers there and then progresses slowly to my pubic hair. His hand is a wand that awakens every nerve, until finally he arrives at the soft folds between my legs. Barely grazing the skin of those outer lips, he pauses—*right* there on the outside—arousing me with the slightest touch.

"How do you know *exactly* where to touch?" He doesn't respond; he just continues to caress that velvety softness. I'm keenly aware that those folds cover the entrance to the most thrilling morsel. He strokes lightly while he pushes his groin against my thigh. I whisper, "This feels *so . . . nice.*"

He kisses me slowly to explore and suck. I get lost in his kiss. When his tongue nibbles my lip it seems like he's directly touching my clit. My groin jumps in anticipation. *Do with me what you will; just don't stop.* I open my legs even more.

He slips his finger between my folds, and finds my clit. I catch my breath and cling to his shoulder with a stronger hand. He stops and holds the pad of his finger right there. What a touch! So restrained. He hardly shifts his finger over my clit—barely moving, then stops and waits; barely moves again, then stops and waits; barely moves—it goes on and on. He owns me. He's *with* me. I never quite know when the thrill of his next shift will come.

When it does, I moan and ache, inflamed by his touch. He slides his finger inside my vagina. I'm deep in the thrall of the sensations he's causing when he says, "Lake Miriam." I'm thrilled that he appreciates my inner flood.

I dip my fingers into my lake and slick up just the underside of the tip of his penis and play with him while he moans. *Yes . . . your moans, they send me higher.* Then I take his cock fully and firmly in my hand, switching between light brushes and firm squeezes. It grows bigger and harder. I relish feeling it leap in my hand. I let go and it arches back to lie on his stomach. *Look what I did.* I'm so powerful. I tell him, "What a sexy view."

He reaches for the condom and rolls it on. I climb on top of him to control the place and the pace of his penis. I slide my labia all along the underside, my slickness caressing his utmost sensitivity. We love our delicious sliding.

We're going slow, slower, slowest today. I cover just the tip of the head with my labia. Pause. Next I barely insert his tip into my vagina. Pause. He likes that first penetration past the tighter opening into the larger cavern beyond. Finally, inch-by-inch, I let his whole shaft slip inside me.

Andrew says, "You're fucking me."

"Yes, I am."

All the while he looks at me and utters appreciative sighs. This is both exciting and sweet. I strip off my camisole. As though summoned, his palms reach up to brush my nipples. He swirls my breasts with the backs of his hands, then his palms again, back and forth. I get more excited and see that he's having exquisite sensations—he never quite knows when or how I'll move next. He looks deep into my eyes and holds my gaze. He says, "You're really caressing me, really fucking me."

The pace is now so slow and so tantalizing that Andrew lightly grasps my hips to guide me, so he can go faster and farther in. But I tease him; *No, no, no—I'm riding you so much more slowly and shallowly today.* He looks at me with urgency, but then releases my hips, giving in to my pace. It's delicious torture and his responsiveness adds to my arousal.

After a long while, I roll over onto my back alongside him. *Okay, you can have your way now.* He climbs on top, smiles, and plunges deep into me. "You're so hot."

"Yes I *am*." It pleases me to hear him say it.

He laughs. "No, I mean literally. You're amazingly hot, deep down inside."

I'm elated that I'm making love with a man who likes to talk during sex as much as I do. It's a turn-on for us both, amplifying our pleasure. Making love and talking about it is a way to taste it twice.

"I'm all the way to your core. I love being this close and intimate with you. And I love that you love it."

He thrusts in so many ways and paces and depths that he helps me feel my vagina at different angles. "Now I'm fucking *you*," he says.

I relish hearing this, but feel challenged to take it for what it is, and not, for so long, what I wished it would be. *You feel this close and intimate with me, and yet you don't want to be my mate.* I have to remind myself that we are meeting in the middle, approaching from opposite directions—polyamory and monogamy. I need to keep that in mind, even in the throes of lovemaking, to both enjoy this meantime *and* to keep looking for my man.

Andrew occasionally checks to ensure the condom is still in place. He treats it as a pause in the action. I think it's a great opportunity for double duty, to graze my clit with his fingers while he checks. *Please, do check the condom more often!*

"It feels like I'm not wearing a condom."

I'm glad. He used to think it was a drag. Why is it better now? I could guess, but I'm just thankful.

Andrew kisses me while he thrusts. Then he smiles into my eyes, a friendly and tender gaze. His thumbs trace each of my eyebrows. *I melt when you do that; I feel so close to you.* A couple of times he gets excited and tenses up but doesn't climax. I ask what he wants to do so he will have an orgasm.

"I'm quite satisfied with these delicious feelings. In fact, being deep inside you and being so intimate almost works against going for an orgasm."

"But surely climaxing would be fabulous." *How could this be enough?*

"I'm often close, but it's not frustrating. It feels great. This must be a little bit like Tantric sex."

Andrew is fine with not climaxing. I want him to, but he demurs. I've learned to respect how far he wants to go in each lovemaking session.

He withdraws and I slip off the condom. I lube him up with one hand, and lube myself with my other hand. *It's time for some ambidextrous fun.* I give him a hand job with my left hand while I touch myself with my right. As I get more excited, I can feel him getting excited.

He slowly, randomly flicks my nipples in an insanely electrifying way. My jagged breath tells us that I'm close. His fingers on my nipples edge me to that primal unleashing. *Don't stop; don't ever stop touching my nipples!* We kiss, and with his nipple flicks, our kiss, the rhythm on my clit, feeling his penis growing harder again—it all builds to a whopping climax.

I recognize the peak arriving and open my eyes. He's been waiting to look into my eyes, with affection and interest. He likes to see in my eyes how the pleasure overtakes me. It's a stretch for me to watch *him* watch *me* be overtaken. His eyes flicker with recognition of the pleasure that is reflected deep in my eyes. His eyes smile an invitation to climax. My eyes narrow as I try to hold his gaze while the explosive bliss overtakes me. *I love showing you my climax!* I grab his finger and slide it back into my vagina so he can feel me jump inside. He enjoys my bucking spasms.

Andrew says, "Welcome home." He offers that eager smile again, greeting me on the other side of my orgasm. He treats it as a gift he cherishes. "I love to witness this. I like the wildness of it."

❅ ❅ ❅

We hold each other for a long time, naked on the bed whose sheets and blankets spill onto the floor. He calls our time in bed a sanctuary. I bury my face in the soft hair on his chest. *I could lie here for hours.* We often do. We visit and watch the pale light of a northern winter day grow to dusk.

I climb on top of him once again. I pin his arms with my legs, sit on his ribs, holding my torso low and close so he can't topple me—it's wrestling time. He seems surprised every time I do this, even though I give him the same sly look when I straddle his arms. *I grew up with brothers; I know what I'm doing.*

"Hmmm, nice view," he says as he lifts his head briefly to nuzzle my breast. Then, in grunting slow motion—with me pressing back on him—he pushes me off and onto my side. "You're *strong*," he gasps between breaths. We pant and laugh our way through a ridiculous yet competitive battle. I'm five foot nine to his six feet, so I can hold my own—for a while. And thankfully my hip doesn't hurt today—I feel carefree as I wrestle and giggle with him. I try to keep myself low on my stomach, so he can't turn me onto my back . . . until he does. Then, with the inescapable push of his hand on my shoulder toward the bed, he pins me and it's over. I'm zero for umpteen million.

We get up with racing hearts to fix "brunch" at 4:30 PM, winding down our time together. After we eat, Andrew gives me a brief kiss at the door and leaves. I feel all melty toward him, drunk on the bonding chemicals of lovemaking. But tomorrow I will continue on my path to meet my mate. Maybe I will email that intriguing man from the dating website, the one I noticed earlier this morning as I drank my morning tea.

MR. SMITH, MS. JONES WILL SEE YOU NOW

D.L. King

"Marge, I'm going to be staying in the city tonight. I've got a meeting with an out-of-town client and it's gonna go late. . . . No, honey, don't worry about me. Dinner? I've made reservations at Antonelli's. . . . Yes, that's right. You just enjoy your evening alone; I'm sure it'll be a welcome break from farting and football. . . . Yeah, yeah, I know, but I'm sure you'll enjoy the solitude anyway. I'll see you tomorrow evening and we'll have the whole weekend to lounge around together. Maybe go see a movie. I love you too, sweetheart."

I closed the cell and my eyes were drawn surreptitiously to the receptionist. She stared at me and smiled. Actually, it wasn't so much a smile as a smirk. The intercom on her desk beeped, and she picked up the handset.

"Yes?" She paused, listening to someone on the other end, and looked at me again. She continued to smirk as she ran a hand over her breast and gave it a squeeze, ending in a nipple tweak. She laughed. "All right," she said, and hung up the phone.

"Mr.," she paused, "Smith?" There was an underlying hint of honeyed contempt. "Ms. Jones will see you now." She licked her upper lip and searched for smudges on her clawlike, neon purple nails. Never looking up again, she said, "I believe you know the way." She pushed a button on her desk and the door lock buzzed.

I walked through the door and heard it close behind me. It felt like going through an air lock—almost like being weightless, crossing that barrier. There was no sound in the hallway at all. I was scared the first time I came here, having no idea what to expect. Now, I can feel the tension drain away with each step. I'd like to come here every week, but I make sure I get here at least once a month. I need it now, to stay sane.

There are four doors on each side of this hallway, and every time I come, I wonder what's behind them. I don't suppose it matters, because my door is at the end. There won't be any other doors for me, unless she says so.

I can't believe it took me fifty-five years. What a fucking waste. Well, I suppose it wasn't really fifty-five years. After all, I couldn't have discovered sexual satisfaction at the age of one or ten, but wouldn't it have been nice to find this before I became a paunchy, balding, out-of-shape man of fifty-five.

She'll get me into shape again. She's probably the only person who could.

At the door, I knock twice and wait for admittance.

Once inside, I close the door behind me and turn towards Ms. Jones. She says, "You'll find your things over there," and points a beautifully manicured finger at the floor in the corner of the room. "I'm very busy today and really should be doing other things, so don't waste my time."

I catch a glimpse of her before sinking to my hands and knees. It will be a good night. She's wearing her tight, black rubber corset: the one that comes up to just below her breasts. I want to run my hands down her sides to feel her delicate frame encased in that shiny, black covering. I spend a lot of time imagining what it would feel like, as I'm never allowed that particular sensation.

Her salt-and-pepper hair is pulled into a severe bun at the back of her head. Her hands and arms are bare right now. They show off the deep red of her short nails. She wears black stockings, held up by garters attached to her corset, and her black calfskin boots, perhaps my favorites. They don't have spike heels to torment me, but the leather's so soft, and they transmit the heat of her skin so readily to my hands and lips. They're completely flat, with smooth, unmarked leather soles, really more like slippers. They encase her legs and rise just past her knees. Sometimes, she lets me stroke her legs through the boots, when I worship her.

Did I see her dark-haired pussy peeking out from under the corset? I can't be sure. She doesn't allow me the luxury of lingering eyes. I take all this in immediately, before casting my eyes down. I keep them on the floor until she tells me otherwise.

In that split second, my cock has detected all it needs. It's painfully pressed against my zipper, with only a thin layer of silk between. It's not like I can get this hard in a split second; I'm not saying that. No, the blood starts flowing as soon as I hear the door buzzer: a true Pavlovian response. By the time I get to the inner sanctum and see her, it's all over. Nothing gets me hard like Ms. Jones. It's like I'm seventeen again, but with the control of age and experience.

I was always drawn to the strict teachers in school or the nurses and hygienists who had a cold, no-nonsense air about them, but I never realized why. My wife, Margie, is the sweetest, most loving and gentle woman I've ever known. She worships me and does everything she can to make my life easier.

I had a talk with her about that once, about my need to be dominated, and she understood. She even tried accommodating me. But she couldn't do it. It made her laugh, and she found it too embarrassing. It just isn't in her. Even if she could pull it off, it would be total make-believe and I'd know it. Make-believe doesn't cut it. I need the real thing.

I crawl to the corner and quickly begin removing my clothes.

"What's that?" she says, when I get my pants off. She walks over to me, carrying a thin bamboo cane in her hand. She runs it up and down the underside of my cock. "Some boys are simply incorrigible, aren't they?"

"Yes, Ma'am." She makes me feel like a boy. I think she must be my age, but she seems so much more mature, more in control.

She's not like one of those young girls who seem to be playing at being dominant; I can never think of them as having true power. Ms. Jones is regal, and her power radiates from every pore.

"Hurry up with those clothes and get ready. I haven't got all night."

"Yes, Ma'am." Quickly, I remove the rest of my clothes and put on the locking, heavy leather ankle and wrist cuffs she's provided. They feel so right against my skin. Is it hot in here? I'm naked; you'd think I'd be cold, but I notice a light sheen of perspiration has begun to form under my arms and on my upper lip. My balls stretch out and hang slightly lower.

My wife, my little Margie, did this for me. That's how much she loves me. She was the one who found Ms. Jones and made an appointment. It was my fifty-fifth birthday present. Can you believe it? And she didn't tell me what the appointment was for; she just told me I had an appointment with a Ms. Jones, at this address after work, as my birthday present. Someone should have taken pictures of my reaction—birthday cake, $29.95; appointment with a dominatrix, priceless!

"All right, stand up."

Ms. Jones uses her cane under my cock to help me up. Once I'm standing, she gives my rear end a quick, playful swat with it. I feel the burn as the line forms.

"It's time for your collar. If there are no objections . . . "

"No, Ma'am." Why, on earth, would I have any objections? But she always asks me. I feel it go round my neck, and her cool fingers fasten the buckle and click the padlock closed in back. I sense the first drop of precome drip from the end of my cock as she takes a dog leash from a hook at her waist and attaches it to a ring on the front of the collar. She drops it, and it bounces off my chest and hangs loose, down past my cock. The metal chain links are cold.

"Sit on your stool and put your kneepads on. I won't have you complaining halfway through the session that your arthritis is killing you." She turns and walks away.

She's left a pair of heavy leather kneepads for me. The insides are soft thick foam, which conforms to my knees. Without these, I'd never be able to hold up.

I always feel invincible in here with Ms. Jones, but there are some things about age that are completely unforgiving.

When I got home that first night, I thanked Margie profusely, and we made love with more passion than we'd been able to summon in years. I never mention it, but I know Margie knows I still come here. I think she's glad, but she doesn't talk about it, so neither do I.

"If you're quite through, come over here."

I quickly drop to my hands and knees and crawl across the room to Ms. Jones's chair. The leash trails between my legs as I crawl. When I reach her, she uses it to pull me into a sitting position.

"What do you think you're looking at?"

I lower my eyes. She's in a high wooden chair, on a dais. Staring straight ahead, I see I was right; she isn't wearing any panties. I am given a lovely view of her pussy, spread slightly open. Thick, curly black hair frames the almost purple interior. Her clit is prominently displayed at the top of her slit. Does she like me, or is it the thought of the games she will play that arouses her?

"I know how much you like that view. You'll get a better one later," she says as a petite, leather-clad foot fills my vision.

She presses the sole of her boot to my lips, and I kiss it, reverently.

"Lick it. Lick it completely clean, and don't forget the heel."

As I bathe it with my tongue, she pulls the leash to her, keeping my face held tightly against her foot. Once she's satisfied, she tells me to stop, and she rubs the damp leather over my eyes, my cheeks, my mouth and chin. She loosens her hold on the leash and pushes against my face with her boot as she rises, pushing me down to the floor.

"On your back," she says. Her voice has a musical, commanding tone I can't get enough of. It really doesn't matter what she says to me; it's that sound—it always sends shivers down my spine, directly to my balls.

When I'm lying on my back, she rubs the foot I've cleaned against my nipples, making them hard. She slides her foot lower and presses against my stomach.

"Are you working out, like I told you? This is not transforming quickly enough. I can see that I'll have to look over your diet again and modify it even more. I'll not have you dying of a heart attack because you have no control over your lifestyle!" She prods my flab. "Do you want to make that charming wife of yours a widow? All this has to go—or you will."

"I'm sorry, Ms. Jones. I'll do better."

"Who told you to talk? Did I ask you a question?"

"No, Ma'am."

"That's right," she says, giving my gut one last toe prod. She slides her foot lower and tweaks my cock with the toe. She moves her foot between my legs and prods my balls, then brings it up to mash my erection against my groin.

I must have moaned, because she stops and says, "What's that, boy?" I don't say anything, and she goes back to grinding my genitals. "Good boy," she says, and I melt.

Eventually, she forces her foot between my legs and slightly under my bottom. She pulls me to a sitting position with the leash, and I find myself sitting on her foot. It is small enough to almost completely fit inside my ass crack. The soft leather feels amazing, and I rock from side to side on it, forcing it further up my crack.

"Stop that."

"Yes, Ma'am."

"Wiggling like that is lewd. I won't stand for that type of behavior. Stand up. Bend over and put your hands on the seat of my chair."

Placing my hands on the chair, I notice she's taken the cover off the seat, exposing the opening. Anticipation of what's to come makes my cock jump just as I feel the cane stroke. I get five hard ones, but I can barely focus on the pain for thoughts of her perfect pussy over my face.

She pulls the leash, breaking me out of my thoughts, and traces the marks on my ass with her finger. "Very nice." She worries one particular welt with a fingernail. "Put your head in the headrest."

Down on the floor, I place my head in a sling, directly under the opening in the seat of her chair, and put my arms down by my sides. I feel her clip my wrists to eyebolts on the legs of the chair and then wrap the leash around both my cock and balls. She brings it up between my balls, separating them and then wraps it around the whole package once more, pulling it tight.

"Put those feet flat on the floor."

I bend my knees and do as I'm told. She spreads my legs apart.

"I want these legs spread as far as possible. What are you waiting for?"

I spread my feet until my hamstrings ache and she fastens my ankle cuffs to other eyebolts, keeping my legs in position. She sits down, confining my vision to only a few square inches of pussy. I breathe her musk in deeply through my nose.

"Now that's a nice view," she says.

You ain't kiddin', I think.

"And good access, too."

The cane slides between my ass cheeks and soon I feel the tip resting on my asshole. Right—her view, her access. For a minute I thought . . . but no, of course not.

"I better not see those knees begin to close. What are you waiting for? Lick!"

I wallow in the taste and scent of her. I really had very little experience providing good cunnilingus before Ms. Jones taught me how to perform it properly. It takes a while, but it's worth the extra effort. I tongue, suck, and lick for a good twenty minutes or more. It takes a while for the first orgasm, but the second follows fairly quickly.

It took exercise and practice, to be able to continue for this length of time. There were some sessions spent entirely on oral exercises and cunnilingus, but it was worth it. Margie has definitely benefited from all the hard work.

Ms. Jones smacks me between the legs with her cane. She gets the underside of my ass and my inner thighs. I know this is just a warm-up for things to come, and my imagination runs wild. There are so many things she could do—has done—with me. Her knowledge supersedes my ability to even imagine. I should probably be punished for these kinds of thoughts. An endless stream of precome dribbles from my cock. It'll be a long night—although, certainly, not long enough.

✳ *A slightly different version of "Mr. Smith, Ms. Jones Will See You Now" appeared under the pseudonym Malcolm Harris in* Pleasure Bound: True Bondage Stories, *edited by Alison Tyler.*

JAGUAR DREAMS

Evvy Lynn

I lie on my belly in the warm jungle grass. I hear his rumbling growl, almost a purr, and then I feel his weight on my back, so heavy, so soft, his paws kneading my shoulders, the tips of his claws pricking my skin.

His fur changes to skin and the claws transform into fingers, strong and gentle at once as they caress my shoulders. His hands move down my sides, then he turns me onto my back. He presses his mouth against mine, probes with his tongue, and an electric thrill runs straight through my body. I feel his hot breath on my face as he enters me, his penis burning with a fire that fills my entire body, and I come, again and again until I can no longer breathe. When my spasms have subsided to tingling, he holds me tightly, then enters me again. My body cries out for him, welcomes him, thrills to the spasms of the whole-body orgasm, deep, unending, as if I have become one with my vagina.

I wake, gasping, trembling. Never before have I had such a dream, so erotic, so real. I keep my eyes shut tight and try to memorize every detail. First, the jaguar. King of the jungle. Lithe, sleek, and smooth, powerful muscles bunching beneath his soft, spotted fur. Then . . . who? In the dream I was unable to see his face.

I don't remember anything earlier in the dream. Nothing before lying in the grass, waiting for . . . something. Feeling a thrill of fear as the great cat pads close to me, feeling the fear turn to desire.

My entire pubic area is still faintly pulsing as I rise and take my morning shower. I half expect to smell the big cat's musky scent on my body, to see scratch marks on my shoulders, but my skin is as it was when I went to bed, unmarked except by time.

It has been a long time since I had sex. But even in the days when I had my choice of men, never was lovemaking so intense, so deeply satisfying. Never in the past did I have multiple orgasms, each one stronger than the last.

As I dress and prepare to go to work, I continue to think about the dream. What could have brought it on? I haven't recently read or thought about jaguars, though I have, I admit, thought a lot about sex. About lying with a man, feeling his warm body against mine, feeling his hardness inside me.

When Rob and I split up after twenty years of so-so marriage, I reveled in my freedom, in the excitement of dating different men, sleeping with whomever I wanted when I wanted. But then I turned fifty and became invisible. All at once, men didn't see me anymore. I once asked my brother why men aren't interested in women their own age. He just stared at me, then laughed. "Well, why do you think, Janice?" he said. "Young women are prettier."

Of course. How obvious. I was "pretty" once—meaning young—with a good figure, smooth pale skin, and long blond hair. Men turned to stare at me on the street. Now, though my figure is still good—I take care of myself—nobody can see past the lines on my face and streaks of gray in my hair.

Stop feeling sorry for yourself, Janice, I tell myself. *You have a good job, a nice house, plenty of friends.*

I head through the lobby for my office at Vista View Retirement Center, past the circle of women sitting on the Santa Fe–patterned sofas in the lobby. I know all of them by name. Some, like Mrs. Anton, with her frizzy gray hair and thick black eyeliner, are always grouchy, scowling at everyone they see. *She must have had a bitter life,* I think. But a few others always seem happy. Tiny Mrs. Miller always smiles over her knitting, although she's crippled by arthritis and has no family. *Is this an accident of temperament?* I wonder. *Which will I be in twenty-five years?*

In my office off the activities room, I try to concentrate on work, planning the next week's events, but the jaguar comes to my mind. His image and the way I felt with him inside me. I glance up at the shelves across from my desk, cluttered with mementos from residents over the years. My heart thuds as I spot a small figurine among the ceramic kittens, personalized coffee mugs, and snow globes. I had forgotten, but now I rise and gaze closely at it:

a small, smooth jaguar carved from shiny, caramel-colored stone. The details are sketchy, but I can see its hard, bunched muscles and the fierce look on its face.

I remember now the jaguar was a gift from Ms. Lemmly, long since passed on. She had obtained it in the Yucatán on one of her many trips there. She was always one of my favorites—active, cheerful, unafraid to travel alone into her mid-eighties—when she suddenly died of a heart attack. Shortly before her death, she had presented the figurine to me. "This is for you, dear Janice," she said. "It is my favorite remembrance of my travels, and I know you are the right person to give it to."

Touched, I thanked her and accepted it, then set it on the shelf among the many other gifts and forgot about it. As I look down at it now, it almost seems to glow. I reach out, pick it up, finger it, feel it grow warm from my body heat, and then nearly drop it as a surge of sexual desire suddenly runs down my arm and through my body.

This is ridiculous! I tell myself. I drop the figurine into my purse, then return to my computer and the morning's mail.

"It may have been a dream, but it was the best sex I ever had in my life," I half-jokingly tell my friend Emily that afternoon over lunch.

Emily looks up from beneath her shiny black bangs. She toys with her mesclun salad for a moment. "You need to meet someone," she decides. "I'm going to a singles thing for over-fifties Friday night. Come with me. It'll be fun."

Fun? I think. *Fun?* Like Internet dating, speed dating, social dance mixers? Like root canal surgery? But against my own good judgment, I agree to go.

That night, lying in bed, I am too tense to sleep. I get up, reach into my purse, and pull out the jaguar figurine. I stroke it with my fingertips. So smooth, almost like skin. As it did when I picked it up earlier, it grows warm, warm as flesh. It seems to vibrate in my hand. I press it against the space between my breasts, then gently move it over my breasts and around my aureoles. I feel my nipples grow hard. I rub my fingers over each nipple, then move the figurine slowly down my chest, my belly, to my pubic mound. I press it there a moment, remembering the jaguar from last night, and I suddenly begin to come, nearly as intensely as I had the night before in the dream. *If only I could have that dream again,* I think, gasping. If I could count on it, say once a week, I wouldn't need a man at all.

The next day I head for the library on my lunch hour. My hand trembles as I pull out a thick volume. *Jaguar* the title says. On the cover there he is, staring at me with his yellow-brown eyes. A jaguar, I read, can be up to six feet long and weigh up to three hundred pounds. I flip through the pages, admiring the handsome, densely muscled cats. I turn to a section labeled "The Jaguar in Myth and Legend," and my breath catches at a drawing of an Indian man standing behind a jaguar. Like the cat, he is muscular but lithe, his skin the reddish brown of the cat's spots. I can't tell his age—he could be in his teens or his sixties—and his dark eyes seem to be looking directly at me. Again I feel that stirring in my groin, so similar to the way I felt when I was fourteen and first began to awaken sexually.

The book tells me that the jaguar first appeared in Olmec legends as a were-jaguar, a cat who became a man by night. According to Mayan mythology, a jaguar symbolized the right of kings, the underworld, rain and lightning, and the god of the night.

God of the night. Oh yes.

※ ※ ※

Friday evening I come home from work early. I shower, set my hair, take extra care with my face. Firming cream, eyeliner, but not too much. Too much makeup is aging. I put on the green silk dress with a plunging neckline that I've never had the nerve to wear before, along with my black bangle earrings. Not bad, I think. Sexy. Maybe I will meet someone tonight.

The party is in the back room of a big Chinese restaurant downtown. As Emily and I enter, I become aware of eyes checking us out. The men's eyes linger on Emily. They slide right past me. Already, I know coming here is a mistake, but I pay my ten dollars, receive a drink ticket, and follow Emily to the area where men and women stand and talk against a suffocating backdrop of red-flocked wallpaper.

I feel dizzy, ready to bolt. Emily takes my hand and pulls me to a small knot of people standing by a potted palm.

"Hi," she says to a silver-haired, handsome man about my age. "Hi," he says, looking her up and down appreciatively. "I'm Brad."

"I'm Emily. And this is my friend, Janice."

Brad doesn't even turn his eyes to me. "Nice to meet you," he says.

"I'll catch you later," I say. I make my way to the patio outside, past the small knots of men and women talking. Not one of the men looks at me.

I stand on the patio breathing deeply as the sun drops toward the pink stucco wall behind the restaurant. Atop a light pole, a mockingbird runs through his repertoire. I think again of all the old women I see in the retirement community. I wonder about the serene, contented-looking ones like Mrs. Miller, or Ms. Lemmly, when she was with us.

What do they have to be happy about? Ms. Lemmly never even married, and Mrs. Miller has been alone for many years. Their kids? Their grandkids? Most of the women I know are disappointed in their children and never see their grandchildren.

"A penny for your thoughts."

I turn. Standing behind me is a man who looks to be in his late sixties. He's not bad looking: tall, with thinning blond hair like Leslie Howard in *Gone With the Wind*. He smiles, revealing very large teeth. "You looked lonely out here," he says.

"Not lonely," I reply. "I was just thinking."

"So was I," he says. "I was thinking that you're a very attractive lady. My name's Ray."

"Hi, Ray. I'm Janice." I offer him my hand. He shakes it moistly. He looks twenty years older than me. To him, I'm a young chick.

"So, Janice, what do you do?" he asks.

"I'm the recreation director in a retirement community," I say.

"Sounds interesting," he says. "I was in one of those nursing homes once."

"It's not a nursing home. It's—"

He interrupts, still smiling. "I had to go there after my first bypass. They told me I couldn't care for myself alone. The nurses were nice enough, but I couldn't stand all the old sick people." Without stopping, he begins to tell me about his second bypass operation. "My cholesterol count's much better now," he goes on. "And the doctor tells me I have the triglycerides of a man in his forties."

This is far worse than not dating. This is far worse than not having a man. I tune out, watch the sunset, try to think about anything but Ray and his bypasses.

"So what about you? What health problems do *you* have?"

I want to laugh. I want to run screaming from the patio and demand that Emily take me home. But instead, I politely excuse myself and go back inside to refill my ginger ale. I sit on a cracked red Naugahyde bench and watch couples dance. Not once in the next fifty minutes does a man approach me. I no longer care.

It's over, I think. *It's really over.*

As soon as I have that thought, I feel a sudden and familiar tickling at my groin. *Stop it*, I tell my body. *No more.*

By the time Emily drops me off, I am exhausted. I remove my makeup and get ready for bed. I look at the jaguar figurine on my nightstand. Then I shut my eyes.

I am lying on the jungle floor. I hear the heavy padding of feet approaching me. I look up to see the jaguar standing above me. As I watch, he transforms into the man from the picture in the book. His dark, handsome eyes fix on me, and his words form in my mind. *You are ready for me now*, he says.

"Ready?"

I am the God of the Night, he goes on. *I appear to all women when it is time. Some women do not want me. They do not remember the dream.*

I nod, beginning to understand.

I am a jealous god, he continues. His rich baritone vibrates throughout my body. *I do not appear to younger women. They are not ready for my gifts.*

I don't answer. I don't need to ask what his gifts are.

As if he has read my mind, he goes on. *You know what I can offer*, he says. *But in return you must promise me your devotion. Your exclusive love.*

"If I promise—" I breathe.

Then I will come to you each night. I will fill you with myself. We will be one. But only as long as you are mine alone. One slip, one promise given to another man, and I will be gone forever.

It's a no-brainer. I promise. And he immediately begins to keep his end of the bargain. He pulls me close, nuzzles my neck, then gently pinches my nipples. I arch my back in response, and he kisses me deeply. Then he slides his hands down my body, caressing my skin with his own, rubbing his strong, smooth body against mine. As I groan with desire, he gently opens my legs and presses into me until I cry out in ecstasy.

❄ ❄ ❄

When I walk past the women in the lobby the next day, the regulars are all there, staring or chatting or hunched over needlework. I notice them in a way I never have before. Mrs. Miller glances up from her knitting. I no longer wonder why she's smiling.

TOAST FOR BREAKFAST

Cheyenne Blue

"Do you ever get lonely, Mum?"

I feel Livvy's eyes boring into my back as I stand at the sink washing the spinach I've just picked from the garden. I don't need to see her to know how she looks at this moment: tall and slender, leaning against the bench, picking at the bowl of raspberries.

I take my time in answering her, dignifying her question with a measured response. *Swish, swish* goes the spinach in the sink as I shake the dirt loose.

"Sometimes," I say. "Do I seem particularly sad to you?"

"Not really," she says. "You're very content with your own company. But sometimes you look sad, as if you've left the planet for a minute. Your hands stop what they're doing and you stare off into space."

I'd stopped swishing the spinach as I listened to her words. The silence is noticeable. Self-consciously, I resume the movement. *Swish, swish.*

"If you're asking whether I miss Dad—yes, I do," I say. "Some days more than others."

I finish the spinach and turn to face her. Her fingers are stained crimson, and the bowl of raspberries contains fewer than I remember.

"I still miss Dad so much," she says. "It must be so much worse for you. I wondered if you'd thought about moving closer to Brisbane."

Closer to her.

"Dad and I worked for this place for a long time." I reach for the feta cheese, chopping it into small cubes. "I'm not ready to give up our dream."

Just because Tom died. The words are like a fog in my brain. I didn't speak them aloud, but they twist thickly in my mouth. I still find them hard to say.

Livvy moves closer and snags a piece of feta. "This place is a lot of work for one person."

"Jay helps." Jay's name rolls off my tongue. It's velvet, smooth, with a hint of fire, just like the fine-sipping bourbon Jay likes. Jay is anything but smooth though. He crackles with life and enthusiasm.

"Jay?" Livvy's frown clears. "Oh, your neighbor."

My neighbor, yes, but so much more. Jay is the man who gave me back myself.

"Are you staying for dinner?" I ask. "If you are, you'll meet him."

Livvy smiles her diffident, gentle-daughter smile. "Actually, I was wondering if I could stay over tonight? I have a meeting in Southport in the morning."

"Of course, honey. Why don't you make up the bed while I finish dinner?"

When she leaves the room, my smile slips sideways from my face. I'd wondered how to tell her about Jay and me. Now the timing is decided. Tonight is our "date night," and there's no way I'm canceling it. Butterflies dance a polka in my stomach. Nerves? I'm nearly sixty, and I'm worried what my adult daughter will think when Jay and I bid her goodnight and retire to the same bedroom. Livvy has a sex life. I found the condoms in her bathroom cabinet when I was hunting for aspirin. She's an adult, nearly twenty-seven years old. I would be more concerned if I thought she was a virgin.

But that is her, and this is me.

She returns as I'm sliding the spinach and feta pie into the oven.

"Sorry, Mum," she says. "I didn't mean to imply you're not capable of living alone here. I just want you to know I'd love you to be closer." Her long hair hides her face. "And it would be okay if you had a companion."

Her words still my fingers as I hang up the oven gloves, and I have to fight hard to suppress a smile. A "companion." Is that all she thinks I need now? Friendship, maybe a hug, someone to share cozy home-cooked dinners—is that what I'm supposed to want?

I turn to face her. "A companion? Do you mean a lover?"

Her eyes widen. "No . . . Yes . . . Whatever." She spins away. "I meant a friend. But—" She breaks off in confusion.

Now would be the time for me to let her know exactly what Jay is to me. I could mention that I don't need to find a lover since I already have one. That he isn't the first lover I've taken since Tom died. That menopause isn't the end of sexual desire—you just have to slow down, be more relaxed about it. But Livvy and I have never shared confidences like this, and I can't find the words.

I let her—and myself—off the hook. "There's a bottle of red in the laundry cupboard."

Jay arrives while she's getting it. He kisses me in greeting, a sweep of beard and soft lips, and hugs me warmly. His breath is moist against my neck as he presses a second kiss there just before Livvy returns.

I introduce Jay and Livvy. Jay smiles warmly. "I've heard so much about you," he says.

Livvy is friendly, but I can tell by her lack of curiosity that she's convinced that Jay is just a neighbor. The conversation meanders, touching on several subjects, delving into others. We devour my pie and the bottle of red wine.

Jay moves into the kitchen to wash up, as he always does when I cook. Livvy dallies with me for a moment longer. "Jay's nice," she says.

She rises from the couch and goes into the kitchen to help Jay. I hear them laughing together.

I'm wondering how to go to bed. There's no point waiting for Livvy to go first; she's a night owl, always has been, while Jay and I are morning types. We generally go to bed by nine thirty, and we are up with the dawn.

Jay comes back out of the kitchen, Livvy behind him.

"Livvy, would you excuse us?" he says, meeting my eyes.

I move to Livvy, kissing her cheek. "Don't wait up, honey," I say.

I can feel her eyes watching us as we disappear into the bedroom and close the door. Part of me longs to rush back to her, to undo Jay's words. But the rest of me longs for my lover.

Jay's in bed before me. He lies with his arms behind his head, the sheet around his waist, chest naked to the slow movement of air from the ceiling fan. His eyes are on me as I shed clothes, letting them lie on the floor where they fall. I climb in next to him, rolling onto my side so that I can use him as a pillow. My fingers toy with the salt-and-pepper hairs on his chest.

"Should we have done that?" I ask.

"I like Livvy and she likes me," he says. The words rumble in his chest under my ear. "She wants her mother happy. Let it go now."

Jay's hand makes exploratory forays, warm, firm sweeps, shoulder to waist. I concentrate on the slide of Jay's hand over my skin. His other hand tilts up my chin, and he raises his head from the pillow to kiss me. It's a long, slow kiss that tastes of toothpaste and good humor.

I raise one leg and rest it on his thighs, high up, just below his groin. His cock presses against my leg. We're at the stage where we can either take this forward into lovemaking, or settle back down for sleep.

My body hums, just a little, a buzz of anticipation. I kiss his nipple, tongue its copper flatness, and press my thigh firmly against his cock. It twitches in response: not erect yet but definitely interested. He reaches down, cups my bottom, and draws me closer while his mouth does wonderful things to mine.

I love Jay's kisses. They're like a stream moving toward a waterfall. A gradual building of momentum, a slow increase, a building of turbulence, of passion, until we crash over the edge together.

We take our time kissing. The urgent rush to completion is absent for both of us. Instead, we're like kids again, and the journey—the kissing, the petting—is as pleasurable as the finale. Jay rolls onto his side so that we're facing each other, and we kiss for long minutes, our hands sliding in slow circles over each other's skin. When he touches my nipple, it peaks into his fingers.

I kiss his flat nipples, one then the other. He winds his hand into my hair.

He's fully erect now. His cock presses against my belly.

"Would you?" he murmurs and presses gently.

I know what he wants, and I'm happy to oblige. I kiss my way down his chest, over his pudgy belly. He's not fat, far from it, but he has a little roll on his tummy, which he hates. I blow into his navel to make a farting sound, as you do with a baby. He shakes with silent laughter, which ceases the second I drop down farther and press my mouth to the tip of his penis. He's circumcised, unlike Tom, and it still seems strange not to have that little extra bit to play with. His penis seems so exposed without it, almost vulnerable, especially when it's limp and hanging loose. Now though, he's hard and purple. I take him into my mouth, pressing my tongue into the slit, tasting his salt. I start the steady sucking motion that he loves so much. His hips undulate in time, never forcing himself into me, content with the gradual buildup.

I withdraw to ease my jaw, which is aching slightly, and he sighs.

"Enough?" I say, and feel his shake of laughter.

"It's never enough," he says.

I smile and move back up to kiss him. Tom hated me doing that; he didn't like the taste of himself on my lips, but Jay doesn't mind.

"What about you?" he asks, when we stop kissing.

I like this about him. He's not afraid to say what he wants, and he expects me to do the same. I consider whether I want his mouth between my legs, but I don't think I do, not tonight. I shake my head and roll over to reach for the tube of KY Jelly in the drawer. I hand it to him.

Jay likes to apply it, and I love it when he does. He squeezes a great gob of it onto his fingers. I raise my thigh for ease of access. The first couple of times he did this, the KY made a huge mess of the sheets when he couldn't get to my pussy quick enough. He's defter now. His fingers part my lips and stroke their way inside. Not too quickly, letting me relax, letting the lubricant ease the way, until I'm slippery, sheened, and as wet as I ever used to be naturally. His two fingers are slipping slowly, in and out. His thumb rubs my clit.

He's patient, and he finds a rhythm that I like. He kisses me, absorbing my little moans into his mouth. I reach down and grasp his cock, wanking him slowly back to full hardness.

When I'm ready, I push him over on his back, and I move up to straddle him. It took me a while to be comfortable making love with Jay this way. I was too self-conscious about my flabby tummy and breasts that are far from perky.

It was different with Tom; we grew old together. Jay and I are suddenly old and exposed to each other. But Jay tells me he loves me as I am, and it certainly doesn't seem to dampen his ardor.

I grasp him and with a shuffle here, fingers guiding there, we're in position, and I sink down. It feels good, having him inside me. I start to move up and down, and Jay pushes up, matching my rhythm.

I guide his fingers to my clit. I need more now than I used to. More direct stimulation, more intensity. Faster, harder, longer. We find our pace and I settle into it, let myself absorb our motion. I concentrate on the feel of Jay's fingers on my clit, how he feels inside me. My hip starts to ache a little.

"Wait," I tell him, and lean over to retrieve my mini vibe from the drawer and thumb it on.

He nods and resumes at a faster pace. The vibe is tacit permission for him to finish at his own pace. He grasps my hips and moves strongly up into me as I play the vibe over my clit, occasionally around the base of his cock.

That little pocket rocket works every time. I press it to the side of my clit and that's it. My flutters become spasms, and I'm coming, a satisfying, deep-felt orgasm. I clench around Jay's cock and he grunts in pleasure. When I open my eyes, his face is scrunched tight. I reach around and run the vibe around the base of his cock.

"I'm coming!" he grunts and his face blooms red, and his hips move in jerky completion.

My hip aches in earnest now, so I bend to kiss him, then dismount, lying down beside him, our bodies aligned. He holds me close and kisses my hair. He's already sliding into sleep; he's a cliché for male response in that way. I don't mind. I'm always slower to drift off to sleep, so I lie and listen to him breathe. He holds me close, even in his sleep. When his breathing rumbles into snores, I move my head from his shoulder and push. He rolls onto his side without waking. The snores stop.

I spoon up against his back and wrap an arm over his waist.

❄ ❄ ❄

I'm up first the next morning. I make coffee and take my mug out onto the verandah to listen to the morning. Jay emerges, pours a mug, and sits next to me. We sit silently together, listening to the birds and enjoying the early morning sunshine.

We're on our second mug when Livvy appears, hair wild and snarled, rubbing the sleep from her eyes. I hand her the remains of my mug, and she drains it one gulp.

"Morning," she mumbles and shuffles back for more coffee.

I rise and move into the kitchen, finding eggs, bread, tomatoes. Livvy comes up behind me, wrapping her arms around my waist.

"Just toast for me," she says.

It's what she says every time. The normalcy of her comment makes me smile. I don't know what I expected from her this morning: a thumbs-up, well wishes for my and Jay's happiness. But this non-reaction is the best. I don't need her approval; I don't even need her comment. Jay and I being together is a good thing, a normal thing. It's nothing that needs pointing out, analyzing, and stamping with approval.

"You need to eat more than toast," I tell her. It's what I always say.

She snorts in denial and takes her coffee back to her bedroom.

I pour another mug and return to the verandah. Jay's mouth quirks into his slow, lazy smile and he pulls me to his side, pressing a kiss to my hair. Together we stand, our lives touching like our bodies, moving forward together.

BY THE BOOK

Rae Padilla Francoeur

There was no sexual revolution back in the day. No women's rights. No touting of the simultaneous orgasm. Songs with lyrics like "to know him is to love him" twisted our synapses and shaped our priorities. As for me, I longed for "him" to rescue me from my unpleasant life. So did half the girls in my hometown.

Growing up in Donaldsonville, Georgia, did have certain advantages. One, you could get both a marriage license and a blood test in the same office in less than five minutes. After that, all you had to do was walk down the hall to the town clerk and finish what you started. I was sixteen and Mrs. Charles Petersham and free to start all over again. It was April 1965.

Too bad I married a man who was clueless about sex. Then, again, so was I. Totally clueless. And sex was not why I ran off with Charles. I just wanted out.

❀ ❀ ❀

Charles and I spent our first married night in a five-dollar motel room in the Georgia woods. The water reeked of sulfur. Freight trains flew by every couple of hours. Dogs howled way out in the swamps. Wow. Even the creaky floors were thrilling. Charles and I were on a great adventure.

Charles consummated our union. I had nothing at all to do with it. As I look back on the loss of my virginity, I remember feeling like an interested bystander. My body hadn't caught up to the reality. That took another several decades, actually.

It was late when I followed Charles into the squat pine cube of a motel room. He put his keys on the dresser and stepped into the bathroom to pee—leaving the door open. He glanced into the mirror over the toilet, caught me looking at him, and winked.

"This is what it looks like," he said, turning around to face me.

"Gosh, Charles."

"Are you scared?"

"No." The real answer was "yes," but why complicate things.

He was about to deflower a virgin, a chore for which most eighteen-year-olds had no skills. He'd better get it right because the next day he had to report to basic training. Charles's family ran a peanut farm. Peanut farming, he said, was a vocation he'd risk going to Vietnam to avoid.

"Okay, then. Go ahead and take off your clothes." His voice quavered. Poor guy.

I slipped the pretty blue dress I sewed for this occasion down over my hips and stepped out of it. Nylons, garter belt, bra, panties—off they went. "Okay?"

He nodded. He eyes caught hold of my breasts and held tight. "Good. That's good. Beautiful, beautiful titties."

I reached out a hand but Charles stepped back.

"No. Just lie down and spread your legs so I can see."

"See what?"

"You know. Where to put it."

I did what I was told.

"More."

He was standing in front of me, at the end of the bed, and he could see more of me than I'd ever seen of myself.

Charles's penis seemed to have a mind of its own. It stiffened and bounced, horizontal to the floor. Because of the harsh overhead light, his penis made bizarre dancing shadows on the pine board wall beside the bed.

"Amazing," I said.

"Please. Be quiet." He dropped to his knees. His breathing was heavy, like he'd been running. I could feel his exhalations pushing against my vagina, like waves washing over me. Again and again. I lay back, closed my eyes. It felt so good and yet there came this rousing need for more.

"I want to wash you," he said, returning to the bathroom to dampen a cloth. His penis, the hyperactive divining rod, let the way to the faucet.

He squatted back down and lathered my pubic hair with a warm, soapy cloth. He slid the cloth between the folds of my labia. He pushed it gently into my vagina.

"Oh Charles."

"Don't move, Rosie. Be still."

He rinsed me off with another damp cloth. And that was it for foreplay.

In two minutes it was all over.

❋ ❋ ❋

For forty-six married years, I conducted an uncomplaining life. Charles, my friend and companion, paid for my degrees in mathematics. I found peace in my work as an actuary. Peace among coworkers deep in problems of probability. Peace in marriage, knowing that Charles would crawl on top of me sometime during or after the eleven o'clock news and conduct some version of our wedding night coupling. It lasted, on average, two or three minutes. All in all, this was doable.

A book changed everything.

At sixty-two, while killing time in a Barnes & Noble in Des Moines, I discovered *The Joy of Sex*. Where had I been all my life? I hadn't even known you could use "joy" and "sex" in the same sentence. This cataclysmic reckoning occurred one hour before I was scheduled to present to an actuarial conference next door on damages to art in museums—higher probabilities than curators would like to think.

I paged through the book in sweaty, uncomprehending shock. I saw pictures of naked, hairy men and women in contorted positions, genitals at the ready, smiling and casually sticking fingers and penises and tongues into each others' impatient orifices as if tongues were intended for anuses and the erect points of breasts.

For a moment, everything froze in place. It was snowing outside. I had on Fruit of the Loom cotton panties and one of those Playtex bras you could wear into the next ice age. Pachebel's "Canon" was playing. I grabbed the book and made a mad dash for one of the fancy stalls in the ladies' room and locked myself in and the world out.

❋ ❋ ❋

Here was the "more" I'd always longed for, suspected, needed.

I placed the book on the changing table and began turning pages. I was entranced. One illustration showed a man and woman having sexual relations with big, sweaty smiles on their faces, eyelids half closed, bangs plastered to foreheads. The woman's neck and back were arched, her nipples reaching for the man's mouth, a mouth half open and honing in as if he could already taste the salt and sweat and, it appeared from her underarm hair, a touch of patchouli oil. I imagined myself arched like that and felt his soft lips sucking, pulling in my nipple. I was desperately hot.

I turned a few more pages in a daze and stopped hard at self-pleasuring. Something told me I'd found what I'd been looking for.

I was in a toilet stall in a mall in the heartland of America. Abortions were verboten here. Obama was a Muslim here. They sculpted cows out of butter here. What the hell were they doing with *The Joy of Sex*? In forty-five minutes, I had to talk to a group of insurance types about incidences of damage to old canvasses on gallery walls. About teenagers sticking gum on the shoe of *The Blue Boy*. About an octogenarian spitting on one of the Sabine women's rapists.

The motto of the actuary really ought to be: Shit happens.

Yes. Indeed.

I was ready to see what Charles saw every night when he commanded me to roll on my back and open my legs. I was ready to do what the book told me to do. Pleasure myself.

I spread paper towels on the floor of the stall. I took off my shoes, my panty hose and my pathetic white panties. I stuffed everything into my leather briefcase, the one my father had carried to and from his job at the bank. I hiked my suit skirt up to my waist where it ringed my naked midriff, crumpled and scratchy. I hung my suit jacket on one of the hooks. I took off my blouse. I pulled down the straps of my bra and my breasts became available to me. I had undressed myself in a bookstore toilet stall in a heat that was taking me where, I couldn't say. Nor did I care.

This stall had a small sink, so I washed and dried my hands. I had moisturizing lotion in my purse, so I rubbed some into my hands. I left the cap off and turned to the diagrams of a woman's vulva.

Now, who was I?

I started with the drawings of a woman's genitals. The woman lay on her back with her legs spread wide. Just like me. Her fingers rested on either side of her genitalia as if framing a work of art.

These frank, head-on depictions shocked me. Here, between the legs of the woman with the scarlet toenail and fingernail polish, I suddenly saw the essence of woman. An exotic, aromatic, deeply captivating force. It's as if she breathed through her vagina. She possessed an allure too primal, too feral for men.

Therein the miseries of women. And the power.

The labia—plump outer lips and thinner inner lips—are, by intent, half protective veiling, half glistening temptation. This woman's dark and moist core, at the joining of her thighs, gave me to understand the word "puss"—said with a wet and hungry pucker of lips that unfurl with the expulsion of *s*'s. Saying "puss" and licking puss are almost the same thing. I could have fastened my lips on hers.

Such purpose in this grand design! And there was the glorious clitoris—merely a temptress in this fleshy assemblage in which perpetuation of our species is all that matters.

At the vortex of this wet and erotic world of wonders lay the vaginal opening, threshold to the vagina itself, whose tufted recesses drew in the eye, the hand, the organ and exuded the life force. My god. This was a deep and complex scheme, the power of which I could not begin to grasp there in a stall in a Des Moines bookstore full of greeting cards and carrying what was clearly an excess of flowery journals begging lonely-hearts for their secrets.

Lonely hearts.

Oh.

What about me? My longing. My own vaginal opening had been touched only by Charles's penis. Touched once a year by my gloved gynecologist with a thumb and forefinger, and only enough to gingerly part the labia in order to insert the metal speculum that filled me the way Charles did—without sensory perception or regard for flesh. In truth my vulva was like the rest of me: wanting.

I squeezed moisturizer onto my nipples and looked at myself in the mirror above the changing table. My little breasts were bulbous protrusions resting on a bony ribcage. Soft against hard, somehow the very definition of sex. A confounding puzzle of opposing forces. I was cold. And hot. Hot for release from this sudden need to touch the parts of myself I hadn't known existed.

There, like the whites of two wide eyes, were two mounds of Jergens moisturizer atop my nipples. No one, no man, no baby, had ever suckled these tight little nipples, now plumping themselves with Jergens.

A virginal portrait. How could I, a woman who had been fucked 16,332 times (there were travel days, and once I was hospitalized for flu-related dehydration), dare presume to call herself virginal? But I was.

Someone rattled the handle to my stall. "Everything all right in there?"

I was addled by want. Delirious. "Yes," I shouted.

I caught sight of myself in the mirror again. All women are beautiful when they are naked. Clothes mask the truth of a woman's beauty. Fat or skinny, young or old. It's the gorgeous woman symmetry, the unbroken line, the perfect alignment of shoulder and breast and pelvis and joining of thighs. From this geometry all math is born.

The soft round mound of my pubis was a beautiful sight. I put my foot back up on the toilet seat and squeezed lotion all over my outer labia. I rubbed it into my mons pubis. My odd nakedness seemed to be saying, "Comfort me. Cup me in your hands."

Oh damn. Just do it.

The book said that direct clitoral stimulation requires utmost finesse. Be gentle. So for the first time in my life, I put the tip of one finger on my clitoris and rubbed it back and forth, visualizing a feather, like in the book, back and forth. I blocked out the sounds of running water just outside the door, flushing toilets, the scuffling of feet on this cement floor. I put lotion on my finger and quickened the pace. Back and forth. It was good the way nothing else was good. A deep, desperate, urgent good. A good that pressed for more. A good that said, "Keep going or die."

A steady rhythm worked best. I was able to witness the whole thing in the mirror above the changing table, in the mirror over the sink, in the reflection of the metal stall walls. I saw my lower abdomen draw in, tightening the muscles in my pelvic floor. I inserted my finger into my vagina and felt it contract. My clitoris tightened, too, growing harder and smaller and more illusive. I chased after it.

What?

I could not believe that Charles's penis invaded this soft, sweet oasis every night without hesitation, without curiosity, without sensitivity. My vagina reminded me of a pomegranate, folds of glistening ruby-like flesh hidden by pale skin that is easily parted for greater access.

I found that I had been holding one finger in my vagina. Like sucking my thumb. Like cradling a marble in the warm palm of my hand. I could live inside my vagina. I moved my hips. I rode my finger. It was delicious.

Another knock on the door.

"Ohhhh," I moaned. I saw myself, the look on my face, the purple vulva, the pelvis that could not hold still. On fire, just like Bruce Springsteen sang. I was on fire.

Another knock. "Hello?"

Oh, fuck you.

"Should I call anyone?"

"No. No!" I practically shouted.

Shit. In thirty minutes I need to be standing in front of sixty-five men and thirty-two women, where I would use a laser beam and PowerPoint to note interesting data on museum accidents. Teenagers on school trips were the worst.

I was a far cry from the lectern.

I put two fingers into my vagina and then stuck them in my mouth. I had never tasted anything like it. Like me. And yet here I was the whole time.

Another knock on the door. "Lady." It was a man's voice.

"What?" I rubbed the Jergens into my nipples, finally, and pinched them till it hurt. I felt a rush between my legs. Fluids dripped to the floor.

The man again. Pounding. "People need to get in there."

"Not yet."

More shouts. "Open up!"

"What?"

"Come out of there!"

"I can't. Not yet."

One hand had found my clitoris again. One hand was rubbing my nipples. I couldn't do it all, by myself, like I wanted. God. Everybody, just go away. Or come in to help me. I can use your mouths, your fingers, your big toes just like the book shows.

I heard wheels squeaking. A baby carriage perhaps. But I was not in a place where I could ever, in a million years, ever stop.

There I was, finally.

Rosie. My fingers in service to my clitoris—queen clitoris—like the queen bee, enfolded, served, expanding as she's fed and nurtured. I was done with gentle. My hips were on automatic pilot. They moved to a rhythm I hadn't known existed. My breasts, red from all the attention I had paid them, took part in this dance. They bounced up and down, up and down. This was how a woman's breasts must move, I thought, when she rode a man like in the book. Now I, once the anonymous Rosie, was on top. All I did was rub against my fingertips and my body knew just what to do. All of a sudden, it was as if my vagina opened up. My fingers slid in and my core clamped down in convulsive spasms. Warmth spread up and through me. I tasted honey. My legs turned to jelly. I peed all over my hand.

In orgasm a woman discovers her power. In orgasm she owns the world. No wonder they cut you to pieces. Sewed you up. Filled you with children.

Fuck all of you.

The man on the other side was pushing against the door. I pushed back. The cold door against my hard nipples made me hot all over again.

❊ ❊ ❊

I walked into my brownstone in Boston right around ten thirty that night. I parked my suitcase by the closet, took off my suit, and showered, entered the bedroom naked. Charles took one look and dropped the clicker.

"Look at me," I said. "There isn't an inch of this body that you aren't going to touch tonight. Or else, I'm out of here." I pointed to the suitcase. "I don't even need to pack."

I reached into my pocketbook sitting at the foot of the bed and pulled out *The Joy of Sex*.

"If you have any questions, here's some reference material."

While I was at it, I tossed a small bottle of KY warming liquid into his lap. "And from now on, use that."

I'd had one orgasm already that day, but I was just getting started.

"Look at me," I told Charles. "There's no such thing as old age to a horny woman. So don't stroke out on me."

BLIND, NOT DEAD

Johnny Dragona

Not getting much attention from my wife, Joann, after forty years of marriage, I joined an organization of people who are blind, in the hope of finding someone with whom I had something in common. I began to correspond by cassette tape with Caroline, who had lost her eyesight as a teenager.

While she usually teased me about my New Jersey accent, I loved her Alabama drawl. She was a woman in her late fifties with a naturally sensuous voice. I had no idea what she looked like, nor had she ever asked for a description of me. We never came on to each other, but there was a gleam in her voice I couldn't interpret. And something about her had me going.

But she was married, and I was married, which was probably what kept our conversations strictly on the social level at first. The only problem with that was trying to keep our taped correspondences on the subjects of trees in our areas, gardening, and what we do on our summer vacations.

Gradually, we began to talk about more personal things. She didn't seem happily married, and I knew my wife just tolerated me. So that was another thing we had in common. Was Caroline reaching out for an extramarital lover? Or did she just need someone to confide in? At best, we could have one of those long distance affairs. But some affection is better than no affection. After all, it would only be words. What harm could that do?

"He's always tinkering with his cars," Caroline said on one tape. "Meanwhile, I just sit around, listening to something boring on television. If I could drive, I'd get into my car and go for a long ride. But that'll never happen."

"Yeah," I agreed on the return tape. "I know what you mean about your husband always having something else to occupy him. My wife is always going to bingo or somewhere with friends. It's getting to the point where she's either asleep on the sofa or out."

Before long, we were talking on the telephone, and Caroline got even deeper into her marital dissatisfaction. "Oh, he likes sex," she said in response to the question I had asked. "The only thing is that he wants me to parade around in front of him in black panties and a black bra." Not being sighted, she didn't appreciate the excitement in that.

"That's interesting," I said. "I've often imagined you in jeans and a loose fitting sweatshirt." I visualized the swell of her breasts under a shirt and fantasized myself kneading them.

"And why is that?" she asked with that honeycomb voice that had often stimulated me.

"I like to use my imagination," I groaned, not having meant to inject a sensuous intonation into my voice. But she had me turned on.

"Oh?" Caroline said and paused, probably not having meant to inject a sensuous intonation into her voice either. "And what else have you imagined?"

"I'll never tell," I said and grunted a laugh. But going down on her had also been one of my recurring fantasies. What the hell, we may have been old, but we weren't dead yet.

"Tell me," Caroline demanded with a soft voice.

"I've often wondered what you look like," I admitted. Actually, that wasn't important. There was something inside of Caroline that attracted me. And I wasn't sure what it was. It was as if there was a passion within her that yearned to be freed, a passion I wanted to help her free.

"Well, if we ever meet, I'll let you feel me," Caroline said and giggled. "Only certain places, though," she added.

"Of course," I agreed, hoping she hadn't meant that latter part. But we would probably never meet.

In June of that year, she asked me to attend a national convention of people who are blind. Knowing we weren't happily married, I secretly hoped something was going to happen—did she? With that soft voice of hers pressing my buttons, I agreed to reserve a room in the hotel in which she would be staying and make the trip to Phoenix.

On the night before I was scheduled to leave for Phoenix, I had to do something to get Caroline out of my mind while I lay in bed. "Hon?" I said to Joann softly, and got no response.

As usual, my wife's back was turned to me. Also as usual, she was sleeping.

Rolling over to face her, or face her back, I slid an arm around Joann and cupped a breast.

Wouldn't you know it? She was wearing pajamas, and the top was buttoned almost to the collar.

I've often said that whoever invented pajamas for women should have been shot. Joann, at sixty, has a luscious, curvy shape. She should only wear mid-thigh-length nightgowns that were low-cut enough to expose as much cleavage as possible. But apparently, she hadn't read that book.

"Hon?" I said again. Hearing no response, I gently kneaded a breast.

"What're you doing?" a groggy voice asked.

"In the mood?" I asked, knowing there was a 99 percent chance she wasn't.

"Tomorrow," she groaned in a way that suggested she hoped tomorrow would never come, as far as sex was concerned.

"I won't be here tomorrow night," I said and circled one of her nipples with the tip of a finger in the hope of stimulating it.

"Where you going?" she asked with an undisguised lack of interest.

"I'll be in Phoenix," I said, hoping to keep her awake long enough to get laid.

"Oh . . . right . . . have a good time." Within three seconds, she was sleeping again.

Rolling onto my back, I considered masturbating, if only to relieve the pressure. Thoughts of what it would be like to sleep with Caroline entered my mind. What would it be like to hold her naked body against mine all night? We could even make love in the shower as the warm water sprayed over us. But that was just a fantasy. And a fantasy would have to do for the time being.

After dropping my suitcase onto the bed, I found the telephone and dialed Caroline's number. Even if we didn't have sex that weekend, which was what I had been hoping for, I expected to have a pleasant time with her. She was comfortable to talk with, and she seemed to like me.

"Hi!" she said as excitedly as a Southern belle can get and still maintain an air of dignity. "Give me fifteen minutes to take a shower and come on up. I'll leave the door unlocked for you."

"Need someone to scrub your back?" I asked to test the water, so to speak.

"I'm perfectly capable of washing my back," she said and chuckled devilishly. "But thank you for the kind offer anyway."

I gave Caroline ten minutes. And sure enough, her door was unlocked. Hearing her humming in the shower, I resisted the urge to ask if she wanted company and knocked on the bathroom door to let her know I was there.

The water stopped. In the middle of a cheerful greeting, she paused. "Oh! I left my towel on the dresser. Will you bring it to me?"

Was that an invitation, or what? It took me a few seconds to find the thing because her room was different than mine. "Okay," I said and tapped on the door with my fingernails. "Here it is. We guys from New Joizie will do anything for a lady."

Caroline chuckled while she slid the shower curtain open. "Are you sure you're totally blind?" she asked and stepped out of the tub.

"The last time I tried to look at a naked woman, I couldn't see her." While a hand touched the towel and took it from me, I decided to throw out a hint. "So she had to let me feel her." That hadn't been true, but it seemed like a good way to let her know what I was hoping.

Caroline must have been drying her face, because she spoke with a muffled voice. "Uh, huh?" Her incredulity was obvious.

We stood so close to each other that I smelled the sweet scent of her flesh. "Want me to dry your back?" I asked. Nothing ventured, nothing gained. Actually, I wanted to dry her everything, but realized it would be better not to rush. If it had been up to me,

I would have carried her to the bed and made love to her just the way she was.

Suddenly, a towel was draped over my face. "Why, that would be nice. I didn't know you Yankees were such accommodating gentlemen."

"I'm sure the pleasure will be mine." Not to seem too anxious, I started with her back, found a slightly tapered waist, a delightful ass, and two legs that had been made to be curled around my neck. Caroline's body was exquisite. I gently spun her around, took care of her shoulders and arms, brushed the towel over her breasts, and had to say something. "You've got nice boobs."

"And you've got a very soft touch," she said with a sensuous voice that obviously wasn't fake. It was also obvious that she wanted me to continue drying her.

"And you've got a very soft body," I whispered hoarsely and spent a few more seconds on her breasts than I had to.

"Thank you," Caroline said and quieted as the soft, fluffy towel glided over her stomach and the front of each leg. Her breathing rate seemed to increase while I dried the inner sides of her thighs. But she broke the silence with a soft moan while I gently patted the underside of her vulva dry.

Putting the towel aside and resisting the urge to knead her breasts without it in my hands, I had to do something. "Um, this goes with the service, too." I lifted her chin with two fingers and pressed my lips to hers. Her feminine, naked body felt wonderful in my arms.

Caroline curled her arms around the back of my neck and smothered my lips with hers. Apparently having felt my slowly developing erection, she pressed her pelvis against it and moaned to signal me that we were going to do more than just kiss that day.

Damn. Her lips were fantastic. And her tender body smelled so clean. I slid the tip of my tongue into her mouth and circled the tip of hers with it. Caroline needed to be loved, and I wanted to make love to her. My only fear was that my occasional impotence was going to cause a problem.

"I think, Sir," she began with her Southern drawl more obvious, "we'd better lock the door."

I kissed her again while holding a firm buttock with each hand and growled before responding. "I locked it when I came in."

"Well, aren't you the sly one?" Caroline chuckled while leading me by the hand to her bed.

I hardly got my shirt off when Caroline's fingers slid over my shoulders and her lips found mine again. We fell sideways onto the bed, wrapped in a hungry embrace while each tongue searched for its mate. Her soft, warm body begged to be loved. Each nipple responded instantly to nibbling lips while my hands explored a delicately tapered waist, rounded hips, and contracting buttocks. That surprisingly torrid woman smelled so clean, so delicious, ready to be eaten. And the way she had been breathing heavily said she was ready for that and more.

"I was hoping we would get the chance to do something like this," Caroline whispered hoarsely while tracing the outline of my lips with the tip of a finger that was as gentle as an angel's breath.

"I'll admit the thought had entered my mind once or twice," I groaned and suppressed a snicker.

"You fibber," she said with a chuckle in her voice and combed her fingers through the hair on my chest, moving her hand downward.

We groaned in unison when the telephone rang.

"I'll be right back." Caroline walked to the dresser, picked it up, and listened for a few seconds. "Yes. I'll be there in about an hour. I'm kind of wrapped up in something now and can't leave just yet."

By the time she returned to the bed, I was completely undressed. She reached towards me and her hand rested on my bare stomach. Startled by my nudity, she stiffened.

"We'll take our time," I told her. "We won't do anything you're not comfortable with. May I use my tongue on you for a while?"

"Yes," she breathed.

I sighed and curled a hand around the base of a breast while she grunted approvingly. The tip of my tongue circled an areola while its nipple expanded and parted my lustfully sucking lips.

Caroline moaned when I switched to the other breast and continued to knead the first one. "My, how you Yankees do carry on," she said with a Southern drawl that was more pronounced than it had been earlier.

For the next few minutes, we touched each other sensuously. My fingertips traced the outlines of her lips, her cheekbones, her jaw. While she explored the muscles in my chest and arms, I slid a palm over a shoulder, a hip, the side of a thigh. I inhaled the intoxicating scent of her flesh and dipped the tip of my tongue into her navel.

"This is wonderful," Caroline whispered and caressed the backs of my shoulders. "I thought these days were gone forever."

Not saying anything and keeping in mind that she had to attend a meeting, I licked a line across the bottom of Caroline's flat, trembling stomach, momentarily savored the scent of womanly arousal, and tasted a honey that was sweeter than her voice. She parted her legs wider and raised her knees. I plunged my tongue inward. I tenderly nibbled her flared vaginal lips, lapped their soft, inner flesh, and lovingly circled her quivering clitoris.

Caroline hissed loudly through clenched teeth, holding bunches of my hair. She ground her sopping pussy against my sucking lips. When she came it was like a dam bursting, a longtime need being satisfied, the fulfillment of a craving.

I held Caroline in my arms and combed my fingers through her shoulder-length hair. She slid a hand down my stomach and found what she was looking for. "My word," she groaned. "They do make them big in New Jersey."

"That's not from New Jersey," I quipped, surprised I had a full erection for a change. But a new woman will do things like that to a man. "It was imported from Italy."

Caroline chuckled while she slid downward. "Good. I just love pepperoni."

I was about to say, "Not sliced, I hope," when her warm, moist lips slid over my glans and glided down about three inches. This wasn't the time for jokes.

While she gently caressed my scrotum with one hand and slowly masturbated me with her other hand, Caroline's mouth and tongue did wonderful things to my throbbing cock. And it was obvious that she wasn't doing it just to accommodate me.

I wanted to spend the next twenty minutes doing that, but twenty seconds was all I could handle. "I'm gonna come," I sighed and put a hand on her shoulder as a tentative warning.

Caroline shrugged it off and took my shaft in to her limit. She sucked harder and rolled her head from side to side while a purring sound came from deep in her throat.

I grunted and felt my entire body stiffen. "Ohhhhh, that feels so good," I groaned, caressing the backs of her shoulders.

While Caroline swallowed my semen, she slid her lips up and down half of my length. It was obvious that she hadn't been a stranger to oral sex.

After about a half dozen passionate kisses, we quickly dressed and went to several separate meetings. We finally met again for dinner, during which Caroline made a few excuses for not spending the evening with other friends. I casually caressed her ankle with mine under the table. "I'm fighting off a maddening urge to kiss you right here."

"Well, we can always go back to my bathroom where it began," Caroline said and giggled.

"How 'bout your bedroom?" I murmured, hoping no one was close enough to hear us.

"My goodness. Are all you Yankees a bunch of sex fiends?" She paused to giggle again. "Maybe we should leave now."

When the weekend was over, Caroline went home to her husband, and I went home to my wife, feeling lively in a way I hadn't in years. Something in my manner must have clicked with Joann, because not only did she respond to my touch, but she let me throw those pajamas in the trash and agreed to buy a few sexy nightgowns. I probably won't see Caroline again, but the cassette tapes we continue to exchange do wonders for my libido!

AFTER DINNER EUPHORIA

Peter Baltensperger

Richard stepped up behind Celia as she was busying herself with the dishes in the kitchen sink, wrapped his arms around her, and took her soft breasts into his hands. Celia sighed deep down in her being and leaned lustily against him, the last plate still in her hands. Richard caressed her breasts through her thin blouse, rubbing and squeezing them until they blossomed in his hands. Then he took her eager nipples between his fingers and squeezed them until they were big and firm. Celia put the plate back in the water and turned around in his arms to face him. She flung her arms around his neck, pressed herself against him, and kissed him tenderly.

Richard held her close while they lingered in the familiarity of their kiss. He ran his fingers through the abundance of Celia's beautiful gray hair. Keeping one arm around her waist, he let the other glide down from her hair over her shoulder, and then slid his hand between their bodies and to her breast. He squeezed and rubbed her soft globes gently until he could feel her hard nipple in his palm and she moaned against his chest.

"Feeling frisky tonight, are we?" she asked with a smile.

"I took a pill earlier," he confessed. "It's allowed, isn't it?"

"It always is, Richard," she replied. "It always is. You know that well enough."

"I do," he concurred. "I certainly do."

It surprised him every time how much they still enjoyed their intimacy after all the years they had shared and how much he still loved her breasts, despite, or perhaps because of, the passage of time. They had been married for fifty-two years, and they still thrived on the tantalizing sensations, the sheer pleasure of kissing and fondling each other whenever they were in the mood.

He remembered as clearly as if it had been just a short time ago when he had held her breast in his hand for the first time.

They had been out on a date, dancing with some friends at a local hall, and he pulled into a deserted parking lot on the way to her parents' house, as he always did at the end of their dates. He put his arm around her shoulder and pulled her close, while she slid over on her part of the front seat and snuggled up to him. They kissed hungrily, snaking their tongues in and out of each other's mouths, tasting each other, and pressing their bodies together with the passion of young lovers. He took her breast into his hand, the way she had let him do almost right from the start.

Only that time, when he let go of her and started to unbutton and then slip off her blouse, she didn't protest—nor when he reached behind her and undid the clasp of her bra. It was the first time in their relationship that he saw her beautiful young breasts with their soft contours, the delicate white skin, the crowning nipples yearning for his touch. He noticed that she wasn't looking at him but kept her face pressed against his chest. Yet when he touched her naked breast for the first time and ran his trembling hand over it, she uttered a deep, guttural groan he had never heard from her before.

She still did that whenever he took off her garments and started to stroke her naked body. It always made him feel special. He wanted her all the more for still reacting with such desire and enthusiasm to his advances. It never took him long to get aroused by her sensuous presence and his desire for her, pill or no pill. The pills just facilitated the process and made it more enjoyable for both of them.

The intensity of their sexual encounters was certainly still there, especially after a prolonged period of inactivity. It was just the frequency that wasn't what it used to be. They didn't mind that at all. They knew enough people, several of them in their own circle of family and friends, who were sleeping in separate bedrooms and, in some cases, had for a long time. They couldn't even imagine not being in the same bed together, let alone in different rooms, despite being together all day.

Richard pressed his erect penis against her belly, pushing her against the sink. He let go of her breast and started to unbutton her blouse.

"Richard!" Celia exclaimed. "I'm doing the dishes!"

"They can wait," Richard brushed her objection aside. "I'll do them later on."

"Yeah, right!" Celia chuckled. "You won't feel like doing anything later on. You'll be sound asleep, and I'll have to finish them."

"All right, then," Richard continued. "If I fall asleep, you can wake me up and I promise you that I'll finish the kitchen."

"That would be nice," Celia purred. She reached for the buttons herself and helped him undo them in eager anticipation.

Together they finished unbuttoning her blouse and pulled it off. She wasn't wearing bras anymore and hadn't in quite some time. They made her feel uncomfortable, she said. He didn't have any problems with that. It just made everything easier. As soon as the blouse was off, he took both her breasts into his hands and let the feeling of her soft contours rush through his body. It was a familiar feeling after their years together, and yet it was always excitingly new as well.

Her bare breasts invariably felt good in his hands, soft globes crowned by roseate beacons, warm skin against his, molded into his hands. It always felt as if it were the first time all over again, especially when she leaned against him, pushing herself away from the sink and into his hands.

He took her hand. "Come," he said, leading her out of the kitchen and down the hall to their bedroom, her breasts beckoning. He took off his clothes while she pulled off her slacks and stepped out of her panties. He couldn't help staring at her gorgeous breasts, letting his eyes travel over her well-shaped body, her titillating buttocks, her slender legs—as if he had never seen her naked before. It was always an intriguing moment for him when they first shed their clothes. In his eyes, she was still the same desirable woman he had married so many years ago, her beautiful skin soft and white, her chiseled features as attractive as ever. Her luscious curves were as inviting and alluring, only more mature, fuller, and more substantial, always an exciting fit for his arms and hands.

"You're beautiful," he beamed and walked towards her to take her into his arms.

"Oh, Richard!" Celia sighed. "You always say that!"

"And I mean it, too." He put his arms around her and pulled her naked body against his.

They kissed, the warmth of her bare skin on his, her breasts against his chest, her pussy rubbing his hard erection, their eager tongues intertwined. She moaned deeply, letting her hands roam all over his body, folding them around his neck, and drawing him deeper into their passionate kiss. He groaned with their shared passion, pulling her closer to himself to deepen the arousal of their kiss. As if on cue, they pulled apart to ready themselves for the next phase of their evening encounter.

"Isn't it time for our shower?" Celia purred.

"I'd like that," Richard agreed. They always loved their shower times together, when they could just be in the cozy retreat of their bath enclosure and enjoy fondling each other's bodies, without any pressure on either of them to do more than delight in their intimate togetherness.

Celia stepped into the tub first and adjusted the water to the proper temperature. He followed her in and pulled the curtain shut behind him. Taking turns standing under the comforting waterfall, they wet their bodies for the next step. Celia was always the one to start the ritual by reaching for their bottle of body wash on the shelf, filling her cupped hand with the aromatic liquid, and rubbing it all over Richard's chest. He stood there quietly, holding on to the curtain rod for balance with one hand and bracing the other against the enclosure.

It tickled when Celia first moved her foam-covered hands from his chest to his underarms, but the feeling quickly turned into the sensuous pleasure of a sensitive body part being stroked and soaped with loving care and attention. Before long, she moved back to his chest, made her way down over his belly, and took his throbbing penis into her hands. He groaned with delight, enjoying the familiarity of her lathering his erection and his balls and covering him completely with the rich suds.

"You're really hard tonight," she commented, stroking his erection with her eager hands.

"The pill seems to be working particularly well this time."

"I'm glad," Celia moaned, lovingly manipulating his penis, watching it grow and harden from her ministrations.

She turned him around in the tub, replenished her hand with the body wash, and went to work on his back, massaging the liquid into his skin, loosening his muscles. He moaned quietly as he felt his back relax under her skilled hands, felt her move slowly down to his lower back and come to his buttocks. She lathered him lovingly, thoroughly, stroking and rubbing his cheeks, running her fingers up and down his crack with great delight and expertise.

He spread his legs and she soaped the insides of his thighs. She rolled his balls between her slippery hands. He loved it when she did that and groaned throatily with appreciation. She gave his balls a quick, playful squeeze, her signal to him that she was done.

"My turn," she gasped, her voice full of excitement, impatience.

He turned around to face her, picked up the bottle of body wash, and poured some of it into his own hands while she anchored herself between the curtain rod and the tub enclosure. Her beautiful body was waiting for him, and he didn't lose any time in reaching for her breasts. He rubbed the creamy liquid all over them, relishing every moment of lathering her breasts and feeling her nipples harden under his hands. He could have stayed like that for a long time, just handling her breasts and spreading the suds all over them.

After pouring some more lotion into his hand, he soaped her belly lovingly before moving down to her pussy. She spread her legs invitingly and he slipped his hand into the proffered space, his other favorite place. Her pubic hair had become quite thin and gray over the years, but he still enjoyed teasing it with his fingers and rubbing the suds into the curls. He continued rubbing the soap all over her belly and her mound until she, too, was covered in bubbly foam. Then he carefully rinsed his hands and her pussy until no suds remained anywhere. He ran his eager fingers all over her dripping labia, into her secret nooks and crannies, into her wet vagina. She groaned with delight as he probed her delicious cave, pulled his finger in and out, stoked her arousal with his intimate exploration.

He turned her around, replenished the body wash, and applied it liberally to her back, rubbing her shoulders and her upper back until she sighed deeply with the pleasure of his massage. He knew exactly what she needed and lathered her expertly until she felt completely relaxed under his hands. Next he bent down again and spread the suds over her lower back to get to her buttocks.

She squealed when he ran his fingers up and down her crack then laughed while he lathered her cheeks, lingering on each one and finally moving down to her thighs. Reaching between them, he massaged them slowly and lovingly. Then he rinsed his hands under the spraying water, cleaned her pussy of all suds, and rubbed it again with great pleasure. She shuddered delightedly. When he felt he had stimulated her sufficiently, he pulled himself to his feet and patted her on her soapy buttocks to signal the end of his routine.

After they rinsed themselves from all the suds, they climbed out of the enclosure, kissed each other tenderly, and toweled each other dry. They returned to the bedroom, climbed on their bed, and stretched out beside each other, feeling relaxed as well as deeply aroused from their shower activities.

Celia reached for the tube of lubricant, squeezed a generous amount into her hand, and rubbed it all over her pussy and into her vagina. Then she took some more, lifted herself up on one elbow, and bent over her husband. With a skilled hand, she lubricated his strutting penis, pulled his foreskin back, and coated his glans with the liquid.

Richard turned over on his side, and she let herself sink down on her back, spreading her legs expectantly. He reached over and put his hand on her slippery pussy. Gently rubbing her excited labia with his skillful fingers he probed her deliciously dripping insides and rubbed her clit. Celia took his lubricated penis into her hand and started stroking his erection until it twitched and pulsated lustily in her hand. They moaned in unison, sharing the joy of their mutual arousal until they were ready for the next phase.

Richard climbed on top of her carefully, keeping the weight of his body lifted up with his arms, and touched the tip of his penis to her opening. Celia shuddered with delight and gasped at the first contact.

"Oh, yes, Richard," she cried out. "I want you so much right now!"

She wiggled into position for Richard to plunge into her slick vagina. As he thrust his penis deeper into her and started pumping, she closed her legs to provide him with more friction and pushed her pelvis against his.

They were breathing heavily, he thrusting and she pushing rhythmically, faster and faster as they worked themselves and each other higher and higher towards the zenith of their pleasure. Richard could feel her internal muscles tightening around him, pulling him deeper inside. It only took him a few more thrusts to get over the top and find his release in a glorious, liberating, and fulfilling orgasm.

He stayed on top of her for a few moments to catch his breath, then rolled off and let himself fall on his back. He didn't rest for long, but turned on his side again and reached for Celia's pussy. He could feel her shiver with excitement as he sought out her budding clit again and began to rub her vigorously and with determination, eliciting visceral groans from her in return.

It always took her quite a while to reach her orgasmic height, but he didn't mind at all. He loved her pussy, loved the slick feeling of the lubricant. He stroked her skillfully until her body began to tense and then shudder with the onset of her orgasm. She grabbed his hand with both of her own and pressed it against her pussy, gyrating and shaking under him. She thrust her pussy into his hand until she began to tremble under him. Her body shivered as she climbed the dizzying apex of her arousal. Her orgasm took hold of her writhing body, and she screamed her way through her glorious release.

She clung to Richard while he kept rubbing her clit to get her up to the top once more. It didn't always work, but he felt that it might this time, and she certainly didn't seem to be ready to stop. She kept pressing his hand into her pussy until she began to tense again and whimpered through a second release, not quite as strong as the first, but clearly quite satisfying, because she smiled happily as her body gradually relaxed.

They collapsed on the bed together after their sensuous exertion, smiling their fulfillment at each other in the delicious afterglow of their orgasms.

After a while, Richard turned on his side and wrapped his arm around his glowing wife and waited for her to fall asleep. Then, true to his word, he climbed out of bed, put on his pajamas, and went out into the kitchen to finish the dishes and clean up the counter. Celia had already done most of it, so it didn't take him long to complete his task. Then he went back to bed and took her soft body into his arms.

"You're so beautiful and sexy," he whispered in her ear. "I'm so incredibly happy that we have such a great love life together."

With that, he fell asleep with a contented smile on his face, Celia breathing deeply in his arms, her body satiated and fulfilled.

THE WACKY IRAQI,
THE SHAMAN LOVER, AND ME

Erica Manfred

At age fifty-nine, my husband of eighteen years dumped me. I emerged after a nine-month mourning period feeling horny as hell. I hadn't had any sexual desire throughout our marriage because I had spent all my sexual energy avoiding sex with my husband. Except for a brief crush on our carpenter, which I wouldn't have done anything about, I had never looked at a man sexually since my wild, single-girl days.

Now I was long past menopause and supposedly long past my sexual prime. My body didn't know this, however. It started twitching every time an attractive man came into the room. All of a sudden I was evaluating every man I saw as a sexual partner. I was on fire all the time, so I joined Match.com.

I agonized over the weight categories on Match. Was I "large," "a few extra pounds," "average," "athletic and toned?" Forget the last category—I settled for "a few extra pounds" since forty was a "few" in my opinion. Some men told me women from five to 105 pounds overweight put themselves in this category, so they tended to avoid anyone who checked that box. My picture was misleading. Since my face was so thin, no one envisioned the size of my rear end.

Harry, whose user name was the *Wacky Iraqi*, first caught my eye. He was the kind of oddball guy who has always attracted me. His photo showed a face like an elderly Norman Mailer on a bad day, but his profile was offbeat and funny enough to overcome the ugly photo. And this is how he described himself:

Most body parts work—some are brand-new and work better than others—and I am in reasonable health. Up to two pills a day! My ideal? An attractive woman with a big smile, twinkling eyes, high center of gravity. All else is optional. Intelligence is a great help to good conversation and discussion when this is necessary. An affinity for Indian or Burmese or Arabic food will make dinner selection easier. A sense of humor is very important—good or bad is irrelevant. Her "get up and go" must not have "got up and gone."

Unfortunately, Harry lived more than one hundred miles from me. Naively I thought distance didn't matter. As it turned out, Harry was also casting a wide net.

Distance was no impediment to emails and phone calls. Harry was an Iraqi Jew from Calcutta, whose parents had fled Burma during the Second World War and walked overland to India. He grew up as part of a small Jewish community in Calcutta. The experience had scarred him in many ways. Seeing people die on his doorstep daily had hardened Harry's heart and given him little faith in human nature. The death of his mother when he was five made him wary of women and commitment, and in his own estimation, unable to fall in love.

I spoke with Harry a couple of times on the phone and liked him better each time. He was very funny, offbeat, and cynical. We dickered about where to meet. I didn't want him to travel all the way to pick me up. I'd have to ask him to turn around and go home if I didn't like him. That kind of distance would put pressure on me to spend more time with him than I might want to. But Harry insisted he wanted to travel to my town, and eventually I gave in.

The minute I saw him, he passed my "Hmm, I could do him" test. He looked younger than his pic, and, though not conventionally handsome, he had a mischievous twinkle in his eyes and a sly smile that charmed me. His self-confidence and his male energy turned me on. He'd only posted a picture of his face on Match.com, but I could see he had an attractive body, fit and strong, if a bit stocky.

He arrived at my house bearing an enormous cake with HAPPY BIRTHDAY ERICA written on it and three cannoli. I asked him why he'd had "Happy Birthday" written on the cake since it wasn't my birthday. He said he couldn't think of anything else. I was charmed by his silliness.

We spent the evening together, talked and joked, went out to a lecture, and found we had plenty in common. Afterward, back at my house, Harry sat on the couch, patted the spot next to him, and asked me to sit there. He cuddled me sweetly, and I sank into his chest. He kissed me passionately, his tongue moving inside my mouth. It had been a long time since I'd been kissed like that. I felt myself swooning in the way that I used to before I got married. My mind left my body, and my body took over, gluing itself to him. I ran my hand up and down his strong back, feeling muscles and a bit of a spare tire around the middle that I found sexy.

I'd forgotten how much I loved men's bodies. Harry's body was luscious. I wanted to touch it everywhere and never stop. But I did stop. I didn't know if the "no sex on the first date" rule was still de rigueur in the dating scene, and I wasn't taking any chances. I pulled away reluctantly, said it was getting late, and told him he had a long drive home. Harry didn't look the least bit put out. He gave me a big hug and said goodbye.

During the next few weeks, we emailed back and forth for a while, but Harry didn't mention visiting again. I kept making my sexual intentions clear in my emails, despite his unexpected protestations that he wanted to be my "friend." This felt like coitus interruptus. How was I going to get him to come back, to take me to bed? I kept making my sexual intentions clear in my emails. *I kinda felt that couch cuddle and passionate goodnight kiss meant you had a bit more than friendship in mind. I sure do. I just try to*

behave on a first date. Next time I'd certainly invite you to stay over.
It's not too often I meet someone sexy who makes me laugh and
listens to my mishegas.

He emailed back:

Sex with a woman at my age? I am considering the priesthood
and celibacy. I have a lot of physical problems. My knees are weak.
My eyes are dim. I have colic. I am not sure what I want. And I
don't know if I can satisfy you.

He was at least thinking about going to bed with me. That
was a start.

Jeez, Harry, you're only fifty-eight, not ninety! Don't worry
about satisfying me—I don't think about sex that way. To me it's the
closeness and touchy feely stuff that I long for, and getting satisfied
is pretty easy, really. There are many body parts for that.

Harry was a bit freaked out by my eagerness, but he agreed
to another visit.

I am not sure I am so good for you. I hate to disappoint. But I'll
enjoy your company if you are so inclined.

Harry showed up very late on our second date night. By the time
he arrived, I was exhausted from housecleaning, food shopping,
shopping for sexy nighties, leg shaving, hair blowing, making up
my face, and all the other tasks I'd forgotten about when it came
to having a man visit.

I had also realized I no idea how to go about having sex with a new man. Was I supposed to take my clothes off first? Get into bed with my bra and panties on and let him take them off? Leave the lights on or turn them off? I decided to take off my underwear and leave my sexy nightie on. It has always turned me on to be naked underneath a flowing gown. The swishing of the fabric against my flesh, having a man snake his hand up under the material, work his way slowly up my legs, between my thighs and inside me, keeps me wet even if we're talking about other things. I was wet by the time Harry arrived, strictly from the fantasies I'd been harboring about him since our cuddling on my couch.

He came in, and we immediately fell into bed, awkwardly. He matter-of-factly took my hand and rubbed it on his body, bringing it down to his cock, which was impressively hard. I was relieved that it wasn't huge. I knew that my days of adoring big cocks were past. No way was I dealing with anything bigger than five inches without a lot of practice.

Harry was very hairy, unlike my ex, who was boyish and smooth. His body was so different—solid, substantial, virile. I wanted him to feel me all over, too, but he showed no inclination to do any stroking. I didn't mind much—just being in bed with a new man was thrilling. He grabbed me and kissed me hard, rubbing that hairy body against mine. Just hugging and clutching him, feeling his cock hard against my belly, was enough.

Actually just about anything would have been enough. That's the beauty of sex with a stranger, especially after a long period of deprivation. All Harry's disclaimers about needing Viagra and not being sexually potent were a total crock. He had no trouble getting hard and fucked like a bandit. Even though I felt awkward and self-conscious and was far from having an orgasm, feeling him inside me was unutterably arousing.

There's something about a male organ plunging into a woman that nothing else sexual can match. It must be a primal, genetic reproductive urge, to take the male inside. Actually, it hurt when he plunged it inside me—it had been so long—but I didn't care. Just having that cock moving up and down inside me, feeling that hairy chest against my soft breasts, sucking on his tongue as it thrust inside my mouth, resting my head on his shoulder afterward, and getting to spend the whole night in bed with him with my arm across his body was all I needed. The whole experience was thrilling and even the pain was exciting. I could make believe I was a virgin again.

Harry was a pretty unimaginative lover by the standards I'd had before marriage—oral sex was anathema to him, for instance, and the missionary position was his only one. But as my first experience post-marriage, he was just what the doctor (and my therapist) ordered. He was the alpha male who grabbed me, threw me down on the bed, and had his way with me. He made me feel desirable, he made me laugh, he wanted me, and he was very male. After eighteen years of a "girly-man," as my ex-husband would call himself laughingly while we watched Hans and Franz on *Saturday Night Live*, a "manly man" was thrilling. Harry fixed things, advised me about my finances, gave me legal advice, and installed my printer.

And, unfortunately, after staying one more night, he left—and never came back.

After Harry, I didn't go dateless for long, but orgasms were few and far between. I became obsessed with Internet dating, spending hours on Match, JDate, and OKCupid. I was like the proverbial kid in a candy store, fantasizing about every guy I saw, wondering if he was good in bed. I found young guys, old guys, guys who wanted phone sex, guys who wanted cybersex, AOL chat room late-night weirdness, men who weren't what they seemed. I slept with a string of unsatisfying lovers.

At the time I was reading *Broken Open* by Elizabeth Lesser and was struck by how finding her "Shaman Lover" awakened her to the life force. As Lesser described him, "Sometimes the Shaman Lover has been sent by fate to blast us open, to awaken the dead parts of our body, to deliver the kiss of life. If we succumb, we are changed forever." I knew I wanted a Shaman Lover to blast me open.

❋ ❋ ❋

After many bad dates, I finally met him through Match.com. The connection was powerful and almost instantaneous. After our first date, dinner at a bar, Bob asked me to come back to his apartment to watch a video, which I interpreted as, "Wanna have sex?" My answer was a resounding yes, yes, yes, yes. A Molly Bloom of a yes.

Bob told me later he actually thought we were just going to watch a video. He never thought I'd go to bed with him on the first date. But I'd learned from my experience with Harry to take my sexual opportunities when I could. To hell with the "no sex on the first date" rule.

Bob had the same kind of masculine energy that I'd found so attractive in Harry. He fucked with a strength, force, and abandon that was thrilling. He didn't ask if he was hurting me, nor did he care. I'm sure he would have stopped if I'd asked, but that was the last thing I wanted him to do. Bob called forth lubrication from my vagina that I thought was long gone. When I was younger, I'd thought I preferred slender men with gentleness and finesse, but I found myself lusting for this short, stocky, powerful tennis player, a Taurus who lived up to his sign—bullish, obstinate, and pushy. Bob reminded me of a seal, with a layer of fat covering a muscular, sleek body. His skin was hairless, white, smooth, and silky to the touch. I couldn't get enough of him.

One delirious night, Bob put his hand between my legs after fucking me and started gently massaging, the way I'd shown him to make me come. I had a strong orgasm, assumed it was over, and prepared to relax—but then another orgasmic wave rolled over me, and then another. At first I couldn't understand why the orgasm hadn't ended, why more orgasms kept rocking my body. I couldn't stop shivering and moaning. I clasped Bob's hand to my crotch and told him not to let go.

"Omygod, I'm having multiple orgasms," I gasped.

"Oh?" He seemed to think it wasn't that big of a deal.

"I never had one like this before—this is the first time."

He grinned. An adorable, boyish grin. "Wow, I'm quite the stud, aren't I?"

I squeezed his penis affectionately. "More than you know."

Here we were, fifty-five and sixty, with as much electricity running between us as teenagers, more than either of us could remember having before. The miracle for me was the mutuality of it. Back when I was single, men I'd wanted this badly usually didn't want me.

Can there be anything sweeter than what he wrote to me after that first meeting:

I was driving back from picking up something for my computer, and I just started thinking of how much I wanted you. YOU, not just sex. Sex with YOU. NOTHING else will do. I didn't think of cumming. I thought of looking into your eyes, caressing your legs, hearing you sound loving and full of desire, feeling that I am making you feel that way. Every sigh of love and scream of pleasure that oozes out of you flows through every vein in my body. There is no better way of giving me pleasure than for you to feel it yourself. Just be a selfish lover and you will have a happy lover in me. Miss you so fucking much I could scream. Please come and spend the night with me. I'm willing to beg.

Bob kept sending me ardent love emails that derailed me. I thought I was going to burst. There was almost no difference between being in love at sixty than at sixteen, except at sixty, I knew I wouldn't die if it didn't work out. Age and divorce had given me enough perspective to know I could survive anything, and that just the experience of having this powerful emotion again in my life was a gift.

It didn't work out. Bob was only a few months out of a seventeen-year marriage, and it was much too early for him to make a commitment. When they say that timing is everything, they—whoever they are—are right. It was too soon after divorce for both of us. We were each other's transitional relationship, the first one after the divorce, and no one ever stays with the transitional relationship. We broke up.

The pain of our breakup hurt more than my breakup with my husband, but unlike my marriage, I'll never regret that thrilling affair with Bob. He was my Shaman Lover, and for that I'll always be grateful.

BEYOND THE DOUBLE DOORS

Sue Katz

It's been many decades since Regina last had automotive sex, although today it is just her imagination taking over as she daydreams in her car, the oldies murmuring from the radio. As a mobile podiatrist, she travels for the elders' health services from senior center to assisted living to nursing home. Today, having arrived too early to this new venue, she is parked outside Kenmore Pines.

She reclines her car seat one more notch and tries to use the extra half-hour to relax. Lately she's been, as they say, "living in the moment." She has a hard time picturing her own future since Ronald passed away. She had often thought they would end up together in a fancy assisted living facility like Kenmore Pines. She shakes her head, preferring to think about the good times. That last year before Ronald died, they had shared some amazing experiences, full of creativity and surprising passion. After he turned sixty, he had started complaining about the unreliability of his erections; then once he got ill, his medications made the situation much worse. But Ronald was more committed to pleasure than he was to his ego, so he had refused to accept his lack of hard-ons as an impediment.

Regina recalls the day he came home with "his and her's" vibrating anal toys and heavy-duty lubricant. Together they discovered a whole new realm of excitement. Her eyes close and she settles more deeply into her seat, as if she were in their king-size bed, while she relives that first time . . .

❊ ❊ ❊

Ronald strokes her with long, firm caresses and bombards her with breath-stopping kisses. As he rolls her onto her side, she hears the familiar snapping sound of him pulling on what he calls his "sex gloves." He slathers his fingers with the new lubricant and begins to gently play with her rear opening. Circling the tender outside tissue with his slicked-up fingers produces an electricity very different from the usual ways he touches her. As soon as she abandons herself to this new excitement, he reaches around her hip with his other hand to pinch the hood of her clit. What a whirlwind of contrasting sensations!

At first he only puts the very tip of his finger into her. But as he feels her pushing back with increasing hunger, he graduates to fucking her anally with his thumb. Her panting is audible, so he decides that she is ready to take her new toy. The pink silicone butt plug is about a half-inch thick and three inches long. It is attached to a battery pack adorned with buttons. Regina feels self-conscious, but committed.

Nudging her onto her hands and open knees, Ronald kneels behind her. He carefully slips the slender toy into her and turns the vibrator on low. Her whole body trembles with the penetrating shivers that spread from her ass to her pussy and down her thighs. Regina moans with ecstatic surprise, afraid to move one inch. She doesn't want this unanticipated new thrill to ever stop. Suddenly Ronald turns the vibrator up higher, using his other hand to work her clit. She comes in an explosion so quick and powerful that she falls over sideways, immobile. "I came in my ass," she sobs to him. "I came back there."

Regina shifts in her seat, half drifting, half conscious, remembering how she had learned to pleasure him with the thicker toy he had bought for himself. He too loved the sensations of anal play and described to her how it made him orgasm without ejaculating. She could hear the echo of those triumphant cries of gratification that had made her laugh with joy. But within a couple of months, he had become too sick to make love at all. And soon after that he had died.

Regina is startled by the buzz of her cellphone alarm wrenching her out of her sweet memories and telling her that it is time to go in and work. Kenmore Pines has lined up two hours of clients for her. She stops at the desk and a handsome man in his early forties comes out of a nearby office. "Hi, Regina. I'm Ted, the executive director, and I welcome you to Kenmore Pines. Let me walk you down the hall to our health clinic." By the time they arrive, she is charmed by his friendly and open attitude.

Two and a half hours later, she has packed up her gear to go. However, her exit is deflected by the sound of a party down the hall. She follows the buzz with curiosity. The noise is almost raucous by the time she approaches the set of double doors to the events room. She's never before heard such high festivity in an assisted living home.

She opens the door to the bewildering sight of a rotund guy in his seventies balancing a tray of plastic glasses while wearing a pink tutu over his jeans, tucked just under his not inconsiderable stomach. Three or four plastic leis in rainbow colors hang from his neck and bounce on his barrel chest. Regina has crossed from the thin, hushed environment of the assisted living to the charged density of a high-energy celebration.

The decorative man stops at the table closest to Regina. There, eight women of a certain age—well, *her* age, actually— reach out to grasp a glass, each with an affectionate quip to her server. Beyond them are at least a dozen more tables, filled with spirited, chattering folks who, despite being beyond retirement age, clearly don't need the residential services of an assisted living facility.

One of the nearby women notices Regina standing uncertainly. "First time here?" she asks with a smile as white and full as her luxurious, wavy hair. "I'm Cherie," she adds, reaching out to shake Regina's hand.

"Actually, I was just leaving the building, but I was curious about all the noise."

"You're just in time for dessert, so sit here next to me." Cherie raises her voice. "Tinkerbell! Bring another glass of champagne for our newcomer!" The guy in the tutu dances back and presents the plastic glass to Regina with a flourish. "Welcome, Madame!"

Regina squeezes in next to Cherie, who tries, over the racket, to introduce her to the animated women at their table.

"You don't know who we are, do you?" Cherie asks, sitting with a confident posture that complements her trim, angular build. Regina looks around, trying to come up with an answer. The lively women from a generous mix of ethnicities and fashion styles seem like old friends. On second glance she realizes that—oh!—there are at least two quite affectionate couples at the table.

Cherie's waiting for her answer. "Not a clue," Regina says.

"We're the LGBT Seniors Dinner Club." Regina knows the acronym—Lesbian, Gay, Bisexual, Trans. But seniors? Cherie continues, "Been meeting here monthly for nearly two years. And the crowd keeps growing and growing. You should see us in the summer, when it's easier for folks to get here. We spill right out there into the garden."

Somewhere in the middle of Cherie's explanation, as Regina is leaning in very close to hear her over the crowd, Regina feels a flush of heat rising from her belly up her chest and neck and onto her cheeks. It's not what Cherie is saying—simple small talk—it's her lips. And the lines at the corners of her mouth. Something about her smile framed by that shimmery white hair with its fabulous lavender lowlights is playing havoc with Regina's bloodstream.

Regina takes a deep breath, realizing that she isn't holding up her side of the conversation. "But why just LGBT elders? Are there special issues?"

The flush on Regina's neck and cheeks does not escape Cherie's notice. "Oh, there are a million reasons," she says, casually putting her arm around the back of Regina's chair. "We're kept out of each other's hospital rooms, even when we have all the proper legal documents. We're excluded from the funerals of our life partners by hostile families or thrown out of the houses we have renovated with our own hands. We're afraid to be affectionate in senior centers or nursing homes in case our caregivers object."

"A toast!" the women at the table cry, and Cherie and Regina realize that they have completely missed the group conversation. "It's true," a woman named Yleana beams, taking the hand of the pretty woman sitting next to her who holds a gorgeous carved cane, "Next month Ruth and I are moving into an assisted living on the north shore that will give us a couple's room." They all drink their good wishes. Regina feels an elation she cannot explain as she and Cherie click glasses. They lock eyes with a growing sense of excited connection.

By eight thirty, people are getting up and leaving. Regina is afraid to lose sight of Cherie. She opens her wallet and peels off one of her business cards. "Here're my details," she says. Cherie slips the card into her back pocket and digs around her own backpack. "And here's one of mine—a bit scruffy, but with all the info intact."

They hug with surprising warmth, and neither wants to break the embrace. Cherie whispers into Regina's ear, "It's been very special to meet you." As the petite woman's lips brush past her earlobe, Regina feels a shivery arousal. But without any other excuse to hang around, Regina exits the double doors back to the car, where just hours before, she had been enveloped in a very different emotional state.

When Regina gets up the next morning and checks her email, there is an invitation to go out to dinner with Cherie. She sends back her answer: "Any time after six thirty, any place in the tristate area! Send details!"

They meet at a quiet, Palestinian-owned café where they sit on beautifully embroidered cushions around tables made of large round worked-silver trays. Sharing hummus and baba ghanoush had never felt so intimate.

"I had a lot of time to prepare for Ronald's death," Regina tells Cherie, as they exchange thumbnail biographies, "but never thought about how to live my life once he was gone. I guess I've been working hard and reading more mysteries than is good for me."

"I understand," Cherie says, laying her hand unselfconsciously on Regina's thigh, "because when Uta decided to go back to Germany after living with me for more than twenty years, I went through a whole bereavement. She's not dead, but she sure is gone."

Cherie walks Regina to her car on the deserted side street. Regina leans her back against the side of her car, pulling Cherie flat against her. Their bodies meld, and for the first time, anticipation transforms into arousal. Regina gasps as Cherie tightens her embrace and then buries her face in the collar of Regina's coat. They remain leaning as one against the car, trembling, and then turn their faces for a first kiss.

❄ ❄ ❄

"Good morning, gorgeous," says the text on Regina's phone the next morning. "No, change that to *great* morning!" Instead of answering and deleting, as she usually does with texts, Regina replies but saves this text, feeling that it marks the start of the transformation of her life. "I'll bring drinks and dessert tonight," she writes, looking forward to her first visit to Cherie's home in Quincy.

❋ ❋ ❋

At Cherie's that evening, dinner is foreplay. Although the chicken is moist and the pasta salad is fresh, the dessert can wait, for the women have sweeter things in mind. For a present, Regina brings Cherie a CD of the vintage Roberta Flack album that had been the soundtrack to their generation's youthful romances. The two women dance to "Killing Me Softly" from the dining corner into Cherie's bedroom, where she has a view of the Boston skyline from Quincy's special bayside perspective.

The moon lights up Cherie's silky white hair, even the edgy lavender stripes in her bangs. The red fairy lights that are draped around the room cast a luscious luminosity over Cherie's light skin. Regina likes the mahogany sheen it gives to her own darker skin, too. Petite but wiry, Cherie shrugs off her own clothes and then crawls onto the bed, smiling. Regina is mesmerized by the woman's beauty and proud of her lack of self-consciousness as she pulls off her own jeans and sweater.

How quickly her own self-image has adapted to this change in her life. She feels so admired and so much a peer that she is happy to reveal more of her body to Cherie than to anyone ever before, including Ronald. And there is more of it to reveal, for she has gained at least thirty or forty pounds since his death, weight that settled in her breasts, her tummy, and her thighs. She had found herself increasingly alienated from her body. That is, until she met Cherie.

Cherie leans over to unclasp Regina's bra and to slip her panties down, murmuring her joy all along. She gently pulls the bigger woman onto her bed, where Regina lies back, exposed, on the white sheet. "Oh, the riches," Cherie says, crawling up and burying her face in Regina's cleavage. Cherie scoops up Regina's breasts from both sides and squashes them against her own ears in a playful gesture that breaks any tension Regina might feel at lying so exposed. But then Cherie sits up on her knees between Regina's legs, saying, "You seem very languorous, my beauty, so I'm going to wake you up." Cherie pinches each dark nipple, drawing up Regina's breasts until they are stretched and distorted, and blood rushes into the tissue.

Regina moans with the mixed sensations of pain and pleasure, closing her eyes tight. With her eyes shut, she does not see Cherie pick up one of two pieces of dental floss that she had laid on the corner of the bed table earlier. Cherie wraps the thread tightly around one hard nipple, circling from base to tip, and then does the same to the other.

"Sit up and look, Regina," she says, and Regina obeys, swinging her legs over the side of the bed so that she won't be straining her arthritic knee. Sitting there, she has her choice of views. She can look down at her fleshy breasts with the tips wrapped firmly in the white thread, or she can look straight ahead into the full-length mirror Cherie had set up and see a frontal view of her decorated nipples, above the tumble of soft rolls of belly.

Cherie crawls around behind her, scooping up her breasts like a push-up bra and then flicking the wrapped nipples with the back of her middle fingernail. Regina gasps at the heightened feeling. The bondage makes her nipples infinitely more sensitive than they had ever been before, and she trembles from the hypersensation. Is she feeling pain? Pleasure? Some hybrid? It doesn't matter because whatever it is, it is doing the job. She is totally aroused.

Cherie scurries off the edge of the bed to come around with a pillow in her hand. She drops it on the floor and kneels between Regina's legs. Regina watches, mesmerized and breathless, as Cherie kisses up her thighs to her outer pussy lips. Unprompted, Regina leans back on her hands to support herself and opens her legs wider. Spreading her lover's inner lips, Cherie uses the flat of her tongue on the hood of Regina's swelling clit. Once she is lapping at the most intimate crevices, she reaches up to knead those substantial breasts. All this Regina watches, as if in a film, as a mirror image. As her excitement mounts, she gazes in the mirror at the curve of Cherie's back and buttocks and the movements of the back of her head.

When Cherie begins twisting her nipples mercilessly, sucking at her clit at the same time, Regina's orgasm builds relentlessly and then cascades in echoing waves. The heap of sensations—the bound and abused nipples, the thump of Cherie's tongue on the hooded length of her clitoris, and, most of all, the spectacular sight of Cherie making love to her—brings on an explosion punctuated by her exultant cries. It takes her some time before she recovers her breath enough to turn her attentions to her lover's pleasure.

❋ ❋ ❋

A few weeks later, Regina parks outside the Kenmore Pines for the second time. As she gets out of the car, instead of carrying her podiatrist's tools, she holds a bouquet of peonies for Cherie. They are meeting at the LGBT senior dinner to celebrate their one-month anniversary.

As she enters the lobby and heads for the double doors, she runs into Ted, the executive director. "Oh, Regina," Ted says, "I almost didn't recognize you. Something's different. Have you lost weight? Did you get new glasses?"

She smiles and shakes her head, but she doesn't stop. She pushes through the double doors, feeling that in exploring another woman's body, she has rediscovered her own. "No," she wants to tell Ted, "I discovered hot sex in the last third of my life, and what you see on my face is happiness. Excitement. Endorphins. And maybe even some love juices."

MORNING

Belle Burroughs Shepherd

I awaken while it's still dark, my bladder urging me to get up. Your white hair is barely visible against the glow of your iPhone clock on the nightstand. With a deep aching in my body, I take my first naproxen of the day.

My bladder made content, I sleepily leave the bathroom. I wonder if it's too early for a cup of tea. A quick glance at the clock and the hint of light coming through the blinds say go for it. Then it's tea, vitamins, and a quick read of my overnight email.

I hear you get up and go to the bathroom, and then head back to bed. You know I will join you again soon. Mornings when you are not working, I am up early as you catch some much-needed sleep. It didn't take long for us to establish our little morning patterns. They just seemed to flow out of our relationship, as easily and quickly as our love reestablished itself.

We never lived together years ago, but the attraction was so deep that it stayed in the backs of both our minds for forty years.

Thank goodness for the Internet, we both say, or we would have never found each other again. My heart skipped a beat when I opened that first email from you four years ago. Every so often over the years, I would dream of you and wonder what had become of my sexy rebel.

I'm awake now from the caffeine and entertaining mail from friends on the West Coast. The aching in my body has lessened also.

It's light enough now in the bedroom to see your face as I crawl back under the blankets. I lie down and drink in the details of your face, as your deep breathing shows me you have fallen asleep again. I gently lay my hand on your cheek. How I love the feel of your rough beard against the palm of my hand. I grin as I remember it against my thighs and pussy.

I remember the photo I have of you sleeping in the hotel room last year, as we took our first tentative steps back towards each other. I smile, thinking of how hungry we were for each other's bodies that first night. You must have made me cum two dozen times—first with your fingers, then your mouth, then your cock. We had been teasing each other for months, ever since you asked me to go to the conference with you. I had been writing erotica for you, and you had seduced me via webcam, so it was no wonder we felt like we had already made love. We were so comfortable together, as if we had never been apart.

You stretch against me and turn slightly. I turn over and settle my back against your chest. One of your arms closes around my breasts, and the other grabs the softness of my belly. No matter how many exercises I do at the gym, that belly that cradled two babies is now a permanent part of me. You don't care though; you love it anyway.

The backs of your fingers are stroking me slowly now, waiting for that gasp, which will let you know that I'm interested. That gasp comes soon, as your touch relaxes and excites me.

The hand on my breast starts to play with a nipple, first just brushing lightly, then as it hardens, pulling and pinching. *Harder, yes,* I think, and as if reading my mind, you do just that. I gasp again.

"Good morning, my love," you whisper in my ear and then give it a playful lick.

Your fingers on my belly are working their way lower, tracing the sparse hair that grows below. I'm making soft purring sounds. One finger slips down into my wetness. I'm moaning now.

"Do you want more, baby?"

"Oh, yes, I always want more."

Your fingers circle around my pussy lips and clit, teasing, keeping me on edge. How do you do that so well? How, in a few short months, have you learned my body so completely?

But then you always did that to me, didn't you? You were my second-ever lover when we came together for the first time forty years ago. You knew exactly what to do with me from the minute you touched me. We were both involved with other people then, but the attraction to each other was overwhelming. Was it the look in your eyes, or your kisses that got to me then? Whatever it was, I remembered it for all those years until we found each other again.

Maybe then it was just sex, but now it is so much more: the conversations where we realize that we are thinking the same thoughts, the complete trust as we reopen our hearts, and the depth of our connection when we look into each other's eyes.

Your fingers have found my center now, and I'm right on the edge of cumming. Your other hand has a firm grasp on one of my nipples.

"Hmm, babe, I'm so close now."

"Yes, yes," you breathe into my ear. I know you love it when I tell you I'm cumming. I turn my head slightly and catch your gaze. I see the love in your eyes, and my orgasm sweeps over me. I hear your laugh as I cum and soak your fingers.

I don't know how many fingers you have inside me now, but I'm crying out, "Fuck me, babe, fuck me hard!" You oblige me, several times, then pull back a bit and play with my clit, which causes me to gasp in a different way. My clitoral orgasms are a little bit harder to make happen, but your fingers know me well now, and your eyes are glowing as one overtakes me.

As I am writing this, you come into the study to look over my shoulder. "I'm working on that story for the senior sex anthology."

"Do you need some inspiration?" you ask, as you swivel my chair around to face you.

Then you are down on your knees and pulling aside my bathrobe, and my legs open wide for you. Your tongue finds my clit im-

mediately, as I sigh and lean back. Just the kind of inspiration I most enjoy. Your fingers slip inside me and I let out a scream.

"More, oh yes, more."

In a few minutes, as I've soaked the chair and your beard is wet and glistening, you look up and stop. "Enough for now?"

The satisfied grin on my face tells you yes.

Time to get back to writing this story, reinspired now.

After so much attention to me, it's time to see what you have been doing, and I reach down to find your cock rock hard. You get so hard just listening to me cum, and now it's your turn. I sit up and climb over you, sinking onto your stiffness. We grin at each other as I move on top of you. If I lean back just a bit, your cock hits that place inside that makes me cum hard. You pinch my nipples as you gaze up at me, and another orgasm shudders through my body.

Alas, your hard-on is losing strength, and you slip out of my pussy before I can give you your much-needed release. Not to worry though, I know what will soon have you up again. I maneuver my way up your body until my cunt is over your mouth. Going to the gym is definitely worth it, as my legs are strong on either side of your shoulders. You grab my ass to pull me into position.

And then your tongue finds my clit and I'm over the edge again, holding on to the headboard. I'm so aroused now that in a minute or so I'm squirting and soaking your beard. I look behind me and see that you are stroking your cock, which is growing solid again in your hand.

I climb off of your chest and turn my body around so that I can lick you. I love the smell and taste of our fluids mixing. The head of your cock swells in my mouth and I tease up and down your shaft with my tongue. I can tell that it won't take you long now.

"Where would you like to cum, babe? In my pussy, or in my mouth?"

"Oh, in your pussy. Yes."

I slide my body around until my back is against you. We maneuver a bit and you push into my wetness from behind at an angle that works wonderfully for both of us.

I reach down to touch my clit, and hearing my moans is the final push you need to let go. I love the way your orgasmic tremors seem to last forever, overtaking your whole body.

The sun is peeking through the blinds now.

"Good morning, my love. Happy?"

"Yes. So very happy. Who knew it could be this good, after so many years of waiting and wondering if I would ever have another lover?"

I stretch out next to you, cradled in your arm. My fingers reach down, and I start to run them all around my pussy lips. Yes, I need just a bit more.

I lean over to find my vibrator by the bedside. As I put the plastic nub on my clit, your fingers reach for my nipples. Just one more body rush as I gaze into your eyes, which are grinning at me. As my shudders stop, you pull up the blankets around me and just hold me.

You are what I have needed my whole life.

ABOUT THE CONTRIBUTORS

PETER BALTENSPERGER, seventy-three, is a Canadian writer of Swiss origin and the author of ten books of fiction, poetry, and nonfiction. His short stories, poems, and essays have appeared in several hundred publications around the world. His erotic stories, poems, and essays have been published in print in *The Mammoth Book of Best New Erotica, Sex in the City—Paris, The International Journal of Erotica, Sinisterotica,* and *Surreal Smut,* and online in *Clean Sheets, The Erotic Woman, Oysters and Chocolate,* and *Every Night Erotica,* among others. He lives in London, Canada, with his wife Viki and their three cats. "With 'After Dinner Euphoria,' I wanted to show the lasting intimacy, the enduring physical attraction, and the beautiful sensuality that can exist in an older couple after many years of togetherness. Also, I wanted to show the comfortable familiarity and open sexuality combined with a sense of excitement and adventure of a couple in a permanent, long-standing, and formalized relationship."

MARYN BLACKBURN has written erotica under various pseudonyms for many years. Her work has appeared in the erotica anthologies *Power Play: Sex and Politics* and *Love Me Tender*. Her horror-erotica hybrid appeared in the e-zine Morgaine from Three Crow Press for its annual erotica edition. Her BDSM stories under a male pen name are still available at CF Publications. She's sold short fiction to regional magazines and *Ellery Queen's Mystery Magazine*. Her plays have won regional playwright awards in her home city. "The mannerisms of a well-dressed older gentleman made me wonder if he might be gay. Then he smiled at a much plainer, somewhat hard woman his age, and I thought, Why not? By the time a person has a great deal of life experience, we see beauty very differently."

CHEYENNE BLUE has lived in the United States, Ireland, the U.K., and Switzerland, but she still calls Australia home, and her writing often reflects this. Her erotica has appeared in over sixty anthologies, including *Best Women's Erotica*, *The Mammoth Book of Best New Erotica*, *Best Lesbian Erotica*, *Best Lesbian Romance*, and *With This Ring, I Thee Bed*. She currently lives in Queensland, Australia. Visit her website at www.cheyenneblue. com. "What is more normal than toast for breakfast? My story, 'Toast for Breakfast,' evolved from a strong belief that sexuality is a normal part of life at any age. However, while the main character enthusiastically embraces this, she's a little concerned how her adult daughter will react."

DALE CHASE has written male erotica for fourteen years and has published approximately 150 stories in magazines and anthologies, of which a number have been translated into Italian and German. She has two story collections currently in print: *The Company He Keeps: Victorian Gentlemen's Erotica* from Bold Strokes Books and *If the Spirit Moves You: Ghostly Gay Erotica* from Lethe Press. Her first novel, *WYATT: Doc Holliday's Account of an Intimate Friendship*, is due from Bold Strokes Books in fall 2012. Chase lives near San Francisco. Check her out at www.dalechasestrokes.com. "I love San Francisco's Castro District, so having my characters meet in Dolores Park felt comfortable. The specific situation presented in the story was born out of the too-prevalent focus on youth."

CHERI CRYSTAL is the author of *Attractions of the Heart*, a 2010 Golden Crown Literary Winner for erotic lesbian love stories. Some of her latest short tales of lesbian lust include "Pandora's Box," "Mirror Image," "Wet and Wild," "Help Wanted: Clitoris Missing in Action," "Conventional Wisdom," "The Ties That Bind," "Keeping Up With Hornelia," "Better Late Than Never," and many more sizzling titles available at www.loveyoudivine. com. Visit Cheri's website, www.chericrystal.com, and join her on facebook.com/chericrystal for details and coming attractions. "My inspiration for 'Better than Vibrators' was spending time toy shopping with my girlfriend in Amsterdam's Red Light District. We had lots of laughs purchasing a new vibrator we dubbed 'the purple penetrator.' I couldn't believe that we were being helped by a young man I could have given birth to."

KATE DOMINIC is a former technical writer who now writes about much more interesting ways to put Tab A into Slot B. She is the author of over three hundred short stories and has been published in *Best Erotic Romance*; *Surrender*; *Yes, Ma'am*; *Indecent Proposals*; *The Mammoth Book of Threesomes and Moresomes*; *Best Women's Erotica*; and many other anthologies. In 2003, her book *Any 2 People, Kissing* was a finalist for a *ForeWord* Magazine Book of the Year Award. Find her at www.katedominic.com. "For over twenty years, my husband has brought me hot chocolate and read over my shoulder while I wrote erotic fiction. Growing older together is fun."

Because **JOHNNY DRAGONA** is totally blind and has an MA in rehabilitation counseling from New York University, his first published articles involved physical disabilities. Switching gears and using pseudonyms, he began to write for adult magazines and has been published in *Hustler*, *Cheri*, and *Playgirl*. His first erotic novel was published in 1994, followed by more than a dozen more. He has a full-time contract to send ten stories a month to a Canadian publisher. He lives in Cliffside Park, New Jersey, with his wife of thirty-four years. "'Blind Not Dead' was inspired by my experience corresponding with another writer who was blind via cassette tape. Her voice with its slight Alabama accent did things to my gonads. But the part about our meeting is fiction."

EROBINTICA is poet, writer, and blogger Robin Elizabeth Sampson. She sent off her first piece of erotica for publication as she turned fifty years old. That story was included in the anthology *Coming Together: Al Fresco*. She has stories in *Best Erotic Romance* and *Suite Encounters: Hotel Sex Stories*. Two of her poems were finalists in the 2010 Seattle Erotic Art Festival's Literary Arts Showcase, and she's read her work at Philadelphia's The Erotic Literary Salon. Robin is at work on an erotic novel with senior protagonists. Her blog is www.erobintica.blogspot.com. "More memoir than fiction, my story was inspired by a night just like the one written. I'd enjoyed the freedom of our privacy that came with our youngest child finally being off at college. In my stories I try to capture the realness of sex in a way that celebrates the quiet and the wild."

RAE PADILLA FRANCOEUR published *Free Fall: A Late-in-Life Love Affair* with Seal Press in 2010. She had fun reading erotic bits for free cocktails and rounds of applause at a packed bar in Manhattan. She publishes fiction and nonfiction, and she works as a journalist and creative director in her arts marketing business New Arts Collaborative. She was creative services director at the Peabody Essex Museum and editorial manager at the Museum of Fine Arts, Boston. Rae started her writing career as a journalist. Later she managed several magazines and newspapers. Learn more at rae.francoeur.com, freefallrae. com, and newartscollaborative.com. "'By the Book' was literally inspired by the book *The Joy of Sex*, by the man with the great name, Alex Comfort. What thrilled me about the book, published in 1972, was its very existence on a shelf in the mainstream bookstore I comanaged in New Hampshire. With its graphic depictions of joyous sexual activity, a page had been turned in American culture. And we had to keep reordering!"

I.G. FREDERICK (www.eroticawriter.net) has traded words for cash more years than she cares to admit and has specialized in erotic fiction and poetry since 2001. She has sold numerous short stories and poems to various electronic, audio, and print anthologies and magazines. Her novels have received high praise from readers, critics, and other authors. In addition, I.G. Frederick is an accomplished book designer, and together with the awesome artist Nyla Alisia (www.nylaalisia.net) and her submissive Patrick (web designer extraordinaire), she provides services to indie authors and small presses as part of Pussy Cat Press (www.pussycatpress.com). "Many of my stories are inspired by people I've met and scenes I've witnessed or participated in. However, truth is stranger than fiction, and only those who were there know which is which."

DOROTHY FREED is the pseudonym of an artist and writer who lives and writes on the coast-side near San Francisco, where she has lived for twenty-five years. She is sixty-seven and is still passionately interested in sex. Her interest in writing erotica came about because art imitates life. Her stories will appear in the upcoming anthologies *Cheeky Spanking Stories* and the *Seattle Erotic Art Festival Literary Art Anthology 2012*. Contact at DorothyFreed@aol.com. "I was inspired to write this story because I am overjoyed and grateful to be still passionately interested in sex at my age, and to have a loving partner who feels the same."

DOUG HARRISON's erotic ruminations appear in more than twenty anthologies, including *Still Doing It, Men Seeking Men, Best Bisexual Erotica, Best Gay Erotica, Best S/M Erotica, Tough Guys, Best Gay Romance, The Cougar Book*, and *Hot Daddies*. His spiritual memoir, *In Pursuit of Ecstasy*, was a textbook at Dark Odyssey Summer Camp. Doug was active in San Francisco's gay and pansexual leather scenes. He appears in Cleo Dubois' groundbreaking S/M video *The Pain Game*, about the "why" of S/M, and in eight other erotic videos. His short stories and essays can be found at www.pumadoug.com. "I'm over seventy. My partner and intimate friends are between ten and twenty years younger. I included the challenges of being HIV positive to raise awareness of the difficulties of this condition, particularly in my age group and especially as it affects staying sexually vigorous. Some of us narrowly escaped with our lives, and despite serious side effects from earlier medication, I remain sexually active."

SKYLER KARADAN, PhD, LMFT, has been practicing (under his real name) as a licensed marriage and family therapist for the past twenty years, focusing on couples' relational issues around communication, intimacy, and sexuality. Both he and his wife have also served as sex educators, co-teaching at the university level. They have been celebrating their honeymoon for the past twenty years. This is Dr. Karadan's first submission of erotic writing, and he applauds the opportunity to creatively highlight senior sexuality. "I wrote this story for my wife as an experiment to see if an erotic tale could be told without crude euphemisms for genitalia and sexual behavior. I also wanted to celebrate the fact that sexual enthusiasm and intimate connection have no age barriers."

SUE KATZ is a wordsmith and rebel who has lived and worked on three continents. She was a martial arts master in the Middle East, traveled the world promoting transnational volunteering for a British nonprofit, and now teaches fitness and dance to seniors in Boston, Massachusetts. She wrote the book *Thanks But No Thanks: The Voter's Guide To Sarah Palin* in twenty-eight days and nights. Sue is working on a collection of stories about elders, sex, and life. Read her edgy blog "Consenting Adult" at www.suekatz. typepad.com or "friend" her at facebook.com/sue.katz. "Not only do I myself work professionally with seniors and elders teaching fitness and dance, I also attend a long-running monthly LGBT senior dinner held at an upscale assisted living center (which appreciates the marketing value of hosting us), one of about a half-dozen such get-togethers in the Boston area. Over the decades, I've written about the suppleness of some women's sexuality and the increasing confidence to try new things as we age."

D.L. KING is a New Yorker and a smut writer, the editor of *The Harder She Comes*; the IPPY Gold Medal winner *Carnal Machines*; *Spank*; *The Sweetest Kiss*; and the Lambda Literary Award Finalist *Where the Girls Are*. Her short stories can be found in anthologies such as *The Mammoth Book of Best New Erotica*; *Best Women's Erotica*; *Best Lesbian Erotica*; *Please, Ma'am*; *Sex in the City: New York*; *Sweet Love*; *Frenzy*; *Gotta Have It*; *Yes, Sir*; and *Yes, Ma'am*; among others. She's published two novels and edits the erotica review site Erotica Revealed. Find her at www.dlkingerotica.blog-spot.com. "I wrote 'Mr. Smith' shortly after my fifty-fifth birthday. I had been playing with my partner, who complained about his knees and that kneeling was becoming painful. I started thinking about what it means to lead an active BDSM lifestyle as we age. Kneepads seemed like a sensible idea."

MIRIAM KURA, sixty, owns her own business and lives in Portland, Oregon. She looks forward to the day when Madison Avenue catches up with the sensuality of the boomer generation and publishes a monthly *Cosmo*-type magazine for juicy over-fifty women. "I wrote this story because I found so little erotica that combines explicit sex scenes in the context of a longer term, loving relationship. Unfortunately for those of us who want both, relationship stories show very little sex, and hot erotica often depicts sex between strangers. I am a big supporter of adding to the emerging 'Hot Relationship Sex' bookshelf."

By day, **LORNA LEE** writes young adult and middle grade novels under her real name while wearing blue jeans and T-shirts. By night, she puts on her black nightie and indulges in her fantasies. She lives in the high desert of Washington State where she also quilts, blogs, and, when time permits, is an amateur photographer. "George is the name I gave to the photo portrait of the nude man that hangs on the wall at the foot of my bed. He is described in this story, and is my most faithful of lovers. How could I not write about him?"

TSAURAH LITZKY's erotica has appeared in over ninety-two publications, including *Best American Erotica* eight times. Her erotic novella, *The Motion of the Ocean*, was part of Three The Hard Way, a series edited by Susie Bright. Tsaurah is also a poet, playwright, art critic, and a writer of book reviews. Her most recent book is the poetry collection *Cleaning the Duck* (Bowery Books, 2011). She has completed an erotic memoir, *Flasher*. Tsaurah writes sexy stories about seniors that she hopes adult readers of all ages will enjoy because she believes in sexual and personal liberation for everyone. Learn more at www.TsaurahLitzky.com. "At a family wedding, I danced with a seventy-nine-year-old cousin (he was some dancer!) who had been a xylophone player in the Paul Goodman Band. He lived in a home for aged musicians on Long Island. He inspired me to fabricate stories about the residents of this home."

EVVY LYNN is the pseudonym of a well-known sixty-eight-year-old writer of fiction and nonfiction. "I always believed that when I hit menopause, I would lose all interest in sex," she says. "I was surprised to discover that was a myth. If anything, I'm more interested in sex than ever, though much more discriminating. 'Jaguar Dreams' began as an actual erotic dream, like the one Janice experiences. I'd been thinking about aging, and how I had become invisible to men, and the story almost wrote itself. I wanted to convey that the jaguar appears to all women when it is time, whether they have a figurine or not. I can't wait for mine to show up again."

ERICA MANFRED is a freelance journalist and author in her sixties who separated from her husband in 2001. Making lemonade out of lemons, she used her own experience, plus interviews with experts and other divorcées, to write *He's History, You're Not: Surviving Divorce After Forty*. Her most recent book is the paranormal romance *Interview with a Jewish Vampire*, which features Sheldon, the first sexy Jewish vampire. Erica's humorous personal essays and self-help articles have appeared in *Cosmopolitan*, *The New York Times Magazine*, *Ms.*, *New Age Journal*, *New York*

Newsday, and many others. Her website is www.ericamanfred. com. "I loved the instant gratification aspect of Internet dating. But it was too easy to get addicted, which I found myself doing in the wee hours when I got lonely. Unfortunately there were too many men who only wanted cybersex. It was hard to find real-life guys for non-virtual sex."

BILL NOBLE is a Northern California writer and poet, a naturalist and teacher, and a great-granddad. He was the longtime fiction editor at *Clean Sheets*. Susie Bright's readers selected one of his short stories as an Erotic Story of the Decade. "I wrote 'Wane of the Moon' in my late fifties. The story grew partly out of a burgeoning personal awareness of aging, but more from witnessing age playing out in the lives of the generation ahead of me, sometimes very poignantly. It was written at a time when my reach as a writer and editor was substantial and I thought I could 'get away' with writing about senior sex and do it in a truthful and empathetic way."

LINDA POELZL has been learning a lot about senior sex for the past ten years, both personally and professionally. She is a fifty-nine-year-old bisexual woman who has been working in the field of human sexuality since 1990 as a sex educator, public speaker, writer, coach, and sexological bodyworker. She is currently writing a book about her career in sexual health and well-being and can be reached through her website at www.waterdragonwoman.

com. "Older men turn me on! Through their eyes, I see the beauty of my aging self. I dedicate this story to all those older men who keep that eternal flame of passion alive within themselves."

BELLE BURROUGHS SHEPHERD has been writing erotic stories for many years, although she has kept most of them to herself. Belle was born in the United States but lived for many years in Canada, where she raised two daughters and helped to raise her two granddaughters. She recently moved back to the East Coast of the United States. When a lover from the past found her, after thirty years of being apart, writing erotica became a way for them to re-explore their sexual attraction. A self-taught web designer, Belle started an anonymous sex blog on Tumblr to further enhance the sexual communication with her lover. "I was inspired to write 'Morning' during the magical first months of our relationship. Since we moved in together, there has been no lack of inspiration for more stories."

SUSAN ST. AUBIN has been writing erotica for nearly thirty years, sometimes as Jean Casse. Her work has appeared in *Yellow Silk, Libido, Herotica, Best Lesbian Erotica, Best American Erotica, Best Women's Erotica*, and many other journals and anthologies, as well as online at *Clean Sheets,* www.fishnetmag.com, and www.forthegirls.com. Her story collection, *A Love Drive-By: Stories of Ambition, Hunger, and Desire*, was published in 2011 by Renaissance E Books/Sizzler Editions. "Since I retired, I've developed the strange new hobby of going to estate sales. My story is an attempt to capture the experience of going into people's homes, pawing through their possessions, and vicariously entering their lives. It's a voyeuristic sensation guaranteed to jog the imagination."

DONNA GEORGE STOREY is the author of *Amorous Woman*, a semi-autobiographical tale of an American woman's love affair with Japan. Her fiction and essays have appeared in numerous journals and anthologies such as *Fourth Genre, The Gettysburg Review, Prairie Schooner, Penthouse, Best American Erotica, The Mammoth Book of Best New Erotica, Dirty Girls, Curvy Girls,* and *Nice Girls, Naughty Sex.* She writes a column for the Erotica Readers and Writers Association, "Cooking up a Storey," about her favorite topics—sex, food, and writing erotica. Read more at www.DonnaGeorgeStorey.com. "'By Invitation Only' is based on a recent lunchtime interlude with my husband of twenty-five years. Our motto is 'you never stop learning,' especially when it comes to pleasure."

HARRIS TWEED is a pseudonym for a published novelist (four books and counting) who has won a national award and received starred reviews from *Publishers Weekly* and *Kirkus.* Harris graduated from Stanford in the early '60s and lived in Italy, New York City, Oakland, and Mexico before settling in Northern California. He is happily married, a parent, and a professional with long careers in mental health and education. "I've always found trains erotic—probably the motion combined with a sense of freedom and adventure. The idea of sex in public with that combination of thrill and vulnerability also excites me. I resist becoming more conservative as I get older—regret is often composed of things never attempted, ideas never explored."

NANCY WEBER kicked up dust in 1974 with *The Life Swap* (Dial Press), about her attempt to become another woman—loving her lovers, doing her work, sneezing from her rose fever—while that woman was (supposedly) becoming Nancy. Her twenty other books include two slipstream novels, YA titles, eight romances, and "$500" fiction about sex workers. On LibidoForLife.com, Nancy writes the advice column and provocative essays. She covers food for NYCityWoman.com. "My first freelance sale, to the humor magazine *Monocle*, was a perverse little essay, 'Why Republicans Are Better in Bed.' The narrator of 'Something Borrowed, Something Blue' is the same girl, fifty years riper, still turned on by starched shirts and, oh God, power ties. (Anxious Democrats, please be assured that I vote with my head, not my libido.)"

CELA WINTER has had various careers, including being a restaurant chef (really). She lives in the Pacific Northwest, where she is at work on a novel. Fifty-something, she calls all people under thirty "whippersnappers" and likes to whack them with her cane. "Who hasn't had a 'what if' daydream about an early love? The return to a relationship after half a lifetime is bound to have some challenges as well as sweet rewards."

AUDRIENNE ROBERTS WOMACK is a native of Washington, DC, who holds a bachelor of science degree in education and a master's degree in public administration. She is an educator in a public school system and also leads women's empowerment/sexuality workshops and sells adult toys and products in her spare time. She is currently writing several projects for children and has published a book of her childhood memories (www.arwomack.com). She has also published several erotic stories in anthologies and a book of erotic poems (see www.lotusfalcon.com). "I encountered many flirtatious younger men who adored seasoned women long before the cougar phenomenon took root. I wanted to celebrate the normalcy of such encounters as a deliberate choice. Having gone through several life-altering surgeries, I wanted to also include that reality to emphasize the ongoing changes that women face, as they continuously reinvent and empower themselves again and again."

ABOUT THE EDITOR

Joan Price calls herself an "advocate for ageless sexuality" and has been writing, speaking, and blogging about senior sex since 2005. Formerly a health and fitness writer (and before that, a high school English teacher!), she switched topics to senior sex with her spicy memoir, *Better Than I Ever Expected: Straight Talk about Sex After Sixty,* written to celebrate the joys of older-age sexuality after meeting her great love, artist Robert Rice, when she was fifty-seven and he was sixty-four.

After hundreds of readers wrote Joan with questions and concerns about their own senior sex life, she wrote *Naked at Our Age: Talking Out Loud About Senior Sex* (Seal Press, 2011), to address the challenges of sex and aging. *Naked at Our Age* received two prestigious awards: Outstanding Service/Self-Help Book 2012 from the American Society of Journalists and Authors, the professional organization of nonfiction writers, and the 2012 Book Award "for a major contribution toward understanding the sexuality of seniors" from the American Association of Sexuality Educators, Counselors and Therapists, the primary professional organization of this field.

Joan's candid, upbeat manner led the media to dub her "senior sexpert." (She has also been called "our mighty, middle-aged Aphrodite," "the beautiful face of senior sex, who turns up whenever the age group is ridiculed," and a "wrinkly sex kitten"!)

Although Robert died in 2008, Joan continues on her mission to change society's view of elder sex, one mind at a time. She continues to talk out loud about senior sex with talks and workshops and offers educational consultations by phone and Skype. Her blog about sex and aging, www.NakedAtOurAge.com, has been ranked in the top twenty-five sexuality blogs for three years in a row, and has received numerous awards from health, aging, and sexuality sites.

Joan also teaches contemporary line dancing—which she calls "the most fun you can have with both feet on the floor"—in Sebastopol and Santa Rosa, California. Visit her at www.joanprice.com, or write to her at joan@joanprice.com.

SELECTED TITLES FROM SEAL PRESS

For more than thirty years, Seal Press has published
groundbreaking books. By women. For women.

Naked at Our Age: Talking Out Loud About Senior Sex, by Joan Price.
$16.95, 978-1-58005-338-9. Full of information from doctors, social
workers, psychologists, and sex experts, this is an indispensable guide
to handling and understanding the issues seniors face when it comes to
relationships and sex.

Better Than I Ever Expected: Straight Talk About Sex after Sixty, by
Joan Price. $17.00, 978-1-58005-152-1. A warm, witty, and honest book
that contends with the challenges and celebrates the delights of older-life
sexuality.

Getting Off: A Woman's Guide to Masturbation, by Jamye Waxman, il-
lustrations by Molly Crabapple. $15.95, 978-1-58005-219-1. Empower-
ing and female-positive, this is a comprehensive guide for women on the
history and mechanics of the oldest and most common sexual practice.

Licking the Spoon: A Memoir of Food, Family, and Identity, by Candace
Walsh. $16.00, 978-1-58005-391-4. The story of how—accompanied
by pivotal recipes, cookbooks, culinary movements, and guides—one
woman learned that you can not only recover but blossom after a
comically horrible childhood if you just have the right recipes, a little
luck, and an appetite for life's next meal.

The Secret Sex Life of a Single Mom, by Delaine Moore. $17.00, 978-
1-58005-386-0. The risqué story of a stay-at-home mom's boundary-
pushing experimentations with sex—and resulting self-awakening—
after a painful divorce.

Mind-Blowing Sex: A Woman's Guide, by Diana Cage. $17.00, 978-1-
58005-389-1. An instructive, accessible sexual guide that will help wom-
en and their partners make their sex life more empowering, exciting,
and enjoyable.

Find Seal Press Online
www.SealPress.com
www.Facebook.com/SealPress
Twitter: @SealPress

Made in the USA
Middletown, DE
22 January 2022

59379874R00201